A REGRETTABLE ROAST

Haunting Avery Winters Book 2

DIONNE LISTER

Copyright © 2021 by Dionne Lister

ISBN 978-1-922407-27-6

Paperback edition

Cover art by Robert Baird

Editing by Hot Tree Editing

Proofreading L. Brodey

 Created with Vellum

CHAPTER 1

I fumbled with the latch on the front gate as I burrowed my head into the top of my umbrella. Fat lot of good it was doing with the rain sheeting on an angle. Only my face and the top of my head were dry. Oh, Monday morning, how I loathed thee.

On Friday afternoon, I'd arranged to interview Mr and Mrs Downs after they'd asked if we'd cover their twenty-year anniversary. The actual day had been yesterday, but since I didn't have to work on the weekend, I didn't.

I hurried to their front porch, lowered my umbrella, and closed it. I was about to knock on the front door, but it was already ajar. Rather than knock, I called out, "Hello! Avery from the newspaper here. Anybody home?" A gust of wind shot along the porch, and I shivered. Summer my arse. It must've been nineteen degrees, windchill factor minus ten. Okay, so maybe I was exaggerating, but still....

A tall, heavy-set man who looked to be in his early forties, who I assumed was Mr Downs, walked into the hallway. He motioned to me. "Come in." He smiled.

Leaving my umbrella outside, I pushed the door all the way open and stepped in, then closed it behind me. I smiled. "Happy Anniversary for yesterday."

"Thanks." His smile fell, and he scratched his head. "You might as well come through." He turned and walked away, so I followed. It wasn't the warmest of greetings, especially since he'd invited me here. What had upset him out of nowhere? Maybe his wife was peeved off about something? Did he not get her a good present?

We walked through a living room and into the dining area. My intuition was telling me something wasn't how it was supposed to be. I stopped just inside the door and stared.

Cripes, not again.

My brow furrowed, and nausea climbed my throat. Mr Downs stood next to the table and gestured to one person on the floor in the foetal position. There were two plates on the table, almost empty, but the remnants of gravy and peas remained. A half-eaten leg of lamb sat on a platter in the middle of the table.

My eyes widened, and I slammed my hand over my mouth and nose to prevent the acrid stench from burning my nostril hairs. What in Hades? I stared at the man on the floor and cocked my head to the side. I moved my gaze to Mr Downs. Back and forth, back and forth. They were definitely wearing the same clothes. I realised what had been wrong earlier—Mr Downs's footsteps had made no sound on the timber floor.

A woman walked in from the next room, which appeared to be the kitchen, if the island bench just visible through the doorway was anything to go by. Cat's bum. This was not good. I jerked my head around to make sure no one else was in the house. I listened intently. Nothing—not from anyone living, anyway. Her high heels were silent on the hard floor.

She looked at me. "Avery, welcome. I'm afraid you're too late."

I shook my head. "What happened?" I was talking to the ghosts of Mr and Mrs Downs. I wasn't sure where her body was, but his was motionless on the floor. This wasn't the anniversary celebration I'd been expecting. This had to be the worst anniversary of all time.

Mr Downs answered, "We'd finished eating our roast lamb when we both felt sick. I had such bad cramps, that I didn't make it to the bathroom. I vomited until blood came out, but after that, I blacked out and woke up like this. Melissa tried to make it to the bathroom. I have no idea if she made it." He looked at her. "I thought it was food poisoning, but looks like it was more than that."

Mrs Downs turned to her husband. "I'd say it was some kind of poison—I've never felt so sick in my life. But it wasn't me. I promise. I was looking forward to our weekend away, and our world trip next year. I love you, darling. I'm sorry we didn't get to go." She placed a gentle hand on his cheek. How sweet. So, love could last into the next life. That was good to know… not that I had anyone I wanted to spend eternity with, but just in case I met the love of my life at eighty, we'd still have lots of quality time together.

"I know, sweetie. It wasn't me either." He put his arm around her and pulled her into his side. He pressed his lips together. "We prepaid those trips too." I blinked. It wasn't like they'd be missing that money now. "But who would do this to us?"

Who, indeed? If they didn't kill themselves, or each other, there was a murderer running around out there. Was this personal or a serial killer? Uneasiness roiled in my gut, and I glanced at Mr Downs's lifeless body. I should probably call the police right now, but this was my chance to get information that might solve the crime quickly. "Who inherits your estate?"

Mr Downs looked at me. "As much as I had nothing to do with my brother, we left a quarter to him, a quarter to my mother, and half to Melissa's parents."

Melissa nodded. "I had no siblings, and Tom and I couldn't have kids." Sadness radiated from her gaze. "At least we didn't leave any children behind."

Mr Downs kissed her forehead. "At least we had each other, and that's all I ever wanted."

She smiled up at him and nodded. He pulled her in for a proper hug. Sensing this was a private moment, I looked around. The familiar tingle in my nose had me blinking my eyes so I wouldn't cry. Two lovely people cut down in their prime. Why? One minute they're calling me to interview them for a happy occasion, the next….

I knew it was probably not legal, or acceptable because who would take pictures of dead bodies, but I wanted to see if I could figure this out. I had a feeling taking photos would help me later. Sometimes the smallest clue was the killer's undoing. Maybe I would see something the police missed? And there was no doubt that as soon as the police showed up, that would be the end of my involvement and information.

I slid my phone out of my bag, walked further into the room, and took photos. I would never get another chance to be at the scene of a murder before the police…. Okay, so this was the second time in a month, but surely this was the last time. I was creeped out, but because I could talk to their ghosts, it took the edge off the horror. Strange but true.

I just had to be careful not to touch anything. I took photos from all angles. "I hope you don't mind, Mr and Mrs Downs. I'll write a story on this later." I didn't want to offend them, but I needed answers. "Were you two fighting about anything lately?"

They both shook their heads. Mrs Downs said, "We were getting along rather well, actually."

"Do you have any enemies?"

They glanced at each other. Mr Downs looked at me, a wary expression on his face. "A couple. My brother is a crazy drug addict. I cut him off financially about a year ago, and he was forever sending me threatening texts until I blocked him. There's also a business associate who I've fallen out with."

"What was his name?"

"Henry Russo."

I pulled out my notebook and pen and wrote it all down. "And why did you guys have a falling out?"

Mrs Downs gasped. She grabbed her husband's arm. "Do you see that?" She stared past me, into the distance.

He blinked. "Yes." He quickly looked at me. "Can you make sure the police don't stop until they discover who killed us, for my mother's sake, and for my wife's parents? They'll be devastated. I know the police will try, but make sure they follow through."

"Of course." Why he was asking me, I didn't know—maybe it was because I was the only one here, and the request was important to him?

"Come on, darling. Let's go." Mrs Downs was still staring at whatever it was over my shoulder. I turned. Nope, nothing. When I turned back to them, they were smiling at each other. Then they focussed on the thing that only they could see—which I was going to assume was the famous come-hither light everyone talked about—and started walking. With every step, they faded, until by the time they reached the wall, they disappeared.

Poop. They were gone, and I had more questions to ask. Might as well get as much info as I could before I called the police. I also wanted to find Mrs Downs's body.

I hurried into the kitchen, which was a mess. They obviously weren't cook and clean-as-you-go people. Oil from cooking the lamb was left in the pan, and a couple of roast potatoes. Dessert might have been in the fridge, but I wasn't putting my fingerprints on anything to check. There was a brown paper bag on the counter near the sink, which had Manesbury Meaty Morsels stamped on the front—they would be worth paying a visit to. A quick scan of the bench didn't offer up the receipt. Hopefully they bought it on Saturday or yesterday and the butcher remembered.

After that, I took some photos. There was no sign of a struggle that I could see, but I wasn't exactly an expert. I needed to find Mrs Downs's body as well.

A door went out to a back patio from the kitchen, but it looked to be locked. Nothing seemed out of place. I wandered the house, and nothing appeared untoward until I reached their bedroom. The timber sleigh bed was neatly made. A hundred useless throw pillows were stacked near the headboard. A scattering of crimson roses covered the bed—how romantic—and a folded sheet of pink paper sat on top of the top pillow. A suicide note maybe? That wasn't quite so romantic.

I stepped close and looked down. It had "to whoever finds this" scrawled on it. I took a couple of photos of the room and note, but I didn't want to spend time reading it right now. Two mobile phones lay on the floor next to the bedside table, between the window and the bed, and a couple of novels and a lamp sat on the bedside table, but nothing else. There was no sign of Mrs Down's body. The most likely place would be the bathroom, so I wandered into their en suite.

Everything was in its place—towels on the towel rack, cosmetics neatly stacked on the vanity, hand towel folded on the vanity top—except the vomit on the floor and Mrs Down's body, which was facedown and in the clothes I'd seen her ghost wearing. Well, she had made it to the toilet, but toilets didn't save lives.

I breathed through my mouth to avoid the stink and took a couple of photos. Maybe I should make it a habit to carry cotton wool in my bag so I could shove it up my nose when I encountered dead bodies—it seemed to be becoming a habit.

I blew a breath out. It was time to call the police. My appointment had been for nine in the morning, and time was ticking. I could say I was a bit late, but if anyone had seen me arrive, I could be in trouble. Best call the police now and not risk it. Not that I'd done anything wrong, but they might frown at the prospect I'd contaminated evidence or taken any.

I called emergency rather than Bellamy direct. "Hello, this is Avery Winters. I'd like to report a murder."

CHAPTER 2

I waited for the police in the entry hall because I didn't feel like freezing my bottom off outside. They kept me for thirty minutes and asked me a ton of questions, which was fair enough; then I headed into the office. When I walked in, I said hello to Bethany. When she answered, I tripped because I didn't expect it. She never reciprocated my hellos. I'd recently found out she was Joyless Joy's sister, which explained everything. Surliness must run in the family.

"You always seem to be at the right place at the wrong time." The way she stared at me implied I must've had something to do with it.

"It's a gift, I suppose." I shrugged.

She narrowed her eyes. "You don't fit in here. All this trouble didn't start till you came."

Maybe if I stand here long enough, you'll cark it too. "Mind if I take a seat?" I looked at the guest chairs in a row along one wall.

She gave me a "what are you going on about" look. Her

phone rang, and she threw me one last dirty glare and turned away to answer it. I smiled. Maybe I could hang around next time and get a result. I snorted as I climbed the stairs to the office. If I was the harbinger of death, she would've been one of the first to cop it. If only I could tell her.

As soon as I stepped into the office, Finnegan and Carina jerked their heads up to look at me. Finnegan leaned back in his chair and smirked. Carina jumped up and hurried over. "Are you all right, hon?"

I gave her a small smile. "I'm fine. I mean, it wasn't great to find two dead bodies, but there wasn't any blood or guts or anything. I'll be an old hand at this in no time." I gave her a "what can you do about it" shrug. If I said I was a bit shaken, she'd hang around and ask more questions, which would only make me feel worse. Besides, I had evidence to chase up.

Finnegan rested a wrist on the table and flicked a pen against the tabletop. *Tap, tap, tap, tap.* "I don't suppose you'll tell me anything else about it?"

I smiled. "Nope. This one is mine. I had to suffer through the discovery. Besides, I was supposed to be covering their anniversary."

"Lovers' tiff?" he asked.

Nope. I stared at him, my gaze all innocence. "I have no idea." I chucked my stuff on my desk and sat. Time to research and write the article before Finnegan got information from Bellamy. While at the house, I'd taken photos of the police searching for evidence, but I'd been careful to take photos of them with a wall in the background—I was mindful not to show what they were looking at. There was no way I was going to post a photo in the article that might have evidence in it—both because of Finnegan and whoever had done it. Generic police-doing-their-thing pics were the safest.

I hadn't read the note on the pillow because I didn't have gloves, which I was considering buying and taking with me everywhere. I had to assume it was a suicide note from the message scrawled on the back, but I wasn't about to believe it since they both seemed happy with each other. Someone could easily have planted it. If only I'd been able to read it. Cat's bum.

Before I started writing, I looked up Mr Downs's company. Firm Base Concreting. Three owners were listed: Tom Downs, Henry Russo, and Jacob Papadopoulos. They owned a commercial property just outside Cramptonbury. I had a bit of other info ready to go from the article I was supposed to do on their anniversary. For now, I'd write about the fact that they'd been found dead, lament that they'd been celebrating a wonderful milestone when they'd so tragically died, give basic background information, and leave it at that. Once that article was in, my real investigations could start, unless the police nailed the case quickly. If that happened, I'd be off the hook.

After a couple of hours, my article was ready to go: '*A Regrettable Roast—Anniversary Dinner Turns to Death for Manesbury Couple*.' I smiled as I hit Send on the email to Mr MacPherson. About five minutes after I sent it, MacPherson hurried through the door. He stopped in front of my desk and grinned. "Great article, Winters. The photo of Bellamy on scene was brilliant. We don't usually get that close to the action."

I smiled. "I figured I deserved something after finding their bodies."

Finnegan stared at me—and, yes, I was all too aware of him looking at me. I'd been here for three and a half weeks, and his attractiveness still unnerved me. "Why are you smiling when you say that? How can anyone smile, then talk about how they found dead bodies?"

Telling him I could also see ghosts and that the couple seemed happy enough wouldn't go down well, so I shrugged. "Maybe the lightning strike fried the part of my brain that makes me act appropriately in all situations. Who can say?"

MacPherson chuckled. He rubbed his hands together. "I forgot to tell you this morning, Winters, but not only did your piece on the land fraud win article of the week for last week, but they ran it in our wider news. You'll receive a second bonus of fifty pounds for that too."

I grinned. "That's awesome! Thank you."

Carina's grin was as wide as mine. "D'at's grand, Avery. D'at one's way harder to get because we're competing against many od'er journalists."

MacPherson nodded. "She's right. So congratulations. Keep up the good work." He spun around and left without a goodbye, which I was slowly adapting to. What he had against goodbyes was a mystery, but if that was the worst of his foibles, I was willing to try and accept it. How big of me.

Finnegan looked at me. "What are you going to do with your bonuses, or is that bonii?" He laughed.

I couldn't help but laugh too. His humour surprised me, which was silly because he was often throwing funny comments around. Maybe it was because Brad had been so straight, and dare I say it, boring. Why I expected all men to be like Brad, I had no idea. As much as it annoyed me that I found Finnegan funny, I was glad. It was refreshing to be around happy people for a change, and I included Carina and Meg in that too. Brad's friends had been all about appearing sophisticated, and when they partied, they couldn't have fun until they were all drugged up or drunk. No wonder I never fitted in. Drugs weren't my thing. I could admit to having a few drinks whenever we hung out with his friends though; otherwise, I'd never have gotten through it. They weren't that friendly to me, and I always felt like they were putting up with me for Brad's sake. Whether I was being overly sensitive, I'd never know. Anyway, I was away from that scene now, and I could breathe. It really was a relief.

"I'm going to buy Meg some flowers because she's helped me so much since I've been here, but don't tell her. I want it to be a surprise. The rest of it will go into savings."

Carina smiled. "Well, congratulations again, lovely. May d'ere be many more bonii coming your way." She chuckled, as did I. Finnegan's word might stick—who needed bonuses when you had bonii?

Finnegan's phone rang. It was an annoying chime sound. He answered it. "Hey, Sid. What's the news?" Cat's bum. He was probably getting some inside information on the deaths. But why was I worried? I'd already written the initial article, which was about the mystery surrounding the deaths and how sad it was. It would be interesting to see if he had anything to say about it when he got off the phone. Maybe Bellamy was telling him what was in that letter? That was something I was itching to know. It didn't look like an obvious murder, maybe a murder-suicide, but they wouldn't have toxicology results back on the bodies. Which meant Bellamy couldn't have too much to impart to Finnegan. Maybe it was about a different case, or maybe he was asking him round for dinner?

It took a few minutes, but he finally hung up and looked at me. "I know what you're going to ask, and I'm only going to tell you if you promise that I get the article when they solve the crime."

As much as it pained me, being a fair person, I couldn't steal his information and write about it. "Of course it's yours. What kind of hypocrite would I be, complaining about my ex stealing my stories if I did the same to someone else?" Okay, so it wasn't exactly the same because he'd stolen stories I'd already written and spent weeks or months researching, but in principle, it was the same, and wasn't I asking Finnegan every five minutes not to steal my articles?

He turned his gaze on Carina and spoke in a proclamatory kind of voice, one you would imagine a medieval town crier to use. "Hear ye, hear ye, let it be known that Avery Winters has agreed not to take this information and use it in a story."

Carina rolled her eyes. "You're an eejit."

He smiled. "Why, thank you."

I cocked my head to the side. "Okay, so I'm waiting. Spill." Even if I couldn't use the info, I needed to know. Keeping me in suspense was totally unfair.

"There was a suicide note on the bed. Mrs Downs was dying of cancer, and he didn't want to live without her, so they poisoned themselves. They're waiting for the autopsies to be done, of course, but there was no forced entry to the home, so Bellamy thinks that's what it was. Bellamy said you found the door open. After an initial inspection, it looks as if they didn't shut it properly, and the wind blew it open. They're going to check if anyone has video footage of the street from neighbours' cameras, but right now, that's where they're at."

"What ab—" Oops. *Shut your mouth, Avery. Idiot.*

Finnegan raised a brow. "What about what?"

"Um, nothing." I'd almost let slip that they had a holiday to go on that was already paid for. How was I supposed to know that information? One of these days, I was really going to put my foot in it.

"No, you were asking what about…. I want to know."

"Well, I was going to ask what about their kids? Surely they wouldn't leave them parentless, but then, I didn't want you to say you weren't going to tell me." Oh, God, that was the lamest excuse ever. I knew they didn't have kids, and that was going to make me look like a dismally bad journalist.

He frowned. "You must think I'm a special kind of simpleton."

"No. I don't. But you are my competition, are you not?"

His expression relaxed, and what looked like regret flashed across his face. "I suppose so."

"Are they going to check if she had cancer? I mean with the doctors, not the autopsy."

"They already did. Bellamy spoke to her oncologist today. She had stage three breast cancer. She was responding to treatment, but the future was uncertain."

"Oh, okay. That's really sad." I wasn't going to argue that at stage three, she still had treatment options, and she was still relatively young at around forty. I didn't know her exact age, but going on how she looked when I'd last seen her, she wasn't old enough to just give up. Surely the doctor would have explained that to the sergeant, yet he was still going with the suicide option at this stage. "But they haven't closed the case, have they?"

He shook his head. "No, of course not. They're waiting on the autopsy, and they want to speak to their family, see if there could be anything else going on, but at this stage, it's looking like suicide."

"Right, okay."

"And you have to admit, dying on their anniversary is poignant, especially if it's because they loved each other and couldn't bear to be without each other."

Carina raised her brows. "Since when have you been such a romantic?"

He smirked. "Never. You know me. Two dates with the same woman is one date too many."

Carina rolled her eyes, then shook her head. "I'm waiting for d'e day when you meet d'e one. It'll happen. Casanova Finnegan is getting old. You want to find d'e right lady before you go bald."

I snorted. "That's some good advice, Carina, but you know some women love a bald head."

Finnegan looked at me. "Are you one of them?"

"Nope, although, there is more to attraction than the hair on a man's head. Never say never."

Carina smirked. "Well, now you don't have to shave your head, Finny. Avery prefers hirsute men."

Finnegan pulled a "what the hell are you talking about" face, and I held up my hand. "I hate to break it to you, Carina, but super hairy chests and backs are out... well, any hair on the back... and it wouldn't matter what his hair situation was, Finnegan is out altogether."

Finnegan jerked up to a rigidly straight sitting position and pouted. "You're mean. Why am I out? Women usually love me."

"I'm sure they do, and I know you don't really care what I think, but I'll tell you anyway. I've dated someone I worked with, and when it all went to Hades, I had to leave." Brad was a lesson learned. Never again. "And, also, you're not my type."

His brow wrinkled. "Why aren't I your type?"

I shrugged. *Because you're a heartbreaker and altogether too good-looking.* "I prefer blonds." Could pretend-me get any shallower? I wanted to laugh at how ridiculous I sounded—especially since I'd just said never say never in terms of a bald guy—but I needed to be believable so he would get off my case. I just hoped I wasn't being rude or hurting his feelings. If he told me

I wasn't his type, I might take that to mean he thought I was ugly. This was altogether a terrible conversation.

Carina stood and covered the short distance to a still-pouting Finnegan. She patted him on the back. "There, there, Casanova. You can't please everyone, you know. There are even some people who didn't like *Harry Potter*."

He looked at her. "The movie or the books?"

"Both."

His mouth dropped open in mock horror, and I laughed. "Okay, now you've forced me to hurt your feelings, can we get back to work? And for the record, I know I didn't really hurt your feelings."

"Oh, but you did." He gave me sad puppy-dog eyes.

Carina rolled her eyes. "Don't worry, Avery; he just has to click his fingers, and a woman comes running. It's about time someone other than me was immune to his charms."

Finnegan gave us both a serious look. "Trust me, ladies; it's a curse." Irritation flashed through his gaze, and he stood. "Who wants a tea or coffee?" If I didn't know better, he was getting uncomfortable and changing the subject. It took one to know one.

"I'm good thanks." I was planning on meeting Meg after doing a bit more research—the police might think it was suicide, but I knew better… at least I thought I did. In fact, I wanted to get those photos onto my laptop and look at them more closely. There might be a clue in there somewhere. The police were probably testing the food too. My guess on the cause of death would be poison, what with the vomit and Mr Downs not even making it out of the room. Mrs Downs being in the bathroom was a huge clue as well. You didn't crawl in there if you were feeling great.

Carina requested a cup of tea, and Finnegan left. She and

I stopped talking and got to work. I set up a document to track all the facts I gathered on the case.

1. *Suicide note—find out what was in it.*
2. *Poison—caused vomiting—blood and the usual—and quick death (they hadn't made it to dessert).*
3. *Enemies—Mr Downs's brother, and Henry Russo.*
4. *Mrs Downs had cancer. But how bad was it really?*
5. *Mr and Mrs Downs were happy with each other and had paid for a holiday.*
6. *No evidence of forced entry. Had they let in the butcher, or had they gone to buy the meat themselves? Had they accidentally left the door open after a friend visited or when they got home from somewhere? If not, how did the killer get in (if indeed there was a killer)?*

Wow, that wasn't a great list, but better than if I hadn't been there. Hopefully, I'd have much more to add to that in a few days. They were a local couple, so maybe Meg, Bailey, or their dad knew them? I'd start there, and maybe a visit to the butcher to see if that's where Mrs Downs bought the meat. It was a longshot, but maybe she'd said something weird or seemed upset. Even though the couple had told me they were happy, ghosts could probably lie, although why they would lie to me and leave a suicide note for everyone else was weird. Unless one killed the other, and the suicide wasn't mutual at all, and they'd literally taken their secret to the grave and beyond. *Argh, way to confuse things, Avery.* I shook my head and set that aside for the moment. As far as my investigation was concerned, it was a murder—whether it was a double murder or not, well, I'd have to keep an open mind.

When Finnegan returned, he plonked Carina's tea on her table and sat without saying a word. As he went back to work, I stood and packed up my stuff. It was time to get to the pub for afternoon tea and a chat with Meg, but I had one place to go on my way.

Petunia's Pretty Petals was a florist on the other side of the high street, opposite the supermarket. The building was a free-standing stone cottage with large glass windows and a slate roof. The other buildings on this side of the road were a mixture of terraces, and two semi-detached retail spaces. All were two stories, except for the florist. It was time to buy Meg that bunch of flowers she deserved.

The day was actually warm, at least for England, at twenty-four degrees, but stepping into the shop with its flag-stone floors and thick stone walls dropped the temp about six degrees, and I shivered, but it did smell lovely. The honeyed scent of summer blooms trickled over me, and I breathed it in, savouring the sweetness.

Large timber trestle tables laden with bunches of flowers and small pot plants filled the middle of the room and the far wall. Plants of various sizes grew from glazed pots that crowded together along the length of a third wall. All manner of pot colours were represented, from vibrant pink to deep blue and terracotta.

"Hello, lovely. Can I help you?" A woman came out from behind a counter to my right. She was taller than me and wore a black apron covered in small rainbows over her white shirt and black shorts. Her frizzy, untamed blonde hair wreathed a smiling olive-skinned face. Her friendly brown eyes regarded me. "Are you the new lady from Australia?"

I smiled. "Yep. I'm Avery." I held my hand out. "Pleased to meet you."

She shook it. "I'm Alison. Pleased to meet you too, and it's about time."

"It is. I would've introduced myself earlier, but things got a bit hectic when I arrived." I didn't bother elaborating because there was no doubt she'd have heard about my dramas via the village grapevine.

"Ah, yes, I heard about all that. Have you settled in okay now?"

"Yes, thanks. So, I'm here because Meg helped me a lot when I first arrived, and I wanted to buy her a bunch of flowers to say thank you. What do you recommend?"

She rested her hands on her hips. "What's your budget?"

"Forty pounds." That was a lot of money, but compared to the petrol she'd probably used ferrying me everywhere, it probably wasn't enough. I didn't want my flowers to look scrawny, like I didn't care enough to get her a good bunch.

Alison smiled. "That's a healthy budget. I'll be able to get you something I'm sure Meg will love. Come and have a look at these." She led me to a trestle table on the other side of the room where flower arrangements in square tubs with bows around them sat. One with shiny black-and-red variegated tulips caught my eye—so dramatic but not quite right. Scarlet roses were too romantic, and I couldn't remember what, but yellow roses were supposed to be bad for some reason—not that I believed in weird rose categorisations, but just in case Meg did, I wanted to choose something else. Then I saw it —*the* bunch.

"I'll have that one please."

Alison grinned. "Excellent choice." She leaned across the table and grabbed a bunch with a mixture of white, yellow, blue, and violet cottagey-type flowers. It was a happy arrangement that spoke of being carefree and joyful. I was pretty sure she'd like them.

As I was paying, I decided to finally involve a fellow villager in my enquiries. "Just a quick question. I hope you don't mind... but did you know Mr and Mrs Downs?"

"Yes. Mr Downs came in here three times a year—once for her birthday, once for Valentine's Day, and once for their anniversary. He was in here on Saturday buying her two dozen red roses. Why do you ask?"

Hmm, she mustn't have heard the news, but I needed to get a question in first. "I'm writing an article on them. Was Mr Downs happy when he came in?"

Her forehead wrinkled, her expression turning serious. "Yes. He was smiling, happy. He couldn't wait to give the flowers to Melissa. So, why are you writing an article?"

"How close were you to them?" Was I the right person to be telling her? Not that I had much choice now. Guilt elbowed me in the side, and I felt the pain. *Bad Avery.*

"Not super close. I've known them for a few years. They were always lovely customers." She eyed me warily. "What happened?"

I swallowed. "They died last night. I'm sorry."

Her mouth dropped open; then she slammed her hand over it, and a sheen of tears glazed her eyes. She lowered her hand. "What? How?"

"They think it was a suicide pact. Mrs Downs had cancer." How would she react to that? I crossed my fingers that she'd give me some insight.

She rubbed her cheek. "But she looked so well. They never said anything. Mr Downs was excited when he came in here. As well as being happy about their anniversary, he said he'd planned a weekend away in London next weekend. That doesn't make sense."

"No, it doesn't, does it? Well, I guess we can't argue with the police. If they find any other evidence, I'm sure they'll chase it up. Maybe don't tell anyone what I told you. I got my information a bit early because I work for the paper. I'm not sure if they've given an official announcement yet as they're waiting for toxicology reports and autopsies."

"Oh, of course." She shut her mouth and made a zipping motion across her lips with her fingers. "I'm a vault."

I smiled. "Thanks. And I'm sorry to have been the one to tell you. It's rather sad news."

"That's okay, lovely. I would've heard about it eventually." She handed me the flowers. "I hope Meg enjoys these."

"I'm sure she will. They're gorgeous. And it was nice to finally meet you."

"You too, Avery. Have a good day."

"Bye."

So, that was interesting. He was definitely happy before their anniversary. Had Melissa killed them both, or was it someone else? I pulled my notebook and pen out of my bag and wrote down what Alison had said and my thoughts on it before I walked into the pub and found Meg.

She was behind the bar pulling a beer, Bailey serving another customer next to her. "Hello." I smiled.

Meg looked up. When she saw me, she grinned. "Hey, Avery." Her eyes widened. "Those are gorgeous! Did someone give them to you?" Bailey glanced my way but gave no reaction before turning around to grab a bottle of rum from the shelf behind him.

"No. These are for you as a thank you for driving me everywhere. You've helped me so much. You really have." She finished filling the glass and put it on the counter. An older man took it, thanked her, and went back to his table. She came out from behind the bar, and I handed the flowers to her.

She shook her head. "You shouldn't have, but they are gorgeous. Thank you so much." She held them in one hand and hugged me with the other. I stole a quick look at Bailey, and he gave me a nod and a smile. I couldn't help but smile back, and when his whiskey-coloured gaze held mine for a beat too long, I didn't look away. A customer calling for his attention broke the spell… thank goodness. What the hell was I thinking, flirting with Meg's brother, or flirting with any man, really? Making my way on my own was a priority, and I wasn't the type of person who could muck around with someone and not develop feelings, and feelings were dangerous. *Stay away from the feelings, Avery. Safety first!*

Meg stared at me. "Avery, are you okay?"

I blinked. "Ah, yeah."

She turned her head and peered towards where I'd been looking, then turned back and smirked. "Were you checking out my brother?"

"Nope. No checking out going on at all."

She raised a brow. "I don't know if I believe you."

I shrugged. "There's nothing to see here. Honestly." Time to change the subject. "Are we having coffee and chocolate pudding or what?" I grinned.

She gave me a quick "I know what you're doing" look, then chuckled. "But of course. Go sit over there, and I'll be back in a jiff." She headed off towards the kitchen, and I took a seat at one of the few empty tables. The lunch crowd was pretty much done, but there were a few stragglers, or were those early birds for dinner, having an afternoon tipple?

Before long, she returned with two cappuccinos and two chocolate puddings with vanilla ice cream on the side. "Oh, wow, yum! Thank you. And you have to let me pay this time, or I'm not ever eating here again."

She pulled out a chair and sat. "Don't be ridiculous."

I gave her my best "don't mess with me" look. "I'm serious. I feel like a moocher, and I hate it."

Meg's expression softened. "Okay, hon, but I don't want you to pay every time. Why don't we make it that you can pay two out of three times?"

"Only for snacks or coffee. If it's a meal, I'm paying for mine ten out of ten times, okay?"

She quirked her mouth to the side. "Argh, fine. You're killing me, just so you know."

"You'll live. Speaking of which, did you hear the news?" I wouldn't normally tell her—or anyone really if I could help it —if something untoward had happened to me because I didn't want any sympathy, but I wanted her take on Mr and Mrs Downs. Meg and Bailey knew pretty much everyone within ten miles because their pub was famous for its craft beer and great food. Apparently, Bailey and his dad had developed a couple of beers that had proven popular with the masses. They even bottled and shipped to other pubs.

"What news? Not about Verity giving Mrs Carver the wrong shade of purple at the salon on Friday?"

I laughed. "Um, no, not that. I take it Verity is the local hairdresser?"

"Yes. She owns the salon, and Kim works for her as well.

They're so good that they're always booked out, but, well, some clients are extremely picky."

"What is the wrong shade of purple anyway? Purple is purple." I shook my head. "I'm taking it you haven't heard. Were you good friends with Mr and Mrs Downs?"

She sat up straighter. "Tom and Melissa? I wouldn't say we were close, close, but I've known them for years. They come in here once every couple of weeks for dinner. Such a lovely couple. Are you talking about their anniversary this weekend?" Everyone knew so much about everyone else's business around here—it was kind of scary.

"I was supposed to interview them about it, but when I went there this morning, the door was open. I went inside when they didn't answer, and I found them both dead."

She gasped. "Oh my gosh, Avery. Are you okay? Was there blood and guts? Carnage? Did you get any on your shoes?"

I wanted to laugh, but that would've been highly inappropriate. "Um, no to all those questions. I think they were poisoned, by the looks of things. Just quietly, the police think it's a double suicide. I'm not sure they're right."

A divot appeared between her eyebrows. "Why?"

"Mr Downs called me on Friday because they wanted an interview this morning and their anniversary mentioned in the paper. Why would they do that, then kill themselves before I'd interviewed them? And when I bought your flowers, Alison said Mr Downs told her they had a romantic weekend booked in London next weekend." I took a sip of coffee. "What I wanted to ask you is, what do you think? How were they last time you saw them?"

She stared at me, maybe assessing. "You know, if you think the suicide angle is suspect, I believe you. You were right about that land thing, and you uncovered who killed Fiona. You have a good nose for these things."

My chest warmed. It was rare that anyone gave me compliments, and even rarer for someone to encourage me and believe in me. "Thanks, Meg. That's nice of you to say. Can we keep this discussion to ourselves? I'm researching this because, of course, I want to make sure it wasn't a murder, but also, I want to write the article if it is, and I don't want Finnegan finding anything out. And if I get anything out of the police, it can't be shared, especially if it's second-hand information from Finnegan. He's the one who told me they think at this stage that it's a suicide pact."

She put her hand on her heart. "Of course you can trust me, but can I ask a question?"

"Shoot."

"You've said it a few times, that you don't trust Finny. Why? He's not a bad guy, you know. Did he do something?"

I spooned a mouthful of chocolate pudding into my mouth, to give me time to think. I knew she wasn't trying to attack me, but it felt like she was asking me to trust him, and I wasn't ready. But how to explain that without coming off like a crazy person? "Um, he hasn't done anything, really. When I first got here, he didn't want to introduce me to anyone, and, of course, he won't share information he gets from Bellamy. But it's more from past experience. I used to work with my ex, and he stole a couple of my stories. The other journalists there, especially the men, were very cagey when they had a good lead. I thought it was normal in that environment, so I've learned to protect my work."

She gazed at me and frowned, maybe figuring out how to respond. "I don't want to tell you how to suck eggs, but Finnegan's a good guy. He comes across as all cocky and arrogant, but it's a front. Don't tell him I told you though. If I'm ever not here and you need help, you can trust him. I promise."

I gave her a hesitant smile. "Thanks for the tip. Please don't hold it against me if I'm slow to catch on. Old habits and all that."

She smiled. "It's fine. I get you've been through a lot recently. Take your time figuring it out."

"Thanks."

"Oh, and you can also trust my brother." She waggled her brows.

I rolled my eyes and gave a small laugh to take the sting out of my words. "Stop already. I don't like to talk about the last twelve months, but suffice it to say, I'm not looking at getting involved with anyone any time soon. I need my own time and space. You know?"

"Yeah, I know. But if you do decide…."

"Ha ha, yes, Bailey will be first on my list. Happy now?"

She laughed. "Yes. Okay, so what else do you have on the deaths? You were there. Surely you noticed something."

"Other than the dead bodies, no. It looked like a normal dinner to me. The kitchen was a mess from cooking. The front door was open though, and I did tell the police." I furrowed my brow. "Surely that could mean someone else had been there."

She sipped her coffee. "Did it look like a forced entry?"

"I don't think so. Nothing looked scuffed or broken, but I didn't have a close look at the door." I lowered my voice, not that anyone else was listening to us, but you never knew. "I had a look around the house, just in case there was evidence I could use in my article. Everything was in its place—it didn't look like a burglary. Surely if someone had broken in, they would've stolen stuff?"

"Unless they were trying to make it look like a suicide."

"I figured that was the case, but I just wanted to make sure. So why would the police discount an open door?"

She shrugged. "They probably think the Downses forgot to close it properly. Other than what you've already told me, is there any other reason you think it's not a suicide?"

If only I could tell her, but I couldn't. "Just a gut feeling."

"Ah, the good old gut." She chuckled. "So now what?"

I swallowed another mouthful of pudding. "I'm going to chat to the local butcher after this. Hopefully they can corroborate that Mr or Mrs Downs was in a good mood. Surely you wouldn't be happy if you knew you were going to kill yourself?"

She wiped a bit of chocolate off the side of her mouth. "Maybe, or maybe not. If that's what you wanted to do, it's possible you'd be relieved and happy."

Cat's bum. She made a good point. How was I supposed to explain this away? Oh, how I wished I could just say that Mr Downs had told me they were in a good place and didn't kill themselves. I sighed.

"Don't worry, Avery. Worst comes to worst, you come to the conclusion that it was what the police say and move on. There'll be other stories."

"True." If only it were that simple.

"Hey, ladies."

I jerked my head up, and Meg smirked. "Hey, little brother. What's up?"

He gave his sister a dirty look and shook his head. "You told me to come by and tell Avery I could help her find a car. Don't act like you don't know."

I added my dirty look to his and raised a brow at Meg. Then I turned back to Bailey. "Hey, Bailey. Thanks. Yeah, I want to buy something reliable, but I can only spend fifteen-hundred pounds, and that is absolute max. Do you think you could find something for that?" I hated asking, but since Meg had put me on the spot and I really needed a car, I might as well just take the favour. I'd figure out a way to pay Bailey back later. Hopefully, he liked cake, and I could bake him a few.

He bit his bottom lip, and it wasn't sexy. Not. At. All. I kicked myself in the shin with my heel as a distraction. *Ow.* Meg must've seen me wince. "Are you okay?"

"Ah, yeah. Just remembered I forgot to hang my washing out this morning."

Bailey's amber eyes stared into mine. "I think it's doable, but you'd be looking at something like a Kia, and it's probably going to be more than ten years old."

"I don't mind. I just need something to run around in. As long as it doesn't break down, I don't care what it looks like. It can even have a few dents."

Bailey grinned. "Not too fussy, hey?"

"Nope. Not when it comes to cars, anyway. Grammar and punctuation are another story."

"You're in luck." Meg smirked. "Bailey's a good speller."

Bailey and I stared at Meg. We managed to be perfectly synchronized when we said, "Meg, stop!" Bailey and I looked at each other and laughed.

Meg, on the other hand, frowned. "Soooory. You can't blame a girl for trying. You two would be awesome together."

Bailey's brows drew down, and he blushed. The death stare he gave her made it clear he wanted to stop her from talking. I knew exactly how he felt.

I thought I'd save Bailey from an assault charge. "Meg, I'm

sure Bailey appreciates your efforts just as much as I do, but I'm not looking to date anyone, and I'm pretty sure if Bailey wanted to date someone, he has lots of other women he'd rather take out. Case closed." This was ridiculous. Were we in high school?

Bailey turned and gave me an apologetic look. "Sorry about my sister. She can be super annoying sometimes."

I smiled. "It's fine."

"So, about that car. I'll start looking tonight after work. When I find a couple that suit, I'll show them to you on the net, and if you like them, we'll go and look."

A kernel of excitement warmed my stomach. Getting a car would mean more freedom and more opportunity to cover stories outside our little pocket of the world. I knew Finnegan wrote stories about people from other villages because our paper serviced all the villages within a ten-mile radius. MacPherson didn't push me to leave the immediate area because he knew my car situation, but there would come a time when he would expect I was settled and ready to cover a wider area. That would also be helpful when the number of stories I was expected to write increased. I had another month, apparently, and my workload would increase by 50 per cent, then later, a hundred.

"That would be great. Thanks! I'm more excited than I thought I would be."

"Why don't you give Bailey your number? I might not always be here, and that way, you guys can organise your-selves." Meg said that with a totally straight face, but I had my doubts as to her motives. But then again, what would it hurt? The more friends I had here, the better, and Bailey seemed like a good guy.

"Okay, sounds good."

Bailey looked at Meg. "My phone's behind the bar. Why don't you just forward it to her."

Meg smiled. "Sure thing." She pulled her phone out, and shortly thereafter, my phone dinged. I put Bailey's contact in, and I was done. "Thanks."

"I'd better get back to work." Bailey gave us a nod and hurried back to the bar.

I finished my coffee and pudding. "I'm not going to hang around. I hope that's okay. I want to talk to the butcher, and I need to make an appointment to interview someone for another article tomorrow."

"Not a problem. I'll get back to work and help set up for the early dinner crowd. The oldies love to eat at five thirty, have a couple of drinks, then get home by eight." She chuckled. "Some days I envy them."

I laughed. "I hear you." I stood, and she did the same. "Thank you so much for afternoon tea."

"Any time." We hugged; then I grabbed my handbag and laptop bag and left. It was time to introduce myself to the butchers of Manesbury. Hmm, that sounded more gruesome than I'd like.

A bell tinkled when I opened the door. The butchery was typical of all the others I'd been in—tiled floors, glass counter displaying meat, and blokey guys standing behind the counter wearing navy-blue aprons. Out of the three butchers, I homed in on the oldest one—a salt-and-pepper-haired man in his fifties. He towered over his younger counterparts. His broad shoulders and muscled physique spoke of someone who wasn't letting themselves go with age. As I waited for him to finish serving an old lady, one of the younger butchers, a curly haired man who looked to be in his thirties asked what I'd like.

"Ah, nothing actually. I'm just here to speak to the boss."

Even if the guy who ran the place hadn't been the one to serve Mr or Mrs Downs, I at least had to ask for permission to speak to his staff. I'd started off on the wrong foot with Bethany and Joy—the sisters from hell—and I didn't want that trend to continue.

He smiled. "Well, you've got the right person. I'm Ben Greaves. What can I do for you?"

I quickly returned his smile, hoping to cover my surprise. Wow, served me right for making a judgement call. How annoying of me to assume. I hated when other people did that to me—assumed I was weak and vapid because I was a young, blonde woman. "Hi, Ben. I'm Avery. I've recently started work at *The Manesbury Daily*, and I'm writing an article about Mr and Mrs Downs. I heard they bought meat from here for their anniversary dinner."

He folded his arms and frowned. "I heard about them dying over their dinner. You're not suggesting my meat killed them, are you?"

My eyes widened, and I shook my head vigorously. "Not at all! I'm sorry. I'm more wanting to know who bought the meat, and what their state of mind was at the time. Was it him or her, and were they happy, cranky, sad?"

He gave me a wary look. "You live in Manesbury, don't you?"

"Yes. Just up the road from here."

"If I find out you're trying to pin this on my meat, I'll never serve you, ever, and you'll have to buy your meat from the supermarket or the next town over. Is that clear?"

I didn't see where the threat was in that, but whatever. "Yes, of course." I'd be more worried about a defamation case. "There's no way I would ever publish false information, and at this stage, I'm pretty sure your meat has nothing to do with why they died." It might have been the vehicle for poison, but as far as I was concerned, the leg of lamb was an innocent bystander.

He shot me one more "don't mess with me" look. "Right, well, Phil served them, so you can ask him." Ben turned to the older butcher. "Is that okay if you talk to her?"

Phil grunted. "Yeah, fine." Hmm, friendly lot.... Not.

I smiled, hoping to disarm his crankiness. "Hi, Phil. Sorry to bother you, but I won't take up much of your time. Was it Mr or Mrs Downs who bought the leg of lamb?"

"Melissa came in. She was in good spirits, smiling, telling us about their anniversary dinner coming up. She was sure the lamb was going to be a hit—it was one of her husband's favourites." His dour expression seemed to dour up a notch at the mention of "husband's." "Surprised me though because I thought she was a vegetarian. Why would you want to serve something you didn't want to eat on your own anniversary?"

"Indeed. I hadn't heard she didn't eat meat."

Ben jumped in. "She turned vegetarian when she got her cancer diagnosis. They thought it would help. I only know because one day, I asked her why she wasn't buying as much meat as usual—I thought maybe our products weren't up to scratch. She admitted she was sick and asked me not to spread it around. Not everyone knew, and she didn't want to have to talk about it all the time." He shook his head. "Meat's good for you. People believe every stupid thing they read."

I wasn't going to argue that maybe her doctor had recommended it, or that when you're sick, you'll do anything to get better, and what harm would it do to try that kind of diet, but I kept those words inside. Instead, I offered other ones. "Mmm, they do, which is why I want to get my facts straight. Is there anything else you remember, Phil?"

He folded his huge arms and looked down at me. "No."

Mmmm, okay. We must be done. "Right, well, thanks for your time."

Ben leaned his forearms on the counter and smiled. "Can I interest you in any of our delicious products?"

When I did my budget each week, I allowed for a certain amount of good-quality food. Some things you could scrimp on, but steak wasn't one of them. A tough, tasteless steak was a disappointment no one should pay for, even if it was cheap. I should probably cook a casserole because cheap cuts were awesome for that, but it was summer, and I couldn't be bothered. I eyed off their meatballs. "I'll take three meatballs, thanks."

"Coming right up." Ben wrapped the meatballs and rung them up. "Four pounds fifty."

I handed the money over and took possession of my meat. "Thanks. And thanks for your help with the other stuff."

Ben smiled. "Not a problem." The other butcher, a young man about my age with short brown hair and blue eyes, smiled. He'd been quiet the entire time, and he wasn't about to break his silence, but at least he was trying to be friendly.

"Bye. See you next time." At least that hadn't gone too badly. I had to live in this town, and the fewer enemies I made, the better.

I didn't have to go back to the office, so I took my stash home. I ever so quietly stepped onto the front porch and carefully put my key in the lock—avoiding Mrs Crabby was a serious business. If I'd thought she was cranky when I first moved in, I'd been in for an education. After being attacked by Crowley, she'd gone from Mrs Crabby to Mrs Crabbier. She'd blamed me for the whole thing, which was kind of right, but not really fair. It wasn't my fault that guy was a psychopath.

Yes, it was my fault he'd come to her place, but it wasn't like I'd started the whole thing.

I turned the key and pushed the door open. As I stepped inside and shut it behind me, careful to only elicit a hushed *click*, Mrs Crabby's door opened. Cat's bum. Sprung.

Mrs Crabby stood in her doorway and scowled. "Oh, it's you. I thought it might be someone else come to attack me, lured here by you."

I couldn't help it—my eyes rolled, and she saw them. She squinted, doubling her scowl power. "Nope, it's just me." There was no point arguing with her. I'd quickly learned that once she made her mind up, that was it. She was more stubborn than a one-ton bull who didn't want to be corralled. Maybe I should get her a big nose ring, and when she annoyed me, I could yank it. I bit back a smile.

"There's nothing funny about the situation, young lady. I still get headaches from where he hit me, and I had to pay for new locks."

As well as being as stubborn as a bull, she was also just as good at headbutting you with guilt. "No, of course not. I'm sorry to hear you're still getting headaches. Is there anything I can get you?"

She pressed her lips together. "No." She stepped back into her apartment and slammed the door. I sighed. I was never going to win with that woman. Thank God I'd signed a year lease, and she couldn't kick me out on a whim.

Oh well, now that I didn't have to be stealthy, I clomped up the stairs. I stuck the key in the lock. Still temperamental, I had to pull the knob while turning the key. It clicked, and I turned the handle and pushed the door open.

Oh God, not again.

You'd think I'd know better by now, but I didn't, and I

screamed. Why did people have to keep getting murdered in my apartment?

A woman lay on the ground, face up. She looked to be young, maybe eighteen or twenty. Blood covered her neck and stained her white top. I gagged.

I gripped the doorframe, my heart racing, and my heartbeat pounding loudly in my ears. Nevertheless, the familiar, unwelcome thud of Mrs Crabby coming up the stairs registered. Cat's bum. She was going to freak. She might even kick me out after what happened last time, lease conditions be damned. At least I knew where the pub was this time.

"What's all this commotion." She frowned, then gazed past me.

The dead woman jerked into a sitting position. Her eyes widened, and she disappeared. You had got to be kidding. She'd pranked me? A ghost had pranked me? And how the bejesus did she get in? I hadn't invited any ghosts into my place, not even my ghostly little assistant, Charles. I might give him the go-ahead soon, but I'd needed time to relax and process everything that had happened without being interrupted every five seconds, especially when those visits would be surprises, not prearranged get-togethers. I frowned.

Mrs Crabby turned to me. "What's wrong with you? Are you going to scream every time you enter your apartment? If you are, I'm cancelling the lease."

My shoulders sagged. "No, I'm not going to scream every time, but there was a mouse." I folded my arms and hardened my gaze. "Maybe I should complain to whatever passes for a renter's advocacy agency over here. We have one in Australia, so I'm assuming you'd have one here. Rats and mice spread disease. Maybe this apartment isn't fit for habitation? I could also leave a review on the internet." The internet was a huge place, and maybe no one would ever see said review, but she didn't know that.

She pursed her lips, then huffed. "I'll leave a mousetrap at the front door for you. You can come and get it later." Her mouth twisted from one side to the other, as if she wanted to say something else, likely mean. Thankfully, she either decided against it or couldn't think of something appropriately horrible and turned and made her way back down the stairs. My money was on her deciding against it—I had no doubt she would never run out of horrible things to say.

I hurried inside and shut the door. After placing my bags on the table, I put the meat in the fridge. I wandered from room to room, looking for the troublemaking ghost. I mean, who did that? Who pretended to have been murdered in a clear nod to a previous murder? My heartrate still hadn't totally slowed to normal.

When I finished searching, I returned to the living area and put my hands on my hips. "Whoever in Hades you are, show yourself." Nothing. "Coward." Was this the ghost Fiona —the previous dead person in my apartment—had been talking about when she said an angry spirit had been poking around the place? Maybe I should invite Charles in and ask him to check it out for me. Ever since he'd offered to be my guide in all things ghostly, I hadn't heard from him since the day I'd spoken to Patrick's best friend. Not that a week was that long ago.

My eyes widened. Come to think of it, could I get Charles to sneak into the police station and spy? If I could do that, I'd get heaps of information on whatever I wanted. Charles wanted to help me and ghosts, so surely he'd agree. Time to forgo my privacy. But how did I do this? Could I call to him quietly in here, or did I have to go outside and shout? I'd never tried to conjure a ghost randomly. If I ever wanted to talk to Fiona, I'd come here where I knew she was, the same with Patrick. Could Charles hear me no matter where he was?

Excitement swirled in my stomach. This could be a game changer—both for my articles and for me helping the dead get justice, and stopping others from being hurt. I licked my lips. Here went nothing. "Charles? Charles?" I held my breath and listened. Nothing. "Charles?" I sighed. Did I have to wait for him to approach me? Maybe he couldn't hear me because I was somewhere he hadn't been?

I grabbed my keys and phone off the table. Hmm, might as well take my laptop, too, so I didn't look sus returning to work. I'd try to talk to him outside the office, but if that didn't work, I'd go inside and ask Erin, the child ghost at the office, how to get in touch with him.

I stepped outside. Wow, that weather had moved in quickly. A charcoal-grey sky loomed above. Should I go back and get an umbrella? I turned. Mrs Crabby stared at me from her living-room window. Argh. No. I wasn't going back in at the risk of having her confront me again. Was it just rain or a storm? Maybe I should stay home.

Mrs Crabby opened the front door and stood in the doorway. "Stop loitering. Either come inside or go."

What the hell was wrong with this woman? I took a deep breath, hoping that the threatening clouds were of the rain-only variety. If it thundered, I'd have a panic attack. Stupid being-hit-by-lightning experience. Was I more scared of potential lightning and thunder or of the guaranteed cranky ogre standing between me and my apartment?

Off I went, crossing my fingers that I made it to the office before the sky drama started.

I passed Anna on the way. She stopped me. "Hey, Avery, right?"

I smiled. "Yes. Hi, Anna."

She returned my smile. "How have you settled in after all that hullabaloo with the estate agent?"

I tapped my foot and swallowed. The longer I stood out here, the more likely the storm would ambush me. "Not too bad, thanks. Slowly getting into the swing of things. Despite a few dramas, I'm enjoying it. I'm glad I came here." I glanced up. The clouds were darker than before, heavier. Ready to explode all over me. Okay, so I was catastrophising, but after everything I'd been through, I deserved some slack.

"If you need anything, let me know. And don't be a stranger—pop into the café and say hello. After that first visit, we haven't seen you since. I hope it wasn't the coffee." Her eyes held concern—she looked legitimately worried.

Should I, or shouldn't I? I gazed at her expectant face. No, I shouldn't mention that Joy was the opposite of her name. I could at least tell the truth… in some form. "It definitely wasn't the coffee. You have awesome coffee. I've just been trying to save money, and I make one at home of a morning, but I'll be sure to treat myself soon."

"You do that. If you get one of our cards, we punch a hole in it every time you get a coffee, and you get the fifth one free."

"That's an awesome incentive. Thanks for letting me know." A flash of lightning strobed over the street. I cringed, and my heart raced. I gripped my laptop bag. My breaths came faster.

"Are you okay?"

Thunder boomed.

I sucked in air, but each breath wasn't enough. *Was my throat closing?* I managed to squeak out an "I have to go," then sprinted the rest of the way to the office, prickles between my shoulders, waiting for the monster to strike. Rather than call out to Charles outside the office, I buzzed and went straight in. Dread followed me. I didn't even bother to annoy Bethany but headed straight up to the bathroom to get hold of myself.

I locked the door of one of two cubicles and sat on the closed toilet lid. After five minutes of slow, deep breathing and visualising golden retriever puppy dogs, the adrenaline come-down began. I rested my head in my hands and squeezed my eyes shut, denying tears of self-pity. When thunder cracked again, my stomach muscles tightened, but I kept with the slow breathing. *You're okay, Avery. You're inside. You're not a lightning rod, and your chances of being hit again are almost non-existent.* I wished I believed myself.

The hinges creaked as someone entered the bathroom. Carina's voice echoed off the tiles. "Avery, are you okay, love? I saw you rush past ages ago."

I swallowed and cleared my throat, banishing any evidence of fear from my voice... at least that was the plan. "I'm fine. Just don't like storms. You know how it is." I laughed nervously. Damn me, giving myself away.

Carina chuckled, but her tone was all warmth and under-standing. "I'm glad I don't know how it is. Don't be hard on yourself. Have you got PTSD?"

"Yes, I guess that's what you'd call it. I'm trying to get over it, but I'm not quite there yet." Nowhere near it, in fact. I stood and opened the door, not wanting to worry her further.

She cocked her head to the side and stared at me. "You okay?"

I gave her a small smile. "Yes. I'll be okay. Thanks for checking on me."

"I told you when you started here—if you need anyt'ing, I'm here for you. Don't forget it."

"Okay. I won't." It wasn't quite a lie, but it would have to be desperate circumstances. Bothering people was on my top-ten list of things I hated doing. Talking to Mrs Crabby was my new number one. It'd just replaced talking to my parents. I hadn't heard from them since I'd moved, and I wasn't about to call them. I was pretty sure my sister had updated them on the fact that I was here and alive.

"You ready to go back to the office?"

"Can I have one more minute? If I don't come soon, you can come back and drag me out." My smile was bigger than the last one as I tried to convince her. I needed to speak to Charles or Erin, and I obviously couldn't do that in the office… or could I? Maybe I could do that on-the-phone thing I'd done twice before?

She cocked her head to the side. "Okay, d'en. You're on. If you're not back in two minutes, I'm coming to get you."

She left. I counted a slow ten after the door shut; then I whispered, "Charles. Hello, Charles, are you around?" I bit my lip. *Please show up.*

A short, grinning form appeared in front of me. Charles gave me a cocky look. "You called?"

"Nice to see you too. And, yes, I called. I have a couple of questions."

"Shoot."

"Can you hear me calling you no matter where I am? Because I tried to summon you when I was in my apartment, and nothing happened, or did you just choose not to show?"

"If you're somewhere I can't access, I probably can't hear you. Also, it depends which dimension I'm in."

Oh, great, now there were multiple dimensions a ghost

could visit? "Um, how many dimensions do you have access to?"

He held up three fingers and pointed at one. "Here." He pointed at the next finger. "The muted reality which mirrors this one. It's where Patrick would have been if he'd managed to escape his little pocket. But that one's dangerous. Scary shadows lurk there, and I don't like it. A ghost can get hurt there. I've only been twice, and that was enough." He shuddered, then pointed to the last finger. "The third dimension is a mirror-image of here, but there are no live people, only ghosts. We gather and hang out. It's easier to be there and no one can hurt anyone. You can talk but not affect anyone else. I wouldn't call it heaven, but it's a place where ghosts don't have to concentrate to exist. It's harder to be here but much more interesting." He grinned. "Also, sometimes, if I'm busy and I hear you, I won't come."

"Oh, right." I glanced at the door. One of my minutes must be up by now. "I have to go in a sec, but I wanted to ask a favour. Can you go to the Cramptonbury police station and spy for me?"

He raised a brow. "You want me to spy?" A thoughtful look settled on his face, and he nodded slowly. "That could be fun."

"Can I invite you to my place from here? I mean, not for now—I'll work in the office for a bit." *Until the storm passes.* "But, I'd like to have a chat with you later, if that's okay."

"Yes, you can. So, you're inviting me into your flat?"

"Yes, I am. Charles, you're invited into my house. Please come later."

"Call me when you're ready because I have a very lax concept of time. If I slip into another dimension, time moves differently."

"Okay. Will do. Gotta go now. Bye." I gave him a smile and hurried out. Carina eyed me as I walked into the office.

"D'at was longer d'an two minutes. Are you all right?"

Finnegan wasn't here, so I could speak freely—not that there was anything much to say, but if he knew the storm had freaked me, he'd either make fun of me or get on my case. I wasn't in the mood for either. "Yes, thanks."

I sat at my desk and pulled out my laptop, then checked my emails. I had another article to arrange for tomorrow. Hopefully there would be no dead bodies when I arrived. I called Ian Jones who contacted the *Manesbury Daily* because he believed a sprite's face had formed in one of his tree trunks. Yep, now I was investigating tree sprites. He answered on the second ring and was amenable to me visiting first thing in the morning. Done.

I looked across the room to the window. There hadn't been a lightning flash since I'd come in, so that was a good thing. Maybe the worst of it had passed. Carina looked up from her computer screen. "What are you t'inking about?"

"Just whether or not I can brave the walk home. I don't mind the rain—it's just the noise. Do you think the worst of it is gone?"

She turned her head and looked out the window. "Maybe, but d'ere really is no telling. It could double back and hit us again. Who knows?"

I gave a wry smile. "Thanks for that helpful information."

She chuckled. "I'm finishing soon. I can give you a lift."

"Oh, you don't walk to work?" I had no idea where she lived. I'd just assumed she lived in the village too.

"Normally, yes, but tonight, I'm visiting a friend for dinner. They live about five miles d'at way." She gave a nod to the east, in the direction of my place and where I'd found Patrick.

"Okay. Since you won't be going out of your way, thank you. I'd really appreciate it." While Carina finished up whatever she was doing, I contemplated the Downses' case. A tingle of excitement replaced the fear in my belly from the storm. If Charles could listen in and maybe even read some of the documents they had at the police station—he'd have to wait for opportune moments, of course—I'd be in a better position than them to solve the crime. Hmm, could he even read? He'd died young. How much could someone learn after they were dead? Maybe he'd just have to listen in.

I was at least confident in what I knew after meeting the ghosts of Mr and Mrs Downs, something the police could never have. But having Charles in the station would be a massive game changer for my articles—both now and into the future. Hopefully, it would be as easy to implement as I thought.

Except, so far in life, easy had eluded me, and it probably would again. Maybe Charles was luckier than me. But then again, he'd died as a child. Was it possible to be any unluckier than that?

CHAPTER 3

The next morning, I turned up at Mr Jones's place at eight thirty and knocked on his front door. His cottage was a bungalow, which meant it was a single-storey home. We didn't use that phrase much in Australia, unless we were specifically naming an architectural period, like a Californian bungalow. Ah, the random information that buzzed through my brain while waiting for someone to answer the door.

I'd met with Charles last night. The plan was for me to do this article and for him to hang out at the police station and see if he could get some inside info on the Downses' case. He was going to find me when he was done.

The door opened, and a short, squat man in his forties stood in front of me, his green eyes on the same level as mine. He smiled and held out his hand. "You must be Avery Winters. Lovely to meet you."

I shook his calloused hand, which kind of felt like bark. Maybe he was super in tune with his trees and there really was a pixie face in the trunk. If ghosts existed, who knew what else was out there that I had no idea about? "Lovely to meet you, too, Mr Jones."

"Please, call me Ian." He stepped out onto the front porch, and I moved backwards. He shut the front door. "Come around the back to where the tree is." He stepped past me, down the two stairs, and around to his right. I followed him through a side gate to a long back garden that contained almost a forest of trees—a small forest, but a forest none-theless. There wasn't much grass because the thick canopy above the many trunks shaded the ground. The ground cover was more dirt and weeds than anything.

His backyard was on an incline that sloped towards the house. I couldn't see a rear fence from where we were, and I wasn't sure how far back his land went. He stopped not far into the canopy and rested his palm on a trunk that was wider than two of him side by side. The deeply ridged grey bark looked like any other oak tree, except for one smoother spot in the middle, which was about the size of a human child's head.

Ian grinned and ran a hand lovingly over the round spot. "Don't you see? Isn't she gorgeous?" He leaned his face towards the round spot and pressed his lips to it. I pulled an "ew" face. Was he going to make out with the tree… in front of me? *Please, God, no.* He pulled away from it before things got too heated. I blew out a relieved breath.

Now that he wasn't crowding the trunk, I could see it clearly. And there wasn't a face. There were knobby bits like lips where you would expect them to be on a face, but that was it. A smoothish oval shape with barky lips did not a pixie face make.

He hugged the tree. "Isn't she beautiful?"

"Um… yes." What else could I say? I didn't want to diss

his girlfriend, even if she was fifteen feet tall and as thick as they came.

"I have a surprise." He dropped his arms from the trunk and stood straight. "Can you take some photographs of this, please? I want them for prosperity, and so I can look back on this moment forever. When I was a teenager, our family house burnt down, and I lost all those memories." Sadness shone from his eyes. "My father died too. It was horrible. I dropped out of school and got a job to help Mum pay the bills."

"Oh, that is horrible. I'm so sorry." It was such a random jump in conversation, but I had a feeling that my superpower of people wanting to overshare was at play. Oh, joy.

He wiped the back of his hand across his eyes, then smiled. "It's okay, though, because now, I've found the love of my life." He stared at me expectantly. Oh, that's right, photos.

I pulled my phone out and brought up the camera app. "Ready to go."

Ian reached into his pocket and pulled out a small purple-velvet box. My eyes widened. Oh my giddy aunt's underwear, he wasn't! Oh, but he was. Ian knelt on one knee and stared up at the love of his life. I clicked off a couple of shots, which was lucky because in my shock, I almost forgot.

He opened the box, revealing a small copper ring with a black stone instead of a diamond inset into it. The earnestness and love in his eyes as he looked up at his beloved was both frightening and sweet. He took a fortifying breath. *Click.* "Pixie of the oak, you've been there for me in my brightest days and darkest nights. I've watched you grow over the last ten years, and I love you now more than ever." I took another photo, but really, I should be videoing this. I doubted I'd ever see anything like this again. "Will you do me the honour of marrying me?"

I wasn't sure what would happen when the tree didn't say anything. Would he take that as a rejection? When the silence continued for a beat too long, I couldn't help it. I put on a high-pitched pixie voice. "Yes, Ian. Of course I'll marry you."

Ian whipped his head around to look at me. "Shush! I can't hear what she's saying. This isn't a joke, you know."

I pressed my lips together. "Oops, sorry."

He turned back to the tree. "Sorry, go on, my love." I bit back a sigh and waited. The breeze rustled the leaves, which must've been the sign he was waiting for. He jumped up and threw his arms in the air as if his favourite football team had just scored a goal. "Yes! She said yes!" He bounced around for a moment, then placed the ring on a small bit of bark that was sticking out. The next storm would surely blow the ring off, but that wasn't my problem.

I held my phone up to take a photo of the lucky couple. "Smile."

⚜

When I got back to the office, no one else was there, not even Charles. It was only nine fifteen, so there was plenty of time for him to spy on Bellamy and report back. Except I had no idea when Bellamy's shifts were. He could have done nightshift for all I knew and was home sleeping already. Surely Charles would come soon and let me know if that was the case.

To distract myself, I got to work on the article. "Pixie in the Tree, Will you Marry Me? Manesbury Local's Flowery Proposal as Love Blooms." When it was done, I laughed as I pressed Send on the email to Mr MacPherson. It seemed as if the level of crazy was escalating, being revealed to me bit by bit. Was it a ploy to keep the nuttiest of the residents away from me until I'd well and truly settled in?

"Hey, Avery."

I jolted back and gasped. "Grrr, Charles, don't do that! You almost scared me to death. If I die, who's going to help the ghosts?" And wasn't that one of the most insane things I'd ever said. Maybe I belonged here.

He smirked. "Gotta keep you on your toes." His smirk faded. Had there been a problem? "I got into the station, but then another ghost kicked me out."

"What? I didn't think ghosts could hurt other ghosts."

"They can't, not really, but they can give off energy that pushes the other ghost's energy away. This ghost was older than me and strong. He used to run that station."

"Ah, I know who you're talking about. I've met him a couple of times. Bummer. Maybe I could talk to him and get him to understand that you're working with me?" Unless he didn't want me getting any extra information either. But why should he care? He was dead.

Charles didn't look convinced. "He was a hard nose. He didn't like me at all. Bad judge of character, obviously." He folded his arms.

If there was one thing I'd learned during my years of being a journalist, people usually had good reasons for how they acted... well maybe not usually. Let's go with sometimes. "Did you do something to upset him?"

He pouted. "Um.... I'd rather not say."

I rolled my eyes. "How are we supposed to get information if you're doing your best to be rude?" He wasn't normally rude to me, but he was cheeky. "What did you do?"

He huffed. "Fine, I'll tell you. He asked who I was, and I

wouldn't tell him. When he threatened to kick me out, I called him a pig."

My shoulders sagged. Why did everything have to be difficult? "Why didn't you just answer him?"

He looked down and kicked the ground with the toe of one shoe. "He would recognise my name... from before."

My brow wrinkled. "What, why?" The ghost policeman's clothes and hair did look like it was from the first half of the last century, so they could've been alive at the same time, but what were the odds of them knowing each other? Or had Charles done something to this ghost after they'd both died?

The young boy shrugged. "Well, I suppose I'll get going now."

I narrowed my eyes. "No, you won't. You didn't answer my question. You offered to help me, remember? If you've changed your mind, say so now, and I'll never call on you again." People had let me down over and over and over again, so it wouldn't take me long to get past it, but I wouldn't lie—I'd be sad. Charles was growing on me, not to mention losing the chance at getting inside information would definitely hurt.

He rubbed his head, scruffing up his brown hair, then finally met my gaze. "I haven't changed my mind. But I don't want you to hate me."

Oh. The guilt and sorrow dampening his features made my heart squeeze in sympathy. He was just a kid. What could he have done that was so bad? And it wasn't like kids had the best decision-making skills. "I promise I won't hate you."

"You can't promise that. You don't know what I done."

"I don't know what you *done*, but you don't seem like an evil psychopath. Just tell me what it is, and we'll figure out a way to get past it."

Before he could answer, Finnegan ambled through the

door. *Ah, cat's bum.* I stared at him. Had he heard me talking? He stopped in front of my table, in the exact same spot Charles had been standing in. The ghost disappeared. Bummer. Would he come back later and tell me what he'd done? What if I never heard from him again?

Finnegan gave me a weird look. "Who were you talking to? You're not on the phone." Okay, so that answered that question.

I looked at my desk, where my phone sat facedown, clearly doing nothing. "Ah, just talking to a ghost." That had gone down so well last time when I wanted him to leave me alone out the front of Mrs Crabby's. Maybe he'd get annoyed at me pulling out the crazy card again and leave me alone.

He frowned. His closed mouth shifted from side to side; then he shook his head and went to his desk. Yikes, had I taken it too far? At least I knew what reaction I'd get if I said it in an honest way—he'd think I was crazy. But then again, if I was ever in a situation where a ghost he'd known as a live person was around, I could back myself up. Not that I wanted to confide in him, or anyone. Okay, so I was lying just a little bit. It would be nice to have someone to bounce this stuff off, to chat about it with. Keeping secrets and making excuses was tiring, and so was irritating others. I'd already pushed Finnegan a hair too far. Who would be next? And, yes, I did get that I'd meant to annoy him earlier, but I didn't hate him, and I didn't want him to hate me. We had to work together and live in the same small village. Making enemies on purpose was stupid.

"Sorry, Finnegan. When I'm stressed, I talk to myself. It's embarrassing, but there it is." My cheeks heated, more for the remembered shame of being wrong and having to admit it rather than me actually being embarrassed in this moment. It took me back to all the times I'd had to apologise after being chastised by my parents or Brad for things that I now realised weren't even wrong. When I ruminated on it, I could see that they kept me in a constant state of insecurity and feeling like a burden. The rush of realisation sent a wave of heat through me that ended in the burn of tears. Damn it; I wasn't going to cry about this. Better I realised these things now than never, though. Growth was painful but necessary, and wasn't that one of the reasons I came here?

Finnegan looked over at me, his expression serious but unreadable. "Oh, right." He eyeballed me for another moment before turning to his laptop and opening it.

I held back a sigh. I'd pushed him too far, but I wasn't going to grovel. My life was what it was, and seeing ghosts was something I had to keep to myself, no matter the stupid things I had to say to hide it and the opinions others would develop about me in the meantime. I was strong. I could do this.

It was time to finish my conversation with Charles. From now on, I'd be more careful. It wouldn't have hurt to have taken my phone out and pretended, which was what I was going to do now. I stood, grabbed my phone off the desk, and went downstairs and outside. I put the phone to my ear. "Charles, hello." That was my way of calling him that didn't look weird. Hopefully he'd turn up.

I wandered up and down the laneway, waiting for him to appear. On my third lap, he materialised in front of the office door, his young face set with all the gravity of a doctor who was about to tell someone their relative had died. He looked up at me, his hands hanging limply by his sides. "I used to steal stuff from the market—mostly food—because we were poor, and I was hungry. He caught me once, gave me a warning, and dragged me home to my parents. My father was mortified.

He belted the living daylights out of me. Said I was stupid for getting caught."

I cocked my head to the side. "That's not so bad… I mean what you did. Your dad belting you though…."

He shrugged like it was no big deal. "It was what they did back then. Weren't unusual. But that's not the bad thing."

My forehead tightened. "Oh." I had a feeling this wasn't going to be good. "What else happened?"

"When the sergeant was there, he told my father off for having no control over me. He also saw my father was wearing new boots and questioned him about where he got them. My dad said he bought them from another village a couple of weeks before. The sergeant couldn't prove he stole them, even though he clearly had—our house was little more than a shack, and neither of my parents worked. Where was he going to get the money for new boots? Anyway, the sergeant said he was going to keep an eye on my father, and that if he stepped out of line, he would throw him in the clink." He rubbed his forehead. "The next day, my father used me to lure him to a quiet laneway—he got me to steal something—and he called the sergeant to dob me in—but I didn't know what he planned, honest." He shook his head, almost to himself. "My dad's mates made sure no one else was there to see, and when the sergeant followed me into the laneway, my dad walloped him over the head with a huge piece of timber so many times until, well…." His shoulders sagged, and his head slumped forward. I almost didn't make out his whispered, "It were all my fault." I was trying to find the words to answer when, without looking up, he whispered, "That night, Dad killed me because he knew I'd tell. I didn't want to keep it to myself. We both knew I'd cave eventually."

I gasped, horror and sorrow expanding inside me until I

thought I'd burst. And now I knew even less what to say.

I thought I'd had it tough. What a whinger I'd been. As bad as my parents were, they'd never killed me to keep me quiet. I swallowed the tingle in my throat that heralded tears. This poor kid. All I wanted to do was gather him in my arms and tell him everything was going to be okay. But he was a ghost, untouchable, and nothing was going to be okay. It was too late.

My voice was gentle. "Charles, please look at me." I waited a moment. "Please." He finally raised his head, his eyes flooded, his cheeks glossy with the overflow. "You were just trying to please your dad and survive. It's not your fault. You didn't deserve that, and neither did that policeman, but that's all on your dad. You didn't decide to kill anyone, and you didn't know what your dad planned... did you?"

He shook his head. "No, or I never would've led him there. But still... it's all my fault."

"No, no it's not. You need to forgive yourself. I bet the sergeant recognised your face, but he doesn't hate you. He likely hates your father. Would it make you feel better if you could apologise?"

"But I called him a pig."

"Why did you do that?"

He shrugged. "I dunno. I was scared, and angry, I suppose, but not really with him."

"With your dad?"

He nodded and sniffed, then rubbed a hand across his eyes.

"So, what do you think? I'll take you and you can apologise? And if the policeman doesn't accept it, that's his problem, not yours. You're a child... or were a child when it happened. It's not your fault."

"But you don't know everything. How do you know it's not my fault?"

I gave him a small smile. "Humans have learned a lot since you died, and one of those things is that children's brains aren't fully developed, especially when it comes to reasoning and assessing the future impact of a choice made now. Not only that, your dad had power over you—you loved him and wanted to do what he said; you trusted him, or you were terrified of what he would do if you didn't obey. If you'd known what he was planning, you would never have lured the policeman there, would you?" If he said yes, I was going to be sad, but still, he'd been so young, and his father was obviously an abusive piece of—

"Of course I wouldn't have. I might've even run away instead. It would've been better than getting killed by my own father." He wiped his arm across his runny nose. He was still such a kid.

"Okay, so I'm right. I'll let you in on a little secret." I looked around as if making sure not to be overheard. My gaze found his again. "I'm usually right." I grinned. I was only half joking. At least coming here had given me room to breathe and realise that I was correct more often than anyone back in Australia ever gave me credit for. "So, whadda ya say?"

He bit his bottom lip and nodded. "Okay, Avery. I'd like to. Thank you for believing me."

"I'm also a good judge of character, and I can tell you're a good person, Charles. It doesn't matter who your parents are… or were—we all still have choices as to who we want to be, and we can definitely be better than they are. We also deserve better from others too. Don't be afraid to expect that." *Look at me, giving great advice.* Now I just had to take it myself.

CHAPTER 4

That afternoon at home, I called out to Charles, hoping we could pay Sergeant Fox a visit. I wasn't sure how we'd manage a conversation inside the police station where everyone could hear us, but maybe we could do it outside in the parking area.

But Charles didn't appear. Rather than being busy, I had the feeling he was avoiding it. I hoped he hadn't changed his mind, or I'd never get the information I needed.

I couldn't let this hold up my investigation though, which was why I'd just gotten off the bus and had walked five minutes to Mr Downs's workplace, a large site containing a huge factory-style red-brick building and oversized car park. Both cars and concrete trucks were parked there, and a delivery truck was dropping something off. Looked like business was booming. It was surprising, considering one of the business's owners had just died. You'd think they'd close for a day or two out of respect, but I guessed customers wouldn't always understand, especially since time was money on a building site. And we all had deadlines.

I stepped through the front door into a roughly five-by-five-metre reception area to the tinkling of a bell that hung above the door. A fish tank replete with colourful coral and fish sat against the wall to my right, and the receptionist desk sat on the wall straight in front of me. A freckled redhead, younger than me, looked up and gave a friendly, albeit subdued, smile. "Can I help you?"

"Hi. I'm Avery Winters, and I'm from the *Manesbury Daily*. I was wondering if I could speak with Henry Russo, or anyone else, really. I know it's a big ask, but I'm doing an article on Mr and Mrs Downs and what they meant to the community." As soon as anyone heard "murder investigation" they'd likely clam up. There was no reason for anyone to know why I was really there.

Her smile fell, and she allowed her sadness to show. "Oh, Mr Russo isn't here right now, but I'd be happy to talk to you, and Shelley from accounting would probably be happy to as well—she was actually quite good friends with Mr and Mrs Downs. They played tennis together once a week."

I took out my pad and pen and wrote it down. "Thank you so much. Do you mind if I sit?" I nodded to a chair that sat just in front and to the right of the table, next to the fish tank.

"Of course, Miss Winters."

"Please, call me Avery." I smiled, hoping to give off the vibe of an understanding, caring party, which I was, of course. As much as I wanted a good article and to expose the murderer, it wasn't for entirely selfish reasons. Mr and Mrs Downs deserved justice, and depending on why they were killed, the killer still might have more victims in their sights.

"Thank you…, Avery. And I'm Sandra. Where should I start?"

"How long have you worked here?"

"Three years. This was my first job out of school. Mr Downs actually interviewed me. He was very friendly back then and has been a good boss ever since." She gave a sad smile, as if remembering kind moments they'd shared. "He was an easy-going guy and always spoiling his wife. She came in once a week, and they'd eat lunch in his office, or he'd take her out." She shook her head. "He was so devastated when they got her cancer diagnosis, but they remained positive. He told me a while ago, that the chemo had shrunk the tumours, so it all looked good. They were really looking forward to their anniversary." She dropped her gaze and stared at the table, then snatched a tissue from the box next to her phone and wiped her eyes. She sniffled. "Sorry about that."

"Hey, no problem. I can't imagine how horrible this has all been. When I turned up, I was actually worried you might've been closed."

She sniffled again. "Ah, my other boss, Mr Papadopoulos suggested it, but…" She lowered her voice. "Mr Russo said we had too many contracts to honour, and he didn't want to lose any of the work. He's always been more of the driving force. When I started here, they were in a place a third the size of this. They bought this and moved last year." She bit her lip. "Obviously, don't put that in the story, please. I don't want to get in trouble."

"Of course not. Don't worry. I promise it will just be the good stuff." I gave her an understanding smile and made more notes. "Also, totally off the books, but just because I'm curious, did Mr Russo and Mr Downs get along?"

Her gaze pinged around the office, and she kept her voice

low. "They were fine until about a year ago." Her brow furrowed. "Actually, just after we moved in here. It was weird because I thought they should be happy they were making so much money and the business was growing, but they started fighting. It was to the point where they only communicated via their secretary or the other partner, Mr Papadopoulos. I don't know what it was about though."

"Oh, okay. So maybe Mr Russo wouldn't be great to talk to if he didn't like Mr Downs."

"Probably not."

The bell above the door tinkled, and Sandra jerked her gaze over my shoulder. She closed her mouth, then forced it into a fake smile—as the purveyor of many fake smiles, I could recognise one at fifty paces. "Um… hello, Mr Russo. I have those files you asked for. Jenny's having a late lunch, but she left them here in case you came in when she was gone." She jumped out of her chair and reached over to grab a small pile of blue manilla folders.

Mr Russo reached the table and stared down at me. His lack of smile could be attributed to the fact that his business partner had just died, or it could be because he was a grumpy pumpernickel. "Who are you?" Looked like Mr Russo was definitely a grumpy pumpernickel.

I stood and offered him my hand. "I'm Avery Winters. I'm here to do a story on Mr and Mrs Downs for the *Manesbury Daily*. I'm sorry for your loss."

He grabbed my hand, gave half a pump, and dropped it. Not the friendliest little possum I'd ever met. If only Mr Downs hadn't gone into the light before telling me why they were at odds. I might never find out now because this guy sure as Hades wasn't going to tell me. "Thank you. I have nothing to say on the matter. I suggest you get whatever you need from his mother. I hear they were close." He turned from me and looked at Sandra. "Why don't you have an afternoon break? I'm sure you need it." *Afternoon break*, in an office? That was a new one.

"Ah, yes, sir."

He looked at me. "Good day, Miss Winters. I'm sure you know the way out."

Argh. Anger pulsed inside me. So rude. I wanted to punch him in the face, but going to gaol for him was totally not worth it. And since when had I become so violent? Maybe since fighting off a killer had me on edge. I pushed those thoughts away and focussed on the now. What was he hiding? "Of course I do." I looked at Sandra who had grabbed her hand-bag. "Thanks for your time." I stood. "At least someone in this place has manners." As I passed Russo, I gave him a death stare. Then I followed Sandra out the door and caught up to her. "Sorry about that. I hope I didn't get you in trouble. Is he always that cranky?"

She kept walking, and we ended up at a green mini. "More or less. Let's just say his issues with Mr Downs weren't the only issues. Anyway, I'm sorry I can't say any more, but I don't want to lose my job."

"Sorry. And I'll keep your name out of the paper. Just in case."

"I'd appreciate it. Thanks."

"Can I give you my number, on the off chance you think of anything else?"

She glanced at the building, probably checking whether the boss from hell was watching. "Sure." She took out her phone, and I gave her my details. "Have a good afternoon, Avery."

"You too, Sandra, and thanks again."

She got in her car and drove off. Maybe I could call and speak to the accountant... Shelley, wasn't it? But not today because Russo was there and on the warpath. I'd leave that for tomorrow. As far as suspects were concerned, Mr Russo was my number one at this point. He certainly had the demeanour for it.

The next interview on my list would have to be Mr and Mrs Downses' family members. Maybe they could shed more light on things. And his brother. Although how safe I'd be trying to interview a potentially aggressive drug addict, I didn't know. I'd start with his mother and go from there.

I hopped on the bus and returned home. Maybe I'd get lucky, and Charles would come visit when I called. Unfortunately, when I walked in the door, there was a ghost waiting, and she was again lying on the floor pretending to be dead, blood and all. I shut the door, ignored her, and stepped on her on my way to the kitchen to put my bag on the counter. I hoped I hid the cringe well when I trod on her stomach—that was creepy, even though I only experienced cold ankles.

My ploy worked. She jumped up and followed me into the kitchen. I took milk out of the fridge and poured it into a coffee cup, followed by coffee I'd made this morning in my Italian stove-top percolator. I put the cup in the microwave and set it for a minute and a half, then turned to face my uninvited guest. "Hello."

She cocked her blood-smeared head to the side and regarded me. I gave no reaction except for boredom. Was this the scary ghost Fiona had warned me about?

Her hazel eyes narrowed. "You can see me, but you're not scared. What's with that?"

I smiled. "I can see ghosts, and since you're already dead, what's there to be scared of?"

She raised her arms and waved them above her head. "Oooooooh." She wailed loudly for another minute.

The microwave dinged. I mashed my lips together to prevent a smile and turned my back on her to retrieve my coffee. I wandered past her and sat on the couch. It was tempting to put on the TV and ignore her a bit more, but curiosity was a persistent beast once she tapped me on the shoulder. The ghost had followed me to the couch. I looked up at her. "Feel free to sit. I'd offer you a drink, but…." I shrugged. A distant part of my brain marvelled at how cool and collected I was being. The Avery I had become was insanely different from the one I'd been a mere year ago… or even a month ago.

She quirked her mouth to the side, then sat next to me. "You sure I can't scare you even a little bit?"

I smiled. "No, not even a little, unless you threaten to drag Mrs Crabby up here."

She wrinkled her brow. "Mrs Crabby?"

"Yes, the lady downstairs who owns this place. She can be frightening sometimes."

The young woman blinked, her expression blanked for a moment. Finally, she smiled. "I hear your name is Avery. I'm Everly. Our names almost sound the same. Match made in heaven? You can call me Ev for short, if you want."

"Okay. Nice to meet you, Ev. Please don't call me Av." I chuckled. I hoped she didn't call me Av to annoy me. Finnegan would do something like that. I resisted the urge to roll my eyes at the thought of him. Gah, why did I let him get to me? Maybe a bit of it was guilt at upsetting him when he really didn't deserve it. I'd tried to make it better, but it hadn't worked. He might be someone who just needed time to cool down. I supposed I'd find out soon enough. "So, how is it that you can come into my apartment uninvited?"

She crossed her legs. As she settled back into the couch, the blood covering her disappeared, as did the angry red wound across her throat. Well, that was much pleasanter. "This used to be my apartment... for a year, anyway."

Oh, wow. "How old are you?"

"Eighteen. I moved in here when I was seventeen and a half. I was killed about a year after I moved in. Here lies Everly—born 1968, died 1986. Ha, funny how the numbers are almost the same." She frowned. "There wasn't enough time in between those dates. I was ripped off."

"Were you killed here, in the apartment?"

She shook her head. "No. I was killed out there somewhere." She waved her hand.

Sorrow for the young life cut short constricted my heart. It looked as if hers had been a violent death too. How horrific and unfair. "Did they ever catch who did it?"

She swallowed and bit her bottom lip. "No, and they never found my body either."

"Oh." Her family must've been devastated. Not only was she taken from them in the worst possible way, they never had closure or any answers. "Do you know where your body is?" Maybe I could help? If she could tell me where it was, I'd be able to tell the police. Figuring out how to get them to believe me would be another thing though. Unless I could "stumble" upon her remains? She'd been murdered so long ago that she'd likely be bones; unless someone had stored her remains in chemicals or something.... *Argh, don't go there, Avery.*

She shook her head. "No. I have no idea."

"Did you want me to try and help you? Is that why you're here?"

Confusion settled on her face. "No. I live here. I come and go, but this is still my house." She gave me an assessing look. "Hmm."

I had no idea what the hmm was for, so I chose to ignore it. I hated playing games. If she had something else she wanted to say, she could say it. I didn't have the patience to guess. "Oh. Okay. So, does that make us flatmates?" I wasn't overjoyed at the prospect. Did this mean I'd never get peace and quiet and time to just chill on my own? This was supposed to be my time to be by myself and learn to deal with things my own way. Would having a companion—albeit a dead one— affect that? If I had a choice, I'd move out and be somewhere by myself, but at this point, I didn't.

She shrugged. "Are you moving out?"

"No."

"Well, then, I guess we're flatmates." She smiled. "I might enjoy having company for a change… well, company that can see me."

My eyes widened as a potential major problem hit me. "Um… we don't have to share a bed, do we?"

She looked at me as if I were stupid. "No. Of course not. I'm a ghost. I don't need to sleep."

"Okay, that's good. I just wasn't sure if… you know, you went through the motions of pretending to be alive. Sorry if that sounds stupid—I'm still getting used to how all this ghost stuff works."

"Yeah, I know you're new to this. I heard you talking to that Fiona woman. Nice work on that case, by the way. You did good." She pulled a silver necklace from under her white top and fiddled with it.

Oh, so she'd spied on us. At least I didn't have to explain everything to her about why I was here in the UK. She'd probably heard some of it when Meg was over, and we were chatting. It also reminded me that I needed Charles to get his act together. It was a genius idea for him to spy at the police station. If only I could convince him to apologise. "Thank you. That's nice of you to say."

She jumped up. "Anyway, nice to meet you. I've got stuff to do. I'll see you later." Before I had a chance to say goodbye, she disappeared. Well, that was... interesting. I would've asked more about who she was, but I hadn't wanted to be invasive, and if she was murdered and lived here at the time, there was likely to be something in old newspapers. I wouldn't ask Mrs Crabby about it though because it was probably a touchy subject, unless she wasn't even living here at the time. Hmm, nope, still not going to ask her. Seeking her out was asking for trouble as much as picking up a funnel web spider was.

I looked at my watch. My curiosity would have to wait until tomorrow because it was after four, and the main library —where I'd imagine the records were kept—would be closing soon, and it was at least a thirty-minute bus ride and walk away. Instead of stressing about it—and worrying about Charles—I looked up the contact details for Mr Downs's mother. She wasn't hard to track down because she lived in Cramptonbury. As devastated as she'd be, I crossed my fingers that she'd agree to talk to me.

As I dialled her number, I ignored the waves of unease breaking inside my stomach. This was the worst part of my job—talking to people who had recently lost a loved one. I felt like a vulture, picking off the flesh of a living being, taking my pound of information, even though I knew it brought pain. But then again, they would've been overcome with grief anyway, whether I'd bothered them or not. That was the only thing I could say that made me feel even slightly okay about it… oh, and the possibility I could help solve the mystery on the off chance the police weren't going to be able to. But in this case, I couldn't say that to Mr Downs's mother since they were still labelling this a double suicide, or at the worst a murder-suicide.

"Hello, who is this?" The woman's voice was tired, as if every word was a major effort.

"Hello, Mrs Downs. My name is Avery Winters. I work for the *Manesbury Daily*, and I'm doing an article on your son and his late wife, about how valued they were in the community. I was wondering if I could make an appointment to talk to you one day that suits you."

The phone went quiet. Guilt jumped up and down on my shoulders, and he was wearing his favourite sprinting spikes. Maybe I should hope she said no because that interview was going to be depressing, and I was going to feel bad for putting her through it the whole time I was there, and probably for some days and weeks afterwards.

She cleared her throat. "Okay, Miss Winters. I'll see you tomorrow at ten. Do you need my address?"

"Ah, yes, thank you." I had it from my online search, but there was no need to say that and scare her. I pretended to write down what she said; then we said goodbye and hung up. Looked like I'd have to drag my guilt cloak around with me a while longer, but it was worth it if I made inroads into the Downses' case.

Who knew? I might be the only person still searching for answers, and after the promise I'd made to Mr Downs, I wasn't going to give up now.

CHAPTER 5

I slept in and got straight on the bus at nine twenty rather than head into the office first. The bus trip wasn't long at all since Cramptonbury was the next village over. As I stepped off the bus, my phone rang. I won't lie—when Bailey's name flashed on the screen, the traitorous butterflies in my stomach took off, flew into each other, then fell in a heap. Argh, the sooner I got over my little crush the better. Not only did I want time to learn who I was, but getting involved with anyone I had to see regularly because we lived so close was a huge mistake. At least 30 per cent of marriages ended in divorce, and I would hazard a guess that the average romantic relationship that never even made it to marriage was even more at risk for a disastrous ending. I could do without that grief in my life and having to confront any dating mistakes multiple times a week as we passed on the street. I had better things to do.

All giddy feelings now squashed, I answered it. "Hey, Bailey." I'd ask what was up, but I was going to assume it was about a potential car, which was kind of exciting. Being subject to sporadic bus timetables was the worst thing about my move —not only was there just one bus in each direction every hour, but sometimes they just didn't show up. Hmm, maybe I should write an article on it—"Exposing Manesbury's Shameful Public-Transportation Underbelly. One woman recounts her tragic story." I smiled. What an exposé.

"Hi, Avery. I'm calling because I found a couple of cars that would be a good fit, and I wanted to know when you'll be available to look at them. We'll need a couple of hours all told because they're both a bit of a distance away. Mornings are better for me because of work. Would tomorrow morning suit you?"

My schedule was pretty flexible, thank goodness, and as long as I handed in my quota of articles, Mr MacPherson was pretty easy-going about how long I did or didn't spend in the office. I supposed we were out and about gathering information anyway, so it wasn't like we weren't doing our jobs just because we weren't in the office. "Sounds good. What time?"

"I'll pick you up at eight thirty, if that's okay."

"Excellent. Thanks so much, Bailey. I really appreciate it."

"Any time, Avery. See you then."

"Bye." And that was that. Ah, Zeus's pyjamas. Why hadn't I asked what type of cars they were? Oh well, beggars couldn't be choosers. If they ran and were the right price, it was what it was.

I put Mrs Downs's address into my map app and started walking.

Five minutes later, I turned right into a street that wound up a hill. Dark timber-framed homes lined both sides of the quiet road. Their grey-slate roofs gave an air of refinement and delicacy, even though the overall colour scheme spoke of rainy days and bleak forests. The bright spot among the pretty sombreness was the green grass in front of most of the homes and colourful flowering plants.

I knocked on the door of number fifteen. It didn't take long for a woman to answer. She was about my height. Her short, silver hair feathered around a slim face. A white linen shirt, sleeves folded to the elbows, fell loosely to her hips, over a pair of khaki calottes. Her expression softened when she saw me, but she didn't offer a smile, and who could blame her? "Hi, Mrs Downs. I'm Avery."

"Please come in." She stepped aside to let me pass. "You'll find the living room just to your left there. Mind the step."

I took one step down onto flagstone floors. Heavy furnishings on two rugs dominated the room, as did the low ceiling beams. As characterful as it was, being so closed in made me want to take a deep breath. There was a difference between cosy and coffin-like.

"Please, sit wherever you like."

I picked a red-velvet armchair opposite a two-seater leather sofa. Mrs Downs sat in it, which would make things easier. "Thank you for speaking to me. I'm sorry for your loss." I was saying that a lot lately. I rarely covered murders in Sydney. I mean, I'd covered a couple, but it wasn't my usual fare. Much of my work back home alternated between feel-good stories and scams or fraud. Lots of research and rarely dead bodies.

She took a tissue out of her pants pocket and dabbed her eyes. "Thank you. What did you want to ask me about?"

"Some general questions about who your son was. Was he into any sports, did he contribute to the community, that kind of thing? Was there anything you were particularly proud of him for? I just want to paint a picture of the person he was." I

71

took out my notepad and pen. I'd save the tricky questions for later. With a bit of luck, she'd say something that could lead me into an "innocent" question.

She stood, went to the fireplace, and took down a palm-sized framed photo. She brought it over and handed it to me, then sat on the leather sofa again. The picture showed a grinning boy of about ten, dressed in cricket whites and holding a cricket bat. "He loved his cricket. Played for the county as a teenager." She smiled. "He won club player of the year when he was sixteen. When he was older, he went on to coach the local kids, but he gave that up about two years ago, about the time Melissa received her initial cancer diagnosis. He wanted to be there for her, no matter what, take her to her appointments, that kind of thing. Unfortunately, the treatment went on far longer than we expected, but she was beating it, finally." She dabbed at her eyes again, then blew her nose.

"He sounds like a devoted husband."

She nodded. "He was." Her brow furrowed.

"What's wrong?"

"She wasn't always appreciative." A frown took over her sad expression. "She cheated on him about a year and a half ago. She was running around with some other bloke for six months when my Tom found out. He came and stayed with me for a few days while he cooled down. She broke it off with the fellow, said she'd lost her mind when she thought she was dying. He forgave her, and they figured things out." Her eyes widened. "He didn't kill her, and he certainly didn't kill himself, if that's what you're thinking." She put a palm to her cheek. "I shouldn't have said anything. Please don't put that in the paper."

I sat forward and gave her my most reassuring look. "It's okay. I won't publish that at all. You probably just needed to talk to someone. What you tell me now won't go in the paper either. Are you still angry at her?"

She bit her lip and nodded. "Yes. How dare she hurt my son like that. He was the best, most loving husband. He'd always wanted children, and when she couldn't have them, he stayed. She was his whole life, and then she threw it in his face." Her lips pressed together in a hard line. "I told him to leave her, but he wouldn't listen. She didn't have to hear him crying of a night when he came here. I don't know if he truly got over her betrayal."

"Do you know who it was with?" Had Mr Downs lied to me? Had he killed her and himself? Had he left the suicide note? People lied, so it stood to reason that their ghosts could as well. Was all this for nothing? If his ghost had sent me on a wild goose—or was that ghost?—chase, I'd be pretty freaking annoyed.

"No, I don't, I'm afraid. I asked him, but he wouldn't say. He said he didn't want me to make a scene at the local shops."

"So, it was someone who worked in Cramptonbury?"

She shrugged. "I assume so."

"Do you think Melissa killed them both?" I would never ask her if she thought her son did it. That would be a question too far, even for me.

"No. They tell me it was a joint suicide—apparently the note was signed by both of them—but I don't believe them. I don't understand why. She was given the news that after some more treatment, she would probably be fine. The chemo was working. And my son would never agree to that. I mean, I wouldn't blame him if he'd killed her, but I can't imagine him killing himself. He'd booked a holiday for them, and a weekend away. He was even planning on going back to coaching the kids at cricket. Last time I spoke to him, he was enthusiastic about the future."

"I'll put that in the article—about your son being happy and looking forward to the future. His business was doing well, too, wasn't it?"

She sat up straighter. "Oh, yes. It was going great guns. He was such a good manager, so skilled at getting clients. Tom took after his father—he was a real people person too." A sigh escaped her lips. "But now I've lost them both, and Tom's brother… well, that's another story."

I opened my mouth to speak but quickly stopped myself. Telling her that Mr Downs had mentioned his drug-addicted brother when I spoke to him would go down really well. *Yes, I speak to ghosts. Mmm hmm.* "Um, so his brother isn't much help? Is he younger or older?"

"It's his younger brother." Mrs Downs placed her hands in her lap and interlaced her fingers. They slowly squeezed together. "He's an addict. He has short periods of being clean, but he always relapses. He wasn't doing too badly the last couple of months, but Tom's death has put him right back there again. I haven't heard from him since I told him the news, and his flatmate called me, telling me he'd gone missing." She shook her head. "I don't have the energy to worry about him too. This whole thing is killing me."

"I'm so sorry. Are you having to take care of your son's estate and funeral by yourself?" An innocent enough question, but maybe I could get more information about who stood to benefit from their deaths. I mean, if both sons died, would she inherit half of the estate all by herself? Not that, that led anywhere. As if she would kill her own son. Sometimes I went down the rabbit hole way too far.

"Yes, but I have a solicitor helping. My other son and I will inherit something, but his will be held in trust. Tom didn't trust him to spend it wisely. We all know he'd buy drugs and likely kill himself." Shoulder's sagging, her gaze moved to the coffee table between us.

"I'm sorry to ask you this, but I went to his office to interview his workmates, and that Russo guy, his partner, well, is he usually defensive and rude?" I couldn't give away that I knew they'd had trouble. Maybe this would shake something loose.

She rubbed her cheek, then shook her head. "I know they weren't getting along, but Tom wouldn't tell me why. He said he'd get angry if he spoke about it. But I know Tom—he just didn't want me to worry, but he might've spoken to his cousin about it—Anson." She smiled. "He's also a Downs—my brother's son. If you'd like his number, I know it off by heart." Her smile fell, and it was as if she realised she'd offered too much. "But why would you put that stuff in the article? My son doesn't need more controversy—his... death... has been horrible enough."

It was my lucky day. "I don't actually want to put that in the article, but I just thought I'd ask. Sorry if I've upset you. It really threw me when he was so awful. But speaking to your nephew would be good—I'm sure he'll have some lovely things to add about your son, which is why I'm here. I want him to be remembered with respect, Mrs Downs, just like you do."

Her chest rose with a deep inhale. She let it out. "Okay, but please do the right thing."

I gave her a reassuring smile. "Of course."

She gave me the number, and I put it into my phone. Her head sank slowly forward, her eyes staring at the floor.

"Are you okay?" Stupid question, considering, but just asking would hopefully make her feel like someone cared. "Is there anything I can help you with?"

Her gaze returned to mine. "Thank you, dear. You've done enough just listening to me complain. You've been such a godsend."

I smiled. "It's been my pleasure. And I won't put anything negative in the article. I promise. Your secrets are safe with me."

"Thank you, again." Sighing, she massaged her temples. "I guess you probably have enough information, and I have a headache. Is it okay if we call it a day?"

"Of course. If you ever want to talk, you have my number. Please use it if you need anything." I meant it. Yes, I sometimes complained that people overshared, but seeing someone suffering brought out the mothering side of me. If we couldn't help each other, what was the point? Community was meaningless without the unity. *Argh, when did I get so cheesy?*

She stood. "Thank you, Avery. That's very kind of you."

I stood and made my way to the front door. Making her ask twice wasn't polite. As I opened the door, she reached me. "Bye, Mrs Downs. Thanks for today."

"Bye, Avery."

As I walked to the bus stop, there was lots to ponder. My phone rang, interrupting my musings. I pulled it out of my bag and frowned. My heart raced. To answer or not to answer. I didn't want to answer. *So, don't answer it, Avery. Put on your big-girl pants and ignore it.*

It stopped ringing.

Phew. Please don't ring again.

It rang. Cat's bum. How long could I ignore it? How many times would she call if I did? I sighed. Maybe I should just rip off the Band-Aid and get it over and done with. If I was an optimist, I'd say my mother was worried about me and missed me.

But I wasn't.

Against my better judgement, I pressed Answer. "Hello." My shoulders tightened as I waited for my parental unit's condescending tone to travel all the way from Australia to here. Technology wasn't all it was cracked up to be.

"Avery! It's about time you answered. And why haven't you called? Your father said you were too irresponsible to move to another country, and you've proven him right... again." My stomach warmed with the familiar zap of adrenaline, and I swallowed. My mind blanked. I didn't know what to say. I wanted to defend myself, but the words had turned to mist and dispersed. "Well? What have you got to say for yourself, running away? Have they put you in a mental home yet? Are you still going on about that ghost nonsense? You should just get on the next plane and come home, stop this stupidity. That's if you even have the money. You were never good with budgeting."

Words, where were they when you needed them? I opened my mouth, but nothing came out.

"Hello? Are you there? Speak to me, this instant!"

The bus stop materialised through my watery gaze. There was no way I wanted other passengers to hear this conversation—not that I was saying much. And I didn't want to cry in public, so I hung up.

So brave of you, Avery. Really taking your life back. Okay, so when it came to my parents, I was a total coward. Baby steps. In another gutless move, I turned my phone off. Knowing my mother, she'd keep calling till she annoyed me into submission. Not today, Satan. Not today.

Because I'd turned my phone off, all I could do while waiting for the bus was to replay my mother's words over and over again and think about what I should've said. One day I'd say the perfect thing to put her in her place, but that day wasn't today. Instead, she'd left me with an adrenaline come-down and fighting the same insecurities as usual. The difference was, today I wasn't going to act on them.

If she wanted me to come back to Australia, she'd have to come here herself and drag me there—not that I'd go quietly into the night. I wasn't usually a superstitious person, but I'm not ashamed to say, I touched the nearest tree trunk. If touching wood was the only thing that would save me, I was in big trouble.

CHAPTER 6

It was a testament to how upset I was that when I hopped off the bus, all I could think about was the need for coffee. Which was how I found myself walking through the door of the Heavenly Brew Café and then being shocked when I stopped at the counter and looked up into Joyless's face. That was my new name for her because, well, if the description fit….

She looked at me, her expression somewhere between bored and irritated. She glanced around before turning back to me. Anna, the owner, was nowhere in sight, so Joyless had the freedom to say whatever she wanted. She already knew I wasn't good at fighting back. Damn my inability to stand up for myself. I really needed to work on those skills. "It's the Aussie bird, back for more." She smirked. Whether she meant coffee or being ripped off, I wasn't sure…. Okay, I kind of was.

I narrowed my eyes, then looked past her to the black-board on the wall, which I should've checked the first time I was here, but I'd been concentrating too much on ordering the right stuff and was nervous. This time, I wasn't going to be so stupid. She was like my parents—give them an opportunity to insult you or trip you up, and they were there for that all damned day. "Hello, *Joy*." *Less*. I smiled because even though she didn't know it, I'd just insulted her. So what if it was only in my head; it was better than nothing. "I'll have a medium cappuccino, please... the three-pound one."

Her smirk widened. "Sure thing."

I did my best not to react because people like her lived for that. My gaze wandered the café for a moment, but then my subconscious screamed, *Never turn your back on the enemy*. I turned around and watched her make my coffee and froth the milk, lest a stray spitball found its way into my beverage. I knew this happened because I'd done it myself once—don't judge me because the person totally deserved it. That's what being passive in the face of continued abuse did. All retaliation had to be carried out in secret. As I said before, it was better than nothing. Hmm, maybe I wasn't as pathetic as I'd thought. Seemed there had always been a bit of fight in me.

As the steam squealed in the milk-filled stainless-steel jug she held at the nozzle, she briefly eyed me. *Good*. I hoped my scrutiny annoyed the bejesus out of her.

When she was done, she put the plastic lid on the cup and slid it on the table towards me. My heartrate kicked up, but stuff it; I was going to say something. "Could you please sprinkle the chocolate on the top?" I'd ordered a cappuccino, not a flat white, and, as much as I loved the coffee part, the chocolate on the top was my favourite.

"I already did." She put one hand on her hip.

I cocked my head to the side and stared at her with a "you've got to be joking" expression. I leaned over, took the lid off, and peered into the cup. "Maybe the evil, *joyless* fairies removed it?"

She pressed her lips together, then grabbed the stainless-steel container that held the chocolate stuff. Making sure she got in a good eye-roll first, she turned the container upside down over my cup and tapped the bottom. When a healthy layer of chocolate was on my coffee, she put the lid on. "Happy now?"

I smiled. "Very. Thank you." Without waiting for her to ask, I handed over the three pounds, picked up my cup, and left. My heart didn't slow until I'd almost made it back to the office. Confrontation was my least-favourite pastime, and I was a rank amateur at it, but I smiled. I'd stood up for myself, said something. And now I had chocolate on my cappuccino. It sucked that she couldn't have given me what I ordered in the first place, but she was contrary, and, for some reason I couldn't fathom, had it in for me. Bethany, her sister, didn't like me either. Maybe it was genetic?

I turned into the laneway. Standing outside the office were Finnegan and Sergeant Bellamy. Hmph. Getting inside information again. Finnegan noticed me first and cut off whatever he'd been saying. Right. Make sure Avery doesn't hear. I sighed but hid it with a smile as I reached them. "Good morning."

"Morning, Miss Winters." Bellamy gave a nod. Would it hurt him to smile? To let his guard down and consider me an insider rather than an outsider?

Finnegan grinned. "Hello, Lightning. How's things?"

"That's such a weird phrase, don't you think? How *is* things when it should really be how *are* things. English is an unusual beast." I smiled. "And things is good, thanks." I looked at Bellamy. "I don't suppose I could have a look at that suicide note, could I? Mr Downs's mother says you're ruling it a double suicide?"

Bellamy pressed his lips together and gave Finnegan a look I couldn't decipher. Finnegan put his hands up. "It wasn't me. If she says it was Mr Downs's mother, it must have been."

"Vinegar's telling the truth. He hates divulging any information." I pulled my best "not impressed" face to reinforce my point. "So, can you confirm or deny?"

"Why are you so interested, anyway? I'm covering the suicides."

"I know. I'm just curious. You do know I'm a journalist, right? The insatiable need to get to the bottom of things doesn't automatically disappear just because I'm not writing the story. I'm the one who found the bodies, remember? I feel like I have a connection to them. I spoke to Mr Downs on the Friday before they died. It's kind of personal." Whilst I was trying to sway Bellamy into giving me information, what I said was true. Only, they didn't know how much more I was connected. After talking to Mr Downs's ghost and watching him and his wife go into the light, I felt a next-level bond. If sharing the most significant moment in someone's life—or death—wasn't a moment that connected you to someone, I didn't know what was.

The men shared a look. Finnegan's nod was subtle. Had he just given Bellamy the go-ahead to tell me something? I resisted the urge to smile. Victory wasn't mine… yet.

Bellamy gave Finnegan a return nod. "I'm going now, lad. We'll talk later." He looked at me. "Good day, Miss Winters."

Cat's bum. I didn't bother keeping the disappointment from my face. "Bye, Sergeant."

Finnegan, the annoyance that he was, grinned. "Hey,

Lightning, why the gloomy face?" At least he didn't still seem to be upset with me.

I took a sip of my coffee—I could count on that to make me feel better, even if it was tainted by the hand of Joyless. "I was just hopeful that Bellamy would finally give me something. Whatever. I'll live." How long did it take to be treated a local around here?

His cheek dimples taunted me. *Stop smiling, dammit.* He chuckled. "For someone who's professing they're not too disappointed, you look like if you had eye lasers, they'd be burning through my forehead right now."

A reluctant smile broke through my irritation. Gah. My reaction would no doubt encourage him. Maybe I should just give up now and accept he was hot, and I was going to be sucked in by his charms. I didn't have to throw myself at him, but I could allow myself to enjoy his company. But maybe that would become a problem—enjoying it too much would be dangerous, and the last thing I wanted him to think was that I was even slightly attracted to him. Give him an inch, and he'd totally take a mile. "Yeah, you'd have a blackened hole in your face right now." Okay, so picturing that was funny, and I grinned.

His grin faltered. "You're imagining that right now, aren't you?"

"Yep." I beamed because my grin wasn't cheesy enough.

"Ha, I knew it. You might want to keep me alive a while longer because I can answer your question. If I tell you and it gets out, he can blame me. He can say I made it up or stole the information or something."

"He's seriously that worried, after feeding you inside information for what I assume is years?"

He shrugged. "You're new, and he doesn't trust you yet.

Not to mention, he only gives me that information because we're practically family. Can you blame him?"

"For not trusting me?" He nodded. As harsh as Finnegan's assessment had been, it was honest and pulled no punches, which I much preferred to bulldust. "I suppose not. You know me about as well as I know you—which is only surface level. I can respect that. Doesn't mean it doesn't pee me off though. It's just frustrating. Surely you can understand as a member of our esteemed profession?"

"As a member of the eternally curious, yes I can, which is why I'm going to tell you about the suicide note."

My mouth fell open. Was. Not. Expecting. That. "Wow, thank you."

His smile seemed genuine. "My pleasure. I know I give you a hard time, but it's just because it's fun to rile you up. And, yes, I'm competitive when it comes to reporting, but I'm occasionally accommodating."

"Ha, *occasionally*."

He waggled his brows. "Hey, I'm still human." He checked his phone. "I have to go in a minute, so I'll get to it. The suicide note was from both of them, but they've analysed the handwriting, and Mr Downs wrote it. They interviewed his mother, who told them her son was upset when he found out she'd had an affair, and then they interviewed his business partner Russo. He told them that Mr Downs had been depressed on and off, that he once said that he couldn't live without his wife. Bellamy didn't tell me all the details, but they're leaning towards it being a murder-suicide."

My forehead wrinkled. "Saying you can't live without your other half isn't exactly proof that you'd kill them. What context was it in? Was it to do with her cancer?"

He raised a brow. "You know about her diagnosis?"

"I'm a reporter. Of course I know. I've spoken to a couple of people about them. Besides, I wouldn't trust Russo. He and Downs didn't get along."

"How do you know about that?"

I rolled my eyes. "I spoke to his mother. Remember me just telling the sergeant?" I wasn't going to mention I also spoke to his ghost.

"Oh, yeah. So you don't trust Russo?"

"Nope." I made a loud pop for the *p*, to emphasise my feelings on that point.

"Hmm. Right. Well, Lightning, I'd love to continue this discussion, but I have to run."

As much as I didn't want to fawn all over him, saying thank you was only polite after the information he'd given me. Because of Finnegan, I could cross number one—find out what was in the suicide note—off my list of facts about the case. "Thanks for that, Vinegar. I appreciate it."

He smiled. "Don't go gushing now. I might get the impression you don't hate me."

"Yeah, don't go that far. Ha ha. See ya." I gave him a wave and buzzed the office intercom. He gave his smirk one more workout, then turned and walked away. *Hmm, since when was his butt so, well, pinchable? Jebers, Avery, stop objectifying the guy.* I ignored the fact that he'd probably love that I stared at his bum, but if he caught me, I'd never live it down.

The door clicked open—Bethany had likely seen us talking on the street through the floor-to-ceiling window. I pushed the door open, called out, "Hello," and kept going. As usual, there was no return greeting. My eye-roll was automatic but probably more for me than her. Why I expected anything more than nothing was beyond me. Meh, from now on, I wasn't going to bother either. A person could only put themselves out there so many times before it became embarrassing. I didn't care if she didn't like me, and I'd made more of an effort than anyone could expect, so my line was drawn. No more greetings to people who didn't deserve them.

As I placed my things on my desk, my phone rang. I fished it out of my bag, ready to ignore it if it was the woman who birthed me again. I blew out a relieved breath on seeing it was Meg. "Hey, lady. How's it going?"

"Hey, Avery. Good thanks. I don't have to work tonight, and I wanted to know if you'd come for dinner, on the house."

"No. I'll come if I can pay for my dinner." Meg and her family had been so helpful and friendly since I'd arrived—well, except for that one incident with her dad—that I couldn't accept any more help. Bailey was taking me to look at cars tomorrow morning, for goodness' sake.

She sighed. "Fine. Drinks are half price… for everyone, not just you."

"Ha, okay. I won't complain about that. I could do with a beer." Bellamy and Finnegan sharing information with me had gone some of the way to making today better than it could've been, but that call with my parental unit had thrown me more than I thought it would've. The irrational fear of being returned to Australia against my will sat like a toxic ball of osmium in my belly. They'd forced me into a hospital psychiatric ward, and that was one of the most horrific, helpless feelings in the universe. One I wouldn't soon forget. If they would do that, what else would they do to control me? I shuddered. In any case, a beer wouldn't fix me overnight, but it would sure help calm my stress.

"Top notch! See you around six?"

"Sounds good. See you then." It felt weird to go out for drinks on a worknight, but I was young and single, why should

I feel guilty? I came here to live my best life, and that's what I was going to do. I smiled.

"Hey." Charles materialised in front of my desk.

I squealed and jumped back. "Jeez, mate. Give a person a heart attack, why don't you?"

His cocky grin was back. "I like to make an impression."

I was still holding my phone, so I brought it up to my ear, in case anyone walked in. I wasn't making that mistake again. "So, have you thought any more about that apology?"

His grin melted into a depressing puddle. "I can't do it." He swallowed and stared at me. "I'm sorry."

Argh. I wanted to be annoyed—I needed that access to the police and their information—but he was just a kid. How much mental growth happened after you died? I cocked my head to the side. He probably wasn't conning me, was he? Hmm. I'd give him the benefit of the doubt... for now. "I'm not happy about it, but I can't force you. All I'll say is that it's the right thing to do—atone for your mistakes, even if you dread the repercussions. And this wasn't even your mistake. You were just a kid with a bully for a father. No sensible person would hold you responsible for what happened." Damn incorporeal ghosts. The urge to give him a hug was strong, but there was no use. I sighed. "Anyway, what else is going on?"

He looked up at me through his long lashes. "So, you're not mad at me?"

"No, Charles, I'm not mad. Frustrated, yes, but mad, no. I have to trust that you'll come to the right decision eventually. In the meantime, we'll have to think of another way around our lack of information." At least Bellamy had fed me something today, and who knew what tomorrow would bring? I'd choose to remain positive. Another solution would hopefully present itself soon. "Moving along, I have a question." As much as I didn't think Mr Downs killed his wife, I needed to consider it, which brought questions. One of which only Charles could answer... if he could answer it at all. "When someone dies, if they go somewhere, is it always into the light? Like, if you were going to 'heaven,' do you get a white light, and if you go to 'hell,' do you get like a red light?" I wasn't even sure if there was a heaven and hell, and since Charles was still here, he wouldn't know for sure either.

"Well, if you want to talk about going somewhere good or bad, I don't know for real, but I think there is. I seen people go into the light, but my dad and mum...." He licked his bottom lip.

"What happened to them? I remember you saying when it was their time that you didn't want to go with them. I thought it was because you wanted to stay here for fun, or because you didn't want to be with them quite yet." Funny how the truth tended to trickle out rather than come in a gush. Things were rarely what you first thought, and people were rarely what you understood from a first impression.

He scratched the back of his head and stared past me. After a minute, he gazed into my eyes. My nape prickled, and goosebumps sprung up along my arms. "I watched them leave. I don't think they had a choice. At the last moment, my mother looked back at me, said she didn't want to go. It was too late."

I released my words quietly, as if I didn't want to alert the monster under the bed. "Did they go into the light?"

"No. It was a shadow that reminded me of a muddy swamp—opaque, thick, oozing, sucking them into it." His breathing quickened, and he gasped for air, not that he needed to breathe. He put a hand to his throat. "It sucked the air away... at least that's what it felt like. It *consumed* them, slid over them until they disappeared. I panicked and ran away. I didn't want it to get me." His glassy eyes revealed his tears.

"I'm so sorry you went through that. Are you scared that's where you'll end up too?" I didn't want to torture him by putting the idea into his head, but I needed to get to the bottom of this. Maybe there was something I could do to help him.

He nodded. "I ain't never leaving." His eyes told the full story—rather than doing the haunting, he was haunted.

"Have you ever seen anyone else get swallowed by the darkness?"

"Yes. When someone dies, they move from the real world to where I am. If you happen to be in the same place—you know, I'm here and you are, but you're on the other side of the invisible wall—the person will come through next to you. I've seen people go to the dark place or go into the light after that."

"Do they always have a choice?"

He shrugged. "I don't know."

His mother was sucked in, but maybe she got too close before she truly made up her mind, and it was too late? But then again, if you were supposed to go to hell, why would the powers that be let you swan around in the in-between, free? And what was Patrick's deal? He'd been stuck. No one had offered him light or dark. Then there were Mr and Mrs Downs—they'd jumped at the chance to walk into the light. It didn't look as if they were forced. And if they were offered the light, surely that would mean he hadn't killed her. What killer got offered a place in heaven, or whatever that place beyond the brightness was? "Did you see the light or dark when you died?"

He blinked, then scratched his cheek. His brow furrowed.

"Neither. I just came here, then nothing." Hope flickered in his gaze. "What do you think it means?"

"I don't know. Maybe no one knows where you belong yet? Maybe you have choices, or maybe you're meant to stay here because you're needed for some reason? Sorry I can't be more helpful. I'm pretty new to this. I wonder if there are other ghosts you can ask."

"Maybe. I've never spoken about it with anyone. I-I was too scared." His cheeks pinked.

"Being scared is okay, Charles. Everyone gets scared some-times. It's normal." I gave him a reassuring smile.

His serious expression was too grown up for one so young. Sadness swelled in my chest and burned the back of my throat. He'd been dead longer than I'd been alive, but he'd died so young. To me, he was still a child. What he'd been through broke my heart. "My dad used to say showing fear was cowardly. He said no son of his would be a yellow-belly or a sissy. I got belted if I woke them up because I'd had a night-mare, or if I cried, so I learned not to."

I frowned and stretched my fingers before balling them up. If that man wasn't already in hell, I would've put him there. What a cruel piece of sh—

"Hey, Avery. How's t'ings?" Carina bounced in with her usual enthusiasm and through Charles, who promptly disappeared.

I said goodbye to the pretend person on my phone and "hung up." "Oh, hey, Carina. I'm good thanks. How are you?"

She smiled and threw her belongings onto her desk. "Oh, what a mornin' I've had! Eejits everywhere. I swear, d'ey give driving licences to any muppet who hands over the money. One old man went t'rough a Stop sign and almost collected me, and *he* had d'e hide to stick his finger up at *me*. D'en a young lass slammed on her brakes a few feet from a street and turned d'e corner wit'out indicating." She shook her head and rolled her eyes. "Would you mind if I wrote an article on how bad the drivers are lately?"

I chuckled. "Go for it. It's a travesty, and something must be said. I've got enough work to keep me busy. I'm sure a good old rant would do well. People respond to that kind of stuff. I'm sure we'll get heaps of letters agreeing with you."

"Darn right we will. T'anks, Avery."

"Don't thank me. You can write whatever articles you like. I'm not worried, as long as you don't write something I'm already working on."

She gave a nod. "It's a deal. Now, I'd better get to work. I have a rant d'at must be done."

I sat down and grinned. She was a good person to have on your side, and she could always make me smile. Hmm. I texted Meg. *Are you friends with Carina White, the woman I work with?*

Her response came back within a couple of minutes. *I know her, but I haven't really hung out with her. She's seems nice enough. Why?*

I was wondering if I could ask her to dinner tonight. She might not even come, but she's a goodun, and I'm thinking you'd like her. If you don't feel comfortable, I won't. Just thought I'd check. Gah, what if she thought I didn't think her company was enough? *I'm totally happy with it just being us two, btw. Your company is awesome.* I added a heart emoji.

She responded with a laughing emoji. *You worry too much. Of course I'm fine with it. It'll be good to get to know another woman in this village. I don't have many friends around here—my best friends from school moved to London as soon as they could. And if she has your stamp of approval, she must be nice. See you at six. Xx*

I started typing, to confirm it was okay, but then deleted it. She said it was fine, so I had to believe she meant it. Argh, why did I have that voice in my head second-guessing everyone's motivations and reactions all the time? I sighed.

Carina looked over. "Are you okay?"

I sat up straighter. "Oh, yes, I'm fine. Just thinking about something. Um, this wasn't what I was thinking about, but I wanted to ask what you're doing tonight. I'm catching up with Meg for dinner at the pub—you know the Meg who owns it with her brother—and we were wondering if you'd like to join us. I'm meeting her there at six."

Carina's smile was wide. "Ooh, I'd love to! It's half-price beve night, isn't it?"

"Apparently so. And that's great! Thanks for saying yes." My cheeks heated. Was that too forward, too eager?

"My pleasure, love. T'anks for asking. I have to go out again later. Is it okay if I meet you d'ere?"

"Of course."

"Good-oh."

And with that, my day was much improved. I hadn't completely forgotten my conversation with Mother Dearest this morning, and the fear that my parents could do something to sabotage the life I wanted still vibrated in the depths of my psyche, but their hold on me was fading. And one day, just like a ghost, it would walk into the light and disappear.

CHAPTER 7

The back of my head hurt from laughing so much. Carina had just finished telling Meg and me a story about an older couple who were naturists getting married in their back garden. She'd thought she was covering a story about the wedding in a garden they'd designed themselves. What she got was a couple and wedding guests who were as naked as the day they were born. She pretended to be cool about it and took lots of photos, which the paper had to edit with lots of little fuzzy spots. When she was done with her reporting, they asked if she wanted to sit down and have a drink with them, but after seeing a naked man get up off the chair they offered her, she politely declined. "I'm not a prude by any stretch of d'e imagination, but ball sweat on my skirt is somet'ing I draw the line at for sure."

Meg and I snorted. Bailey chose that moment to see if we wanted more drinks. "Evening, ladies… and Meg."

She rolled her eyes. "Ha ha."

"Can I get anyone another drink?"

"Hey, Bails!"

Bailey turned to the new arrival. "Hey, man, how's it going?"

It was the quiet but friendly butcher. "Same old, same old." He looked at Meg and blushed. I hid my smile. "Hi, Meg."

She smiled. "Hi, Luke. Long time no see."

He put his hands in his jean pockets. "Yeah, been working and looking after Mum. Her arthritis is getting worse." He gave a casual "what can you do?" look. What a nice guy, though, looking after his mother.

Meg frowned. "Oh no. That's awful. Say hi for me. I noticed she hasn't been around in the village lately."

Before Luke could answer, Phil, the cranky butcher, joined us. He gave Bailey, Meg, and Carina a nod, then looked at Luke. "We'll sit over there. You get us a table, and I'll grab the drinks."

"Sure thing." He looked at us one at a time and smiled—unlike Phil, he didn't ignore me. "Maybe we can catch up later. Enjoy your evening." We all said goodbye, and they walked off. Hmm, had I done something to get Phil offside? I seemed to have that effect on half the people in this village.

"So, ladies, another drink?"

"I'll grab another one of your light ales, please. It's really good."

"One Blond Bombshell coming right up." Bailey grinned, and I assumed it was because I was blonde too. But it was a clever name for a beer.

Meg and Carina each ordered a glass of sauvignon blanc. I didn't mind wine, but beer was my favourite. There was nothing like the tang of cold beer on a hot day. I looked at Carina. "Did you get your rant done?"

She smiled. "I did, t'ank you. D'e rant is done and dusted. MacPherson's going to run it tomorrow."

"Ooh, what rant? The lack of parking at the church, or the cost of re-thatching your roof? Or is it that there are too many *naturists* running around Manesbury?" Meg snickered.

I couldn't help but laugh. Carina snorted. "It's about the daft drivers around here. Honestly, who's giving out licences? I reckon d'ey're giving them out free at d'e supermarket when you spend over fifty quid."

Meg turned to me. "Are you still working on the Downses' article?"

"Ah, yeah." How much should I tell them? I wasn't supposed to spill information to other people about what was told to me in confidence. Although, was Finnegan going to mention that suicide note thing in his article?

"What's wrong?" Meg's brow furrowed.

"Ah, I just can't discuss some of the things I know. Finnegan and Bellamy were kind enough to offer me information today, and it's confidential. But, let's just say that I don't agree with where the police are going with the investigation." I'd probably said too much, but I needed someone to bounce my theories off. I knew I could trust Meg… at least I thought I could. Could I trust Carina not to go running to Finnegan with whatever I said? Hmm, probably not. They'd been working together for about three years, from what they'd said. Her loyalty—if she had loyalty to anyone—would be to the person she'd known the longest, logically speaking, and they seemed to get along well.

Carina nodded slowly. "D'at's interesting. Can you say why?"

I bit my lip. I wasn't going to spill, but how to frame that without saying I didn't trust her? I must've delayed too long because Meg jumped in. "Her gut told her. Isn't that right, Avery?"

"Yes, partly. I don't know. It seems like they were both happy—from what everyone I've spoken to has said. Her cancer was getting better, and they had a weekend away booked for this coming weekend too. So why would they kill themselves? It doesn't make sense. You guys know them way better than me. Well, I didn't know them at all, except for a brief telephone conversation with Mr Downs on the Friday before it happened. What do you guys think?" And after speaking to their ghosts on Monday. Ha ha. If only I could be honest about it all.

Bailey came back and placed our drinks on the table. "Ladies." He said that whilst staring at me with those lionish amber eyes.

I smiled, and my stomach did a little flip. I'd have a word to it later—not only did I not want a boyfriend in general, imagine if things went pear-shaped. I still wanted to be friends with Meg. It would be mega awkward if Bailey and I were on the outs. "Thanks."

Carina twirled her blue hair around her finger, and she and Meg shared a look. Bailey left and went back to the bar. I rounded on Meg and Carina. "Stop it with those looks, you two."

Carina chuckled. "Avery and Bailey sitting in a tree." She made kissy noises. Meg laughed.

"Gah. You two are killing me. So, back to Mr and Mrs Downs. Have either of you got any insight?"

"I do." I tried not to focus on the woman standing behind Meg because that would just look weird, but I flicked her a glance to let her know I'd heard. Meg's grandmother gave me a gentle smile and said, "I'll talk to you later." She disappeared, thank goodness. Well, I hadn't thought to ask other ghosts, but of course they might know something. They weren't always around to hear what was going on, but surely they were sometimes. I tried to sit still as the excitement of what this could mean for my investigation sank in.

Meg shrugged. "Nothing to add since last time. They seemed happy every time they came in here. I tend to agree with you—either of them wanting to kill themselves is strange."

Carina sipped her drink. "I don't agree. Maybe Mrs Downs's cancer came back more aggressively, and they didn't tell anyone. They could've decided they couldn't live without one another, and to get it over and done with before she became too sick."

If I didn't know what I knew, I could see that as a legitimate theory. "Is there any way we could get her medical records?" It was a stupid question. There was no way, unless I managed to wrangle the information from the police, which was never going to happen. Poop.

Meg sat up straighter. Her mouth opened in a surprised *o*, and her eyes widened. "Ooh, ooh, I know! Mrs Downs went to the local doctor. I mean, she was obviously seeing a specialist for her cancer, but her regular doctor is here, in Manesbury. The receptionist was a good friend of my mother. Dianne might help us out, but then again, she's an honest person, so she might not break that confidentiality."

Carina frowned. "She could get into a lot of trouble. I don't know that we should even ask her." The warm fuzzies hit my chest. *We.* They wanted to help me figure this out. I wasn't used to being part of a female-friend *we*. Or maybe I was making too much out of it. She might've just said it because tonight we were together chatting about it, and I wasn't about to ask. I might not have grown out of my teenage insecurities, but I wasn't stupid enough to actually voice them out loud. That would be even lamer.

Meg quirked her mouth to the side. "Hmm, you're probably right." She scratched her chin. "Still, they're both dead. It's not like anyone is going to sue if they found out. And they won't find out."

Carina shook her head. "I don't know. It just doesn't seem right. Maybe we could ask Fin?"

I snorted. "Getting anything out of him and Bellamy is like pulling teeth. They have their own 'old boys' club going. And to be fair to Fin, he is just doing his job. He managed to get a good information source. It gives me the irrites, but there's not much I can do about it."

Meg's brow furrowed. "The whats?"

I chuckled. "Aussie slang. Sorry. Irrites is short for irritating. So it annoys me, basically. But, like I said, I can hardly blame him. I'll just have to deal." I swigged a mouthful of beer. "Seriously, Carina, we're a couple of journos. Surely we can think of something." I looked at Meg. "We might have to go with your idea. It might come to nothing, but I still think we should."

Carina looked at me. "You're potentially risking Dianne's job, and for what? A hunch? It isn't unheard of that people suicide together."

Frustration bubbled in my gut. I couldn't fault her for being devil's advocate though. If she had reservations, so would others, and I needed to consider all angles. *But none of them had spoken to the couple after they died.* I had to believe I'd seen them for a reason, and not just because I could see them, but the powers that be had seen fit to have me meet them before they went into the light. That had to count, right? Okay, so it didn't really, but I had to believe something right now. "I agree, but what if it wasn't a suicide? There's enough evidence for me to have doubts. What if someone killed them? That would mean there's a killer out there getting away with it. Not only is that not fair, it leaves them free to maybe kill someone else. It might be personal, or it might be random, but we don't know."

Carina twirled her blue hair around her finger again. "Okay, I'll give you d'at. Unfortunately, we can't decide eid'er way because we don't have enough evidence. And if we can't get d'at evidence, you'll have to give up on d'e t'eory and move on."

Meg bit her bottom lip, flicking her gaze between Carina and me. "Argh, you both make sense. Look, what if I ask Dianne but not put pressure on her? Who knows, she might be able to help by suggesting another way? Hmm, you could also speak to Melissa's best friend, Catherine Bickford."

Carina smiled. "That's a great idea, Meg!"

I smiled too. "Carina's right. I knew you guys would help. I'm not used to living in a place where everyone knows everyone, so I didn't even think of it, which is pathetic for a journalist." I was probably focussing too much on how I could get information via my ghostly contacts, and I forgot about the living. "It's so much easier to get access and knowledge about close friends of victims in a place like this. In Sydney, you can fall down the rabbit hole searching for connections, especially when the police won't give out that info, and significant others usually clam up when they have their phones ringing off the hook with questions from the media. So, how do I contact Catherine?"

"She's a vet at Cramptonbury Veterinary Hospital. I'd just call tomorrow and make an appointment to talk to her." Meg's phone dinged with a message. She picked it up off the table and looked at it. She frowned and typed a message back to whoever it was.

Yes, I was nosy. "Is everything okay?"

She looked up at me. "Um, it's Chris."

"Oh, the guy you've been dating?" She'd said things were going well, but maybe something changed.

"Yeah. He's had a job offer in Scotland, and he's just decided to take it." Her shoulders sagged.

"Oh no. I'm so sorry." I got up from my chair, went to hers, and bent to give her a quick hug. At least she was real, and I could comfort her properly.

"Oh, honey, d'at's bleedin' awful. I'm sorry."

Meg took a deep breath and let it out. "We haven't been seeing each other that long, but we're going to try and make it work long distance, but I can't see it lasting. As much as I like him, neither of us want to upend our lives for the other— our relationship's too new. I don't know. I'll see what happens."

"It still sucks." I put my hand on her shoulder and squeezed gently, then sat back down.

Her grandmother appeared behind her, sadness in her eyes. "My poor lass." She stroked her hair, and Meg shivered.

Meg's phone dinged again. She read the new message and blew out a breath. "He wants to catch up for dinner tomorrow night. He's leaving in two weeks, apparently." She answered the message and put her phone back on the table. She picked up her wine and skolled the last of it. "Sorry for ruining our night."

We reassured her that it was all good. Carina looked at her phone. "This has not'ing to do wit' you, honey, but it's ten, and I have an early start tomorrow. Why don't we get together again on Saturday night if you're free? We can help console you wit' a few bevvies."

I looked at Meg. "I'm in for sure. If you're spending that time with Chris, let us know, but if not, we'll be here six thirty Saturday. How does that sound?"

She nodded, her face glum. "Thanks, ladies. You're the best. He wants to call me, but I said I was somewhere noisy. I suppose I'll go up to my apartment and call him."

We all hugged goodbye, and I went to the bar to see Bailey. He smiled as soon as he saw me. "After another blond?"

"Ha, no. Three's enough for a weeknight. Just heading home, but I wanted to say thanks again for tomorrow, and I'll see you in the morning."

"Do you want me to walk you?"

"Huh? I thought we were driving."

He laughed. "No, I mean now… home. It's late."

My cheeks heated. *Argh, idiot, Avery.* "No, I'm fine. But thanks for offering. So, I'll meet you here tomorrow at eight thirty."

"I was going to pick you up."

I waved a "don't be silly" gesture. "I like to start my day with a bit of exercise. I'll see you here tomorrow morning." His gaze lingered on me for a moment before a patron snagged his attention.

Ignoring the butterflies in my stomach, I turned and left. Maybe agreeing to let him help me was a bad idea. But it was too late now. Pondering my dilemma of being in the car alone with him for a couple of hours and having to ignore how attractive he was, I didn't hear the man approach me until he called my name.

"Avery, please wait."

I turned, ready to defend myself, which was stupid since if

someone was going to attack me, they wouldn't warn me first. Not to mention that I was still in front of the pub, and people inside could potentially see me, even under the dim street lights. "Oh, hello, Luke."

"Hi. I'm sorry to bother you. Um, you know how you came in asking about Mrs Downs?"

"Yes." Ooh, maybe he had something important to say. I crossed my fingers.

"Well, I know Phil said she was normal, happy, whatever when she came in, but I saw her the day before, standing outside the post office, crying. It was when I went for my lunch break, so it was just after twelve thirty. When she saw me, she pretended to smile and put her sunglasses on, then left."

"Was she by herself?"

"Yes, and I have no idea why she was upset, but, well, I thought you should know. It was niggling at me, so I wanted to tell you. It's probably nothing, and I know you're just doing an article on her, but, anyway." He gave me an apologetic smile.

"Thanks, Luke. I appreciate you telling me."

"There you are, lad." Phil came out of the pub and approached us. He gave me a nod—which was better than nothing—and slapped Luke's shoulder. "Time to go. Early start tomorrow."

"Bye, Avery." Luke gave a wave.

"Bye. Luke… Phil."

The two men wandered the opposite way to where I was headed. Well, that was interesting. Had *she* killed both of them for some reason, and Mr Downs hadn't realised? But then, if she had, how did she still get to go into the light, and didn't the police confirm it was Mr Downs's handwriting? Argh, this was getting more complicated.

Oh, cat's bum, Meg's grandmother wanted to tell me

something. I looked at the pub door, only forty feet away. If she saw me, Meg would wonder why I was back. Maybe I'd use the excuse of needing the bathroom. I hurried back and stuck my head in the doorway to the bar area. Meg wasn't there, thank goodness—she'd probably gone up to her apartment to make the phone call. She lived onsite, and Bailey lived in a cottage about five-minute's drive away, so I'd been told.

Bailey was clearing a table, the place only a third full since it was close to closing time. There was no way I'd avoid him seeing me, so I walked straight in and waved.

"What are you doing back here? Did you decide to take me up on the walk home?" Was it wrong that I was a tad happy that his eyes flashed hopefulness—well, I thought they did, but I was so rusty at flirting and dating, it was probably wishful thinking?

"Ah, no. Decided the toilet couldn't wait till I got home." Argh, how embarrassing, again. Even though I wasn't telling the truth, he didn't know that.

"Oh, right. Yep."

"Okay, bye." I turned and hurried out the door that led to the hallway and back door to the car park. Before I got that far, I turned right into another hallway and then into the first door on the left—the Ladies. All three cubicles were empty. I got my phone out—just in case—and held it to my ear.

"Mary, are you around? Hello, it's Avery."

Meg's grandmother appeared in front of me. "Hello, Avery. I thought you'd forgotten about me."

"Sorry. I almost did. Thanks for offering me information. I appreciate it."

She smiled. "Think nothing of it. It's nice to get involved, make a difference. I like to stay around to see my family, but I can never do anything. Watching becomes tedious after a while when you see someone needs help and you're helpless to do anything about it."

I returned her smile. "I know all about it. I'm properly here, and sometimes I still can't do much when I want to."

She rubbed her hands together. "So, what do you want to know."

"When was the last time you saw Mr and Mrs Downs?"

She put her fingers on her closed lips, likely thinking. Eventually, she let her hand drop. "I'm sorry, but time moves differently for those of us in the in-between. I would say that it might have been about a month ago. It was cold enough at night that our patrons wore their spring woollens, but during the day, the flowers started emerging. Bob, Meg's father, hadn't returned from his travels. It was only a few days before he came back... at least I think so."

"Okay, that's good. Where did you see them?"

"Just out the front. I don't wander far from the pub, but they'd stopped to chat to a friend. They were telling their friend that Melissa's treatment would likely finish by September, and how excited they were to go on holiday afterwards. They were going on a two-month trip. They were holding hands, and if they were having problems, I couldn't tell." She nodded. "That cancer treatment you have these days is wonderful. Things have come a long way since I died. It's a wonderful time you lot live in now." She shook her head slowly. "Mobile phones, computers, things I could never have imagined. I wish I were still alive to experience it all."

"It is wonderful. I think we all take it for granted. Anyway, I can't talk much longer—Bailey will wonder what the dickens I'm up to in here. So, do you think they killed themselves, or that one killed the other?"

"Oh, no. Not at all. I will say that I have life experience, and Meg got her sense of reading people from me. They looked like a couple who wanted to live, and there wasn't any tension between them. But we ghosts aren't omnipresent. We can move from one place to the other quickly, but if we're not somewhere, we can't see or hear what's going on there. I can't read minds either. So, whilst I don't think I'm wrong, I might be."

I smiled, remembering when I'd first encountered Mary and thought it was my own brain, or maybe that if she were a ghost, I could talk to her mind to mind. That hadn't worked out. "Yes, I've learned that through trial and error." I chuckled. "Well, thank you for your insight. I tend to agree with you, though—I think someone else was involved, but I have absolutely no proof and only the word of Mr Downs, which counts for nothing, especially since ghosts, like live people, can lie."

"Yes, lass, they can. Did they go to the light?"

"Yes."

"Well, again, in my experience, whenever I've been present to see a person transition, those who went to the light always seemed like nice folk. If one of them had killed the other, I don't think that would've happened."

"Do you know for sure?"

Her kindly smile held a note of regret. "Unfortunately, no. I'm in the dark as much as a living person when it comes to whatever's on the other side of the portal to the next realm. I can tell you some things about the in-between, but what comes after remains a mystery."

"Bummer." Nothing was easy, it seemed. Even dying wasn't enough to find some things out. "Thank you again. I'd better get going."

"Don't be a stranger, Avery. It would be nice to chat again."

"I won't. Next time I get a chance, I'll come and say hello… in private."

Her quiet laugh was as sweet and light as fairy floss. "Indeed. I understand. All right, Avery, have a lovely night, and stay safe."

"I will. Thanks." She disappeared, and I slid my phone into my bag. Right, time to walk home. Hopefully Everly, my ncw ghost, wouldn't be there to keep me awake.

Navigating a new job, ghosts, an annoying landlady, new friends, dead bodies, murderers, unexplained deaths, and tempting men—I didn't think my life could get any more complicated.

Boy was I wrong.

CHAPTER 8

The next morning, on the way to the pub, I stopped at Heavenly Brew to grab a couple of coffees. I'd checked with Meg, and she told me that Bailey liked flat whites. When I walked into the café, an interesting sight greeted me. Joyless had her hand on Finnegan's shoulder and had pulled him halfway across the counter. Her mouth was right up to his ear. Mmm, cosy. I had no idea what she'd whispered, but his cheeks were red. When I walked in, he scrambled back, and she gave me a charming smile. "Avery! So great to see you again. Are you going to have the usual?"

For a moment, my speech centre refused to work. I glanced outside to check that things hadn't frozen over. I turned back to her. "Yes, thanks. Can I also get a medium flat white?"

"Ooh, who's it for?" If she didn't knock off the fake syrupy-sweet, I'm-your-new-best-friend tone, I was going to vomit right there on the café floor.

She was the last person I wanted to tell my business to, but it would be rude of me not to answer. "Bailey. He's taking me to see some cars this morning. I really need some wheels."

Finnegan had finally stopped blushing. "Bailey's a good choice for you, Avery. He knows all about cars."

"Excuse me?" I stuck my finger in my ear to make sure nothing was stuck in it.

"What?" His striking blue eyes emanated confusion.

"You called me by my correct name. Are you feeling okay, Finnegan?" If he could use the right name, so could I.

He smirked. "Sorry, Lightning, it's early, and my brain hasn't started functioning properly."

"Maybe it's lack of blood flow?" It was my turn to smirk as I glanced from his crotch to Joyless.

"Oh, that's right; you were hit by lightning, weren't you?"

I warily eyed the barista. She'd been fakely nice so far, but I could sense something coming. Rarely were bully's questions innocent. "Yes."

"Oh, that must be what that scar on your forehead is from. I wouldn't worry, though. It's not that obvious."

I touched the faint two centimetre scare near my hairline on my right side. It was so faded, I didn't even notice it anymore. It was from me falling off my bike when I was four. She was so full of it, and she'd said it in a way that Finnegan wouldn't realise she was being a cowpat. I smiled serenely. "Actually, that's not from lightning. I got that one a couple of years ago. There was this chick bullying my friend, and I head-butted her. That's from her two front teeth, which broke clean off. She had to have implants."

Her mouth fell open, and she quickly covered it with both hands, maybe fearing for the safety of her own teeth. Finnegan was holding back a laugh, but he watched me with an assessing gaze.

I looked at the two takeaway cups she'd just placed on the counter. "Are those mine, or Vinegar's?"

Her brow furrowed. "Whose?"

I jerked my head at Finnegan. "That guy."

"Oh, ah, no. These are for you. He hasn't ordered yet."

"Great. Thanks." I paid with the right change and grabbed the cups. "Have a lovely day, both of you." I managed to hold in my snort until I was out of hearing distance. Okay, so I hadn't directly threatened her, but it was nice to put the idea in her head that I was a touch crazy and possibly rather violent.

When I went into the pub, Meg was pouring coffee for a couple at one of the tables, and Bailey was behind the bar, his back to me, restocking one of the small fridges. I went to the bar. "Morning. Ready and reporting for car shopping."

He placed a few cans in the fridge, shut the door, and straightened. He turned to me, and wow, his smile was something to behold. I managed to hold in the happy sigh threatening to give me away as I handed him his coffee. If I pushed my feelings away long enough, they'd leave for good. Independence was important. "Oh, thanks. Flat white?"

"Yep. I sussed out your beverage preferences with Meg."

"I'm surprised she didn't tell you to get me a green tea. I can't stand the stuff." He grinned, and I couldn't help but return it. "Anyway, I'm keen to show you what I found. I had a look at a few more online last night, and I honestly think these two are the pick of what's around in your price range at the moment—at least within an hour's drive."

"Fair enough. I don't want to put you out any more than I already am, and like I said—I just need something that won't break down."

"There are no guarantees, unfortunately. But if whatever

we buy does give you trouble, I can fix it, so don't stress." He was just as nice as his sister. I was lucky to have landed here, among people who were actually decent and caring.

"Okay, thanks, but I don't want to abuse the friendship." Unless the cost to fix something on the car was ridiculous, there was no way I was going to ask him to help out again. I owed him too much already.

"I like to help. Chances are that we'll get you something reliable. If either of these cars today aren't right, I'll just keep my eye out."

"Okay, thanks. So, I suppose we should get to it?" I didn't want to be pushy, but the sooner we got this over and done with, the better. Spending a couple of hours with him was going to be a lesson in self-control. For someone who wanted to avoid dating, my hormones were being ridiculous, so minimizing contact with the opposite sex was probably more sensible. Kind of like when you were dieting and didn't buy junk food to keep in the house. If it wasn't there, you couldn't eat it.

Meg had served her customers breakfast and came over, a smile on her face. "Morning, Avery. Ready to buy a car?"

"Yep. How did last night go? Did you talk to him?"

Her smile fell. "Yeah. I'm going to his place tonight to hang out. It's a really good job offer. It's his dream promotion, and he'll make an extra twenty thousand a year. As much as I'm going to miss him, even I had to insist he should take the opportunity. I don't want to be someone he resents later because he missed out on this, and, as you know, we haven't been together long enough to know whether this is going to last long-term. We'll play it by ear, but I'm sad."

I stuck my bottom lip out in sadness solidarity. "Carina and I will keep you busy so you don't have time to miss him. Okay?"

"Is that a promise?"

I nodded. "Yep. I promise on chocolate pudding."

She grinned. "So, if you break your promise, you'll never eat it again?"

"Yep, and you know I love my chocolate pudding." I gave a short laugh.

"As much as I do. Thank you, Avery." She gave me a tight hug.

"Okay, ladies, I hate to break it up, but we have to get going." Bailey had come out from behind the bar and stood next to us.

"Okay, little bother. Take good care of her."

I snickered. "Bother? Ha, nice one."

Bailey looked at both of us and shook his head. "This is the thanks I get?"

We laughed; then I waved goodbye to Meg as we left. I followed Bailey out to the back car park. "Ooh, nice car." It was a lipstick-red, two-door classic car. I had no idea what it was, but it looked kind of sporty.

"It's a Volvo P 1800. Made in 1967. I bought it a few years ago and restored it." He placed his hand on the roof and caressed it.

"Well, she's gorgeous." I didn't care that much about cars, but this one was super pretty and stylish, so much so that I found myself wanting one. But it would be well out of my price range, so I didn't even ask what it cost; plus he might think I was being rude asking how much his car was worth.

He unlocked his side, got in, then unlocked my door. No central locking for 1967 cars. I slid into the light-tan leather seat, careful that my coffee didn't spurt out of the little hole at the top. "Wow, it's low." I felt like a 1960s movie star. Shame I wasn't dressed like one. Someone hand me a sparkly floor-length gown, white gloves, and a cigarette in a cigarette holder.

On the drive to the first one, we chatted easily… about the pub, his growing up with Meg, his craft beer, and his interest in cars. He'd asked me a few questions, but I didn't want to share what a train wreck my life had been before here, so I was vague and kept steering the conversation back to him. I didn't want his sympathy, but I also didn't want him realising what a naïve, weak person I'd been—letting toxic people control my life. It was embarrassing. Thinking of how my parents had treated me… still treated me… made me feel like I was ten and had no control over my life. Since I'd arrived, I'd had several nightmares about waking up back at their place, trapped for eternity. No thanks.

When we finally pulled up outside the house for the first car, I bit my tongue. *Oh, that's one ugly car.* Maybe it wasn't the one for sale?

"That must be it—a Nissan Juke. They're not the prettiest car out there, but they're reliable for the price."

"You're not wrong. The front is so… lumpy, the headlights are just ew, and it's baby-poo brownish green. What even is that colour?"

"I think the hue you're looking for is mustard." He chuckled.

Oh, goodness, I was sounding like a right prat. He'd gone to a lot of trouble for me, and I was being finicky after I'd said I had no preferences. "Sorry. That's just my initial reaction. Maybe it's nicer inside?"

He threw his head back and laughed. "You're a classic, Avery. You're allowed not to like it. I probably should've shown you the pictures first. But I do think it will be a good car. Let's just look at it. Also, do you like yellow?"

"Bright yellow, yes. Mustard yellow, no. Just in case you weren't sure." I gave him a sheepish smile.

"Well, the next car is canary yellow. Just thought I'd check before we drive there." He opened his door. "Come on. Let's go have a look. You need a starting point, in any case."

"Agreed."

After checking it out from top to bottom and taking it for a test drive, we said goodbye to the owner and hopped back in the Volvo. Bailey started it and turned to me. "I can polish out those scratches, and I know the seats were worn, but that's an easy fix with some seat covers. So, what do you think?"

I shrugged. "Um, I suppose it might do. Can we look at the other one, and maybe some more another day?"

"You can say you hate it. I won't be offended."

I pressed my lips together and counted to five. *Be polite.* Argh, who was I kidding? I let the words burst forth. "Okay, it's the ugliest car I've ever been in. Everything was lumpy. How did they manage that? Like the outside *and* the inside. Bumps everywhere. And the colour. Maybe they were going for a vomit theme—poo green and rounded chunks. I'm sorry. I just can't do it." I hung my head in shame. I was such a bad person to try and help. I lifted my head and looked into Bailey's eyes. "I didn't realise I was so picky. I'm usually not." He raised his brows. "Honest!" As evidenced by my previous choice of boyfriend.

He laughed. "It's okay. The next car is definitely not lumpy and is not an homage to vomit. Based on your different reactions to that car and this Volvo, I think you'll like it."

Bailey wasn't wrong. The next car was a cute canary-yellow Peugeot 207. As we got out of Bailey's car, I gave him a thumbs up. "This one is lovely. I like it."

"Hallelujah. Let's have a closer look and take it for a drive, and I'll let you know whether it's a goer. Also, they're asking fifteen-hundred pounds. I'm happy to negotiate for you if you decide you want it."

"Okay." He was clever about all things mechanical, so I'd trust his judgement, and I had no interest in trying to negotiate. I always felt guilty for asking for a discount, so me trying to get a good deal would not end well for me.

We had a look at the car, took it for a drive—we both had a turn—and when we got back, we sat in his car for a chat. "I like it."

"Are you sure? It runs well, and there are only a couple of scratches. I'll polish them out."

"You don't have to do that. As long as it gets me from A to B and doesn't look like a huge lump of crap, it's all good. In fact, it's quite a cute car. I think I'll call it Daisy."

He looked at me as if I'd gone mad. "You're going to name it?"

"Yes. Do you have a problem with that?"

He put his hands up. "No. Not at all. You do whatever you like. So, what's your top price?"

"Well, I couldn't spend more than fifteen-hundred pounds, so anything less than that is good. More than a hundred pounds off would be brilliant."

"I'll see what I can do." He gave me a smile and got out of the car. As he chatted to the owner, I drummed my fingers on my thigh. This morning, I didn't have my heart set on anything, but now, I really wanted that car. It was such a happy colour, and it was comfortable to drive. It would also mean more freedom for me. I was surprised to realise I'd be disappointed if I couldn't get it. Maybe I should go out and just say I'd pay full price. It was within my budget, after all. I put my hand on the handle and was about to open the door when the men shook hands.

Did that mean the car was mine? Should I get my wallet out?

Bailey turned towards me and waved "come on." Ooh, ooh, it was mine! I jumped out and walked over, trying not to bounce. This was the most exciting thing that had happened for a long time. Not that moving to a new country wasn't exciting, but there was mega stress that came with it. This was just fun... except the parting with so much money bit, but that couldn't be helped, so I wasn't going to dwell on it. "So, what's the damage?"

"Thirteen hundred and fifty." Bailey had his back to the seller and winked at me.

I grinned at him, then looked at the seller. "I wasn't sure if I was buying something today, so is it okay if I give you a five-hundred-pound deposit and bring the rest around tonight?" Whilst I'd known I might buy a car today, I wasn't sure, and I didn't want to wander around with that much cash on me.

Bailey shook his head. "That won't be necessary. I have the rest. You can pay me back when we go home. I'd rather do it this way than come back." My mouth fell open. Who carried that much cash around on a whim? He smiled. "I don't usually have that much cash on me, but I knew you might buy something. I wanted to be prepared... just in case."

Could he get any sweeter? His kindness blew me away. Was he for real? "Are you sure?"

"Of course. I wouldn't have offered if I wasn't. I know you're good for it." He made a decent point. He knew where I lived and worked. It wasn't like I could avoid him forever.

"Okay, then. We're good to go." I handed my money to the seller, and Bailey handed his over. We filled out the logbook paperwork, and Bailey sorted the insurance for me. The seller gave me the keys. Oh my God! I was the proud owner of a car. I stared at the keys. All mine. "Thanks." I turned to Bailey. "I guess I'll follow you home."

He grinned. "Let's go." He shook the guy's hand again. "Thanks, mate."

I got in my car and waited for him to start his; then I followed him home. The only disappointing thing about the day was that I didn't get to share the car trip home with him. I was way more disappointed than I should've been.

Oh, Avery, what am I going to do with you?

I honestly didn't know.

CHAPTER 9

On the way back to Manesbury, I stopped at the bank and took out the money to repay Bailey. Then we met at the pub where I gave it to him and showed an excited Meg the car. She was all squeals and congratulations. How had I lucked into such a wonderful friend? She'd put aside her sadness at her impending separation and was genuinely happy for me.

After that, I parked the car near the alley that led to Mrs Crabby's and walked back to work. As excited as I was to have Daisy, I had calls to make. The Downses' case wasn't going to solve itself. Okay, so the police were trying to figure it out, and they would probably get to the answer before I did, but until then, I'd keep going.

I buzzed the intercom at work, and Bethany let me in. My initial plan of killing her with kindness had fallen by the wayside. The energy it took wasn't worth it, so now I basically ignored her unless there was a specific reason to talk to her. It wasn't ideal, but you couldn't force someone to be friendly, so I accepted it and moved on.

Finnegan and Carina were in the office. "Hey."

They both looked up and returned my greeting. Carina smiled. "So, did you buy a car?"

I grinned. "Yes, I did! Bailey did such a good job finding one—he really knows what he's doing. And he was so nice to take me. It was almost an hour's drive away."

Finnegan stared at me, his expression serious while Carina was practically bouncing in her seat. "So, what did you get? What colour is it?"

Finnegan rolled his eyes. "Why do women always ask what colour the car is, as if it's the most important part?"

We both looked at him and answered in unison, "Because it is!" He shook his head.

I addressed my answer to Carina since Finnegan apparently didn't care about this information. "It's bright yellow and cute. I love it! It's a Peugeot 207. Bailey says they're very reliable."

"What did you call her?"

Finnegan looked at Carina like one looked at someone who'd just announced the world was flat. "What? Cars don't need names. They're all she, and that's it."

It was my turn to roll my eyes. "Her name is Daisy, and I'll give you a lift any time, Carina." I shifted my gaze to Finnegan. "But if *you* ever want a lift, you'll have to apologise for being such a grumpy pants."

"Thankfully, as you know, I have my own car, so I won't be imposing on you any time soon. Oh, and I've submitted my article on the Downses. The police have confirmed it was a murder-suicide. Mr Downs killed himself and his wife."

My mouth dropped open. "What?!"

"They've got some of the toxicology reports back—it was arsenic, which they found in his back shed and in the lamb. He wrote the suicide note, and even though Mrs Downs supposedly signed it as well, their handwriting expert said she didn't. Mrs Downs spoke to a friend of hers a few weeks ago and said they were having trouble and she was worried he might do something crazy."

I pressed my lips together. Had Mr Downs lied to me? Ghosts were just people, so they'd have the same flaws, but still, he went into the light. Something wasn't right. "So that's it? They've closed the case?"

"Yep. Done and dusted. My article's already on the net, and it'll be in tomorrow morning's paper."

Wow, way to kill the mood. "Right. Okay." I plonked into my chair. Now what? Did I keep digging, or was it a waste of time? Was I wrong in my assumption of his innocence?

"Don't worry, love. We can't get it right all the time." Ah, Carina, trying to make me feel better.

"Thanks." I'd keep digging because my gut was still unsettled, but I didn't have to tell anyone—if I was wrong, I'd like it to be in private. "Well, I have another story to work on, so I'll get to it." I gave them a fake smile and got out my laptop.

Hmm, traditionally, women used poison to kill people. Men were more for violence, like knives and guns. So that was another strike against him having done it. Not that it was an impossibility, but still. Also, I imagined it was a painful death. It wasn't sudden, like a bullet. I googled death by arsenic and wrote down the facts. It was odourless and practically tasteless. It could kill within thirty minutes, or it could take hours. There was vomiting, diarrhoea, muscle cramps, abdominal pain. Yeah, not pleasant. Why would you choose to die that way? Apparently Agatha Christie enjoyed killing her characters with it. I thought back to those novels on the bedside table. Hmm. I took out my phone and scrolled through my photos. One book was on top of the other, so only one title was visible. It was a David Baldacci novel, *One Good Deed*. So, it was a thriller. That told me nothing.

Whatever evidence the police had found led them to believe he killed her, so if there was a third party involved, they either left no evidence behind, or they were never in the house with the couple. Maybe they had accidentally left the door open, but maybe someone exited in a hurry and left it open. I scrolled through all the pictures and zoomed in, just in case something jumped out at me.

It didn't.

Cat's bum.

Was I wrong? If I was, looking into it further was going to be a colossal waste of time. I sighed. I felt like there was more to this, but was that only because I'd spoken to Mr and Mrs Downs, and they seemed fine together? There was no evidence of a break and enter. No evidence of a third party killing them… well, I couldn't see any, and the police hadn't found any. Had Mr Downs lied to me?

Without access to police information, and with nothing else to go on, maybe it would just aggravate Melissa's best friend for me to interview her? Was it time to accept defeat and move on?

I opened my emails and grabbed the information on someone else who wanted their time in the sun. I'd think about the Downses' case and decide tomorrow—it wasn't as if I could save their lives and time was of the essence. I had to pay my bills, so I called the proud parent of a super-intelligent— no doubt precocious—ten-year-old who'd just won some spelling competition and gotten the school award for maths. Boy oh boy was this going to be fun....

Karen Wilkinson was the thirty-five-year-old mother of Aiden —the boy smashing all records, according to her, anyway. I glanced down at my phone. Sitting in her conservatory, we were on minute twenty-two of how smart she'd been as a child, how ahead of her age she was, and how he'd taken after her, and I hadn't even gotten to ask him anything about the spelling competition or his maths award. "And, of course, all the other mothers are jealous. I've seen the looks they give me. Honestly, you'd think being smart was a crime. It's not my fault their lack of intelligence is a bore. They never ask me to anything, but I wouldn't go anyway." She rolled her eyes. Ooookay.

I used the pause to get a word in. I looked at Aiden. "So, did you do much study before the spelling awards?"

Aiden smiled. "Ye—"

Karen tittered, cutting him off, then gave me a "don't be absurd" look. "He didn't have to study. He's naturally intelligent."

Aiden's little face fell. She was taking his moment away from him. If he'd worked hard to achieve his goals, the least she could do was acknowledge it. Stones of anger ground against each other in my stomach. Bullying took many forms, and I was attuned to all of them. I ignored her. "Aiden, I think you did study and work hard, and I say congratulations to you for putting in the effort." I smiled. "You should be so proud of yourself."

He gave me a grateful smile. His voice was quiet, but at least he got it out. "I am. Thank you, Miss Avery."

"And how did you feel when you won the maths award?"

He grinned, but his mother answered, obliviously selfish. "Oh, I expected it, but my husband and I were so pleased. He gets his talent from me, you know."

Right, did I ask you? I pointedly stuck my gaze to Aiden. "How did you feel, *Aiden*?" And just in case she didn't get it, I looked at her, my patience done. Her mouth was opening to speak, but I cut her off. "I'm not asking you. I'm asking Aiden. Please let him answer."

Her mouth dropped open, and her hand flew to her chest, as if I'd mortally wounded her with my sharp, but necessary, words. Finally, she was speechless.

I turned back to Aiden and smiled. "Go on."

He grinned. "I was excited, and my friend Briony was too. She clapped the loudest. I just missed out on the award last year, so getting it this year was the best. My dad even gave me ten pounds. I'm saving for a puppy."

I returned his grin. "That's excellent, Aiden. Hard work always pays off, and you deserve that award. I'm so pleased for you! Why don't we get a photo of you with your spelling trophy?"

"Okay." He picked the small bronze-coloured trophy of an open book from the table and held it up near his face.

I turned a flinty gaze on his mother but kept my tone even, so as not to upset Aiden—I'd probably already shocked him by speaking to his mother as I had. Maybe it wasn't professional, but she'd not only snapped my last straw, she'd chewed it, spat it out, and stomped all over it, sprayed it with lighter fluid, and torched it. "I'd like to get a picture of just him, and after that, I'll take one with both of you in it." She nodded but said nothing. Was she scared of me? I couldn't help the evil smile that crept into existence. Good. She'd probably never had anyone stand up to her before. The other mothers at school obviously avoided her for their own sanity rather than get into a pointless argument with her. I looked back at Aiden. "Smile big for the readers!" *Click*.

After that, I took a photo of Karen with Aiden; then I left. I already knew what I was going to call the article: "Aiden Wilkinson Proves Hard Work Reaps Rewards." I wasn't going to give his mother the credit—she had that covered. My article would be all about what a modest, lovely boy he was, and how he'd studied hard and dreamed of achieving those goals. His mother might not give him his dues, but someone needed to.

I returned to the empty office, typed the article, and pressed Send to Mr MacPherson. After that was done, my phone rang. Tom Downs's mother. "Hello, Avery speaking."

"Oh, hello, Avery. I don't know if you remember me, but I'm Agnes Downs… Tom's mother."

"Of course I remember you. Is everything okay?" She sounded a little breathless, stressed.

"Well, I've just read the article in your online paper. The police didn't even inform me of their findings. I called them to complain, but I'm just beside myself. They're wrong. My boy couldn't have killed Melissa, or himself. He just wasn't that person. He would never physically hurt someone else, let alone the love of his life. As much as I didn't particularly like after she betrayed him, I accepted that he loved her. When he was younger, I swatted a fly, and he cried about it. He wouldn't use fly spray either—it drove Melissa crazy that he would let the bugs be. That's the sort of man he was. I can't accept their findings. I just can't. I won't. There must be another answer."

So, I wasn't the only one who questioned the outcome.

Admittedly his mother would be on his side, but still…. "I'm so sorry, Mrs Downs." I had to be careful what I said, because I didn't want her complaining to Mr MacPherson that one of his journalists disagreed with a story he'd approved. It would be different if I had proof, but all I had was my gut, and as far as I knew, it had authority over nothing, and its reputation had still to be proven. "It must be terrible to hear that. I'm not sure why you're calling me though. I can't change their findings." As much as I wanted to. Although, I should be mindful—reporting the truth was still my passion, and I shouldn't let my feelings get in the way of that. I had to accept that he could be guilty.

"I'm desperate, Miss Winters. Melissa's parents have called and abused me, blamed me for the whole thing. But I don't even mind that so much. It's what everyone thinks of my boy. He's not a killer. I can't bear that everyone who knew him, and people who didn't, think he could kill someone. He did so much good when he was alive, and it's all come to nothing. When I spoke to the police, they were less than helpful. I fear I'll get no help there. You just seemed so nice, and I've looked you up online. Your investigative work is impressive. You've cracked some cases wide open for the police back in Australia, and I saw that you solved that estate agent's murder just a couple of weeks ago. Please help me. I can pay."

I rubbed my forehead. It was one thing to see what I could find because I was curious, but it was another to have someone relying on me. If I took this on, it might lead to disappointment for her—not that it would be my fault, but I hated disappointing people, especially a grieving mother. Also, I'd just about run out of leads. There was really only the best friend to talk to, and maybe, if I was lucky, someone else at his work to get the lowdown on Russo.

But if I said no, she'd be just as upset, and she had no one else to turn to. Cat's bum. I was so bad at saying no to people. I huffed out a breath. She wasn't the first person to go to a journalist for help, and I dared say she wouldn't be the last. "Okay, Mrs Downs. I'll help you. But I can't guarantee anything, and I won't accept your money."

"Please, I'm happy to pay."

"No. If it turns out the police were wrong, I'll have another prize-winning article, and my boss will pay me. I can't take your money. As long as you can agree to that, I'll help."

"You drive a hard bargain, Miss Winters, but okay. Thank you so much. You have no idea how relieved I am that you'll help. So, what do you need me to do?"

"Right now, nothing. I wanted to interview Melissa's best friend. So why don't I do that first, then I'll be in touch."

"Okay. Please let me know if you find out anything in the meantime."

"I will, and you too."

"Okay. Speak to you soon."

"Bye, Mrs Downs."

"Goodbye." She hung up.

I looked up the vet where Melissa's best friend worked and crossed my fingers because after this, I had nothing except maybe begging Bellamy for answers as to why they'd declared it a murder-suicide. As far as my ghost connections were concerned, I'd exhausted that angle for now. Until Charles wanted to make amends, I'd be stuck.

I called the vet, my stomach muscles tight with trepidation. What if she refused to talk to me? At least the receptionist had put me through. In a few seconds, Melissa's best friend picked up the phone. "Hello, Catherine here. Avery Winters, is it?"

"Yes. I'm sorry to bother you, but I'm doing an article on

Mr and Mrs Downs for the *Manesbury Daily*, and I was wondering if I could chat to you about them. I only need five or ten minutes."

"Oh." Silence invaded the line until it became uncomfortable. I was about to ask if she was still there when she said, "I saw the article today. What could you possibly have to talk to me about after the fact?"

"That wasn't my article. I'm doing a personality piece—how their lives were integral to the Manesbury community, and how sad their friends and family are that they're gone. I figured since you were Mrs Downs's best friend, that you might want to say something, but if you don't, it's okay. I understand. I just figured that it would be a lovely tribute to her for you to share a memory or two." Hopefully the guilt-trip method would work.

"Mmmmm." She sighed. "Fine. I don't like talking about it because I still tear up, but if you can bear with me, I'll do it. I have time tomorrow morning at ten. You can come to the clinic. It's then or never." Wow, she was... I didn't actually know. She was giving me an interview, but she wasn't making it easy.

"I'll be there. Thank you so much. I'll see you tomorrow at ten."

"Goodbye, Miss Winters." She hung up before I had a chance to say goodbye. Was she a prickly person, or was this just her exhibiting grief? I guessed I couldn't expect everyone to hold onto niceties when they were upset.

"Afternoon, all!" Mr MacPherson strode through the door, his voice enthusiastically loud. He halted abruptly when he noticed I was the only one in. "Where are the others?"

"Ah... I have no idea. There's not a rule that they have to be in here right now, is there?"

"No, no, of course not. I just wanted to make an announcement." He shrugged. "No matter. I can do this twice." He reached into his trouser pocket and pulled out a shiny blue key. "This is for you. It's the front-door key. Bethany's complained about having to let you in every time you buzz, so I figured I'd get you all your own keys. I'm sure I can trust you lot not to lose them."

My brow furrowed. "Did she just complain about letting *me* in, or everyone?"

He rocked from heel to toe and back again. "Just you, come to think of it, but I'm sure she meant everyone. In any case, here we are. You get your own key. Isn't that wonderful."

Wonderful? I was pretty sure we had different definitions of wonderful, but anyway, he was trusting me more, so I'd take that for the positive it was. It also meant that I wasn't about to be fired. I smiled "Yes, Mr M——, ah, Julian; it's extremely wonderful."

"Good!" He slapped his hands together. "Tell the others to come see me when they get in, and I'll give them their keys." He gave a firm nod. "See you later."

"Bye."

He hurried out the door, leaving me with the spoils of Bethany's disdain. I pulled my house—and car, hooray—keys out of my bag and tried to push the end of one ring through the hole in the key. It slipped, and I wrestled with it until I got it on, almost scraping my finger. Three tries must be my new record. Surely there was an easier way? With all the technology in the world today, these metal rings were the best mankind could do? Society had a right to be disappointed.

I checked my phone. It was midafternoon, and other than book in tomorrow's interview, I had nothing left to do. Hmm. I had Tom's cousin's phone number. It might be time to call him. Even though I'd probably get the same story from him as Tom's mother, it wouldn't hurt to call. Even one new piece of information could help.

I dialled Anson Downs. He answered on the third ring. "Anson speaking."

"Hi, Anson. My name's Avery Winters, I—"

"Ah, my aunt said you might call. I'm happy to talk to you. Anything to help."

It wasn't always this easy to get people to talk—well, trivial stuff, yes, but serious stuff, not so much—so I allowed myself a moment of relief. I'd been interviewing a lot of bereaved people since I arrived in England, and my shoulders were constantly tight. It was as if I was only a few words away from an argument. And my inherent nature of not wanting to upset people didn't help. Treading lightly was hard work. "Thanks so much, Anson. I really appreciate it. I'm not even sure if you'll have anything new for me, but let's try."

"My aunt mentioned you were trying to help her figure out what really happened. For what it's worth, I knew Tom incredibly well—we were more like brothers than cousins—and he wouldn't have killed Melissa. There's no way."

"What about her affair?" He'd said he wanted to help. It was time to see how much.

"It killed Tom. He wanted to do whatever it took to fix things." He paused for a few beats. "He forgave her quickly... too quickly if you ask me. I was waiting for her to do it again, you know, because where were the repercussions? As much as I loved Tom, he was a pushover as far as she was concerned. The moment he met her, he never looked at another woman. He always did whatever she wanted. That's partly why he had a falling out with one of his business partners."

Things just got more interesting. Could this be the key to the whole thing? "You mean Russo?"

"Yes."

"Just a quick question before you continue. Did the police interview you?"

"No. I haven't heard from them."

"Okay, thanks. Anyway, please go on." How many people had the police spoken to? I knew they'd spoken to Tom's mother and Russo, but other than that, had they bothered to interview anyone else?

"When their business grew and they needed to buy another premises, Russo wanted them to put their houses up as collateral for the bank. Melissa refused, and in order to get the deal done, they had to pay a higher interest rate because their loan-to-deposit ratio was too high. They almost missed out on the property. Russo had words with Tom and Melissa. After that, Melissa was on the war path. She knew he was having an affair and told his wife of eleven years. She left him, took their three kids, and he lost his house. Admittedly, he's a bully, and his wife is probably better off without him, but Melissa created an enemy that day. Russo said if she ever came near him again, she'd better watch out, and he lost all respect for Tom for not standing up to Melissa. Russo and Tom barely spoke after that. They went from being best friends and business partners to just shy of enemies."

"Wow, what a mess."

"Indeed."

"So, Russo might have had motive to kill them?"

His tone sounded unsure. "Possibly, but you would think something would've had to trigger that. As much as they didn't speak, they'd settled into a toleration of one another. I would've thought if Russo wanted to off them, he would've done it ages ago."

"Maybe he's good at the long game and didn't want to be too obvious, or maybe something else happened recently?"

"Maybe. If it did, Tom didn't say anything to me."

"So, if the police didn't speak to you, and Tom's mother didn't know, Russo would hardly have said how much he disliked Tom and Melissa. Someone at the office would've said something to the police, surely?"

"I can't say."

I rubbed my forehead. From what I'd seen on my visit, the staff were scared of Russo. Maybe they all kept quiet for fear of losing their jobs... or worse? Argh, now I really needed to speak to someone else there. I sighed. This case was complicated. "Do you know who Melissa had the affair with?"

"Yes. Phillip Granger. He lives in Manesbury and works as a butcher."

My mouth dropped open. Could it be Phil, the guy who'd sold Melissa the meat? "Does he work at Manesbury's Meaty Morsels?"

"Yes, that's the guy. Tom complained to me that he couldn't step foot in there any more. He'd promised Melissa he wouldn't make a big deal out of it, but if he'd gone in there, he probably wouldn't have held his tongue."

I drummed my fingers on my table. "Do you think Phil could've killed them? Do you think she was still seeing him?"

"Not that I know of, and as for him being capable, I don't know. I haven't had any dealings with him. I only know from everything Tom told me."

"Okay, thanks. Is there anything else you can think of? Anyone else that might've had it in for both of them?"

I waited a few seconds for his firm answer. "No. That's it.

If I think of anything else, I'll let you know, but Russo and Phil, well, based on what I just told you, either of them could've done it."

"Okay, thanks, Anson. I really appreciate you talking to me."

"Any time, Avery. Thanks for helping us out."

"Not a problem. Speak to you soon." Argh, why did I say that? I should've just said bye. I likely wouldn't be speaking to him soon. Automatic niceties could be embarrassing.

"Bye."

So, Phil the butcher, aye. If his borderline aggressive demeanour was a clue, he definitely could've done this. Although, again, I'd see him more as a violent person. Still, whoever did this had pulled off the perfect crime. Just because men could be violent, didn't mean they were stupid, and if poison got the job done and you avoided suspicion, I guessed it was logical that they'd choose to do it that way.

I wrote everything in my notebook. Thanks to Anson, I had new information—much more than I thought I'd get. Lucky I made the effort. If there was anything this job had taught me, it was that information could come from unlikely sources, and all you needed was one nudge in the right direction for things to completely change.

So, my suspect list, if I included Tom, had grown to three when I included Phil. No wonder he'd been less than friendly towards me. He was probably hoping I wouldn't find out he'd been getting it on with Melissa. It seemed to be a well-kept secret. So, what did I do with that information? Should I tell the police... assuming they didn't already know. Should I interview Phil again? Hmm, I didn't know what the point would be. He was already trying to tell me as little as possible, and admitting to him that I knew he'd had an affair with Melissa wouldn't make any difference.

Well, sitting in the office wasn't going to help me, so I decided to go home and look at my car. Eek! I had a car! Tomorrow, I could drive myself to Cramptonbury. No more bus for this little possum.

Excitement zinged in my belly as the happy yellow of Daisy became visible when I was only part way up the hill. My brow furrowed, and I walked faster. "Hey, Vinegar! You'd better not be hurting my new car."

He planted his hands on his hips as I reached him. "This isn't new. It must be at least ten years old."

I rolled my eyes. "Very funny. It's new to me. And why are you skulking around her?"

He raised an eyebrow. "I'm not skulking. I was just wondering whose car it was. I should've known it was yours. Why did you park in my spot?" He folded his arms.

"This isn't *your* spot." I wandered around the car, perusing the ground. "There's no sign that says Annoying Manchild."

"This has always been my spot. I've parked here ever since I moved in."

"Why did I see a white van parked here yesterday? And whose green Renault is sometimes here? Your car is here like a third of the time. And what's the big deal, anyway? You have to walk a further, what, ten or twenty feet if you park behind me or the next spot down?"

"That's not the point, Lightning."

I cocked my head to the side. "So, what is the point? And don't cry. It won't work." I smirked, knowing full well he wasn't going to cry.

"It's just… well…. It's mine. I was here first."

I smiled. "Apparently, I was here first because I got this spot." I stroked the roof of my Peugeot. "Isn't she pretty?"

His face was no less gorgeous for being stained with the grumps. He'd get over it. "No. She's not pretty—she's annoyingly in my spot. Her owner's annoying too."

"Oh, for Zeus's sake. Get over yourself. Are you always this immature?" I narrowed my eyes. "You must be an only child—used to getting your way."

"No, I have an older sister."

"Send her my condolences. Having to grow up with you must've been a trial. Anyway, I have stuff to do. See ya."

His eyes widened. "You're not going to move it?"

I looked at him as if he'd just suggested I invite Mrs Crabby over for dinner. "You're out of your ever-loving mind. Your car is two car lengths away. You've already walked the distance to here." I narrowed my eyes, then smirked. "Ha! This isn't even about the car any more, is it? You just can't stand not getting your way." I shook my head. "I'm going to enjoy eating dinner tonight and lying in bed waiting to go to sleep because I'll know you're next door crying into your pillow and hating that my car is where you wanted your car to be and that you're fuming over losing. Poor baby." This was the most ridiculous conversation I could remember being involved in for a long time... well, except for the guy who married the tree, but my expectations had never been high with Ian.

Before it became even more insane, I gave him a wave, turned, and walked through the narrow laneway to home. Now I had to work out how to get that spot more often because there wasn't anything quite as much fun as annoying Vinegar.

CHAPTER 10

My interview with Catherine wasn't until ten, and the next village wasn't that far away, so I got up early and walked to work. I ran into Sergeant Bellamy outside the café, which was fortuitous and would save me a phone call. I'd tossed up whether to speak to him or not and decided I might as well—I had nothing to lose and everything to gain if he took me seriously. "Morning, Sergeant. How goes it today?"

His lips moved slightly, but I would've said it was more of a grimace than a smile. Oh well, you couldn't win them all. "Morning, Miss Winters. I'm well, thank you. How are you?"

"I'm good thanks. I wanted to talk to you about something, actually."

A distinct "oh no, not again" look hijacked his face. "I'm in a bit of a hurry. Maybe we could chat later?"

"I'm sorry, but I need to tell you now. Did you know that Mrs Downs had an affair a little while ago? She was dating Phil Granger, the butcher. He sold her that meat… you know, the poisoned leg of lamb. I hope you interviewed him in depth about his feelings for her. We all know what can happen when a lover is scorned."

His expression shuttered, and police mode was activated. "I'm not at liberty to discuss who we interviewed." Hmm, that might be code for they didn't know or talk to him, or it might be that he just didn't want to tell me. If only Charles would apologise to the dead policeman.

"Weeeeeell, if by any chance you haven't spoken to him, maybe you should."

His bushy eyebrows rose. "Is that so?"

I smiled. "Yes. Not telling you how to do your job,"—okay, so I was totally telling him—"but Tom's mother doesn't believe he's capable of killing anyone, and I promised I'd help. At least I can tell her that I asked you about it. It gets me off the hook." Lies were becoming my forte, but only at work. It was always good to add new skills to one's repertoire.

He cleared his throat. "Right. Well, is that all, Miss Winters?"

I gave him my most innocent smile. "Yes, Sergeant. Thank you for your time. Have a lovely day." His response was a grunt. I really wasn't making friends around here. Maybe it really was me? Carina and Meg might just have a high tolerance for annoying people? If I was a dog, I probably would've been one of those small, persistently yappy ones. This self-reflection left me deflated; however, I wasn't going to change what I was doing. When it came down to it, I'd rather help someone and get to the truth than make friends. Sergeant Bellamy would get over my interference, and I might as well acclimatise him to how it was going to be.

Feeling brave, I ducked into Heavenly Brew to grab a coffee. To my delight, Joyless wasn't in. Anna, the owner, was there by herself. It was altogether a pleasant experience. Maybe today was going to be a good one.

I spent an hour in the office and teed up another article interview for tomorrow for a new fitness club opening two villages away. At least that wouldn't hold any surprises. A simple promotional article with no narcissistic parents, dead bodies, or foliage fetishists. What a novelty!

Once that was done, I walked home to grab Daisy. There was a note on the windshield, under the windscreen wiper. I unfolded it, and in big letters, it said, "You suck more than a commercial vacuum cleaner." It was signed, unsurprisingly, by Finnegan. I laughed. It was worth parking in this spot, just for the note. I was pretty sure he was mucking around, but who knew? There were enough nutty people around here that maybe I'd finally exposed Finnegan for the crazy person he was. I hoped not because it would be such a waste of a gorgeous guy. Oh well.

I scrunched the note up and put it in my bag. I clapped my hands together. Woohoo! I was going to drive my new baby. Thankfully, she started first go. There was no reason she shouldn't have, but I usually expected the worst so I wouldn't be disappointed when it happened. It had been a good strategy in Sydney, but maybe I didn't need it so much here? I wasn't quite ready to ditch that habit yet, and habits took a while to unwind, so I'd worry about it later.

I drove with the windows down, the warm summer air whooshing in and mussing up my hair. The radio was on, upbeat tunes cascading out of the speakers. Boy, was this way better than the bus. I grinned, the feeling of just being alive sending a joyful warmth through my veins.

Cramptonbury Veterinary Hospital was on the main road, so it wasn't hard to find. A single-level white brick building, it looked like a repurposed seventies government building. I parked in a spot that had a vacant space on either side. My car wasn't new, but I didn't want her getting dinged on our second day together. She was my first possession bought without interference from those who wanted to control me. Yes, I'd had advice from Bailey, but it was offered with kindness and knowledge. He hadn't said it to boss me around, and I'd had a choice. As I got out of the car, it sank in how truly controlled I'd been. How had I not realised it back then? A subject to consider at another time. Right now, I needed to focus on getting more information to help Agnes Downs. That's what mattered today.

The waiting room was brightly lit, but the grey-and-white vinyl floor tiles had seen better days. A few owners and their animals waited to be seen by one of the vets. Their website listed five vets. If I ever got a pet, I'd know where to take them. Even though the floor could do with a retile, the reviews were good.

One of the two vet nurses manning the reception desk looked up as soon as I reached it. "Hi. Can I help you?"

"Yes, thanks. I'm here to see Catherine Bickford. I have an appointment. My name's Avery Winters." She looked at my vacant arms and gave me a weird look. I only just stopped myself from saying, I'm here for my worming tablets and flea treatment.

"Is your pet in the car?"

"No. This is a personal matter."

"Oh, okay. Hang on a moment." She stood and left down a long hallway, which led to many doors. After a minute, she returned. "She can see you now. It's the second door on the left."

"Thanks." I crossed my fingers that she'd have information that would help.

Her office door was open, so I knocked and went straight in. She stood and reached her slim, white-coat-clad arm across the table. "Hello, Avery. Lovely to meet you." I shook her hand. At least we were off to a good start. "Please sit." She gave me a tired smile. Photos sat on the shelf behind her. A photo of her and Melissa, and one of her, Melissa, and Tom. There were also photos of dogs and horses.

"Thanks so much for talking to me today. I'm so sorry you've lost your best friend."

She pulled a piece of red wool out of her pocket and twirled it around her fingers. "Thank you. Yes, it's come as quite a shock. She was beating her cancer, making plans for the future. It's just such a waste. I can't believe that Tom would do such a thing when they both had so much to live for. Just goes to show that you never really know a person." She pressed her lips together. "I'm still quite angry at him. Fair enough if you want to kill yourself, but why did he have to take Melissa with him?" She tugged on the wool, and it snapped. Her forehead wrinkled, and she leaned under the table, presumably throwing it away. She reached into her pocket and pulled out another one. Maybe she'd recently given up smoking or biting her fingernails? It didn't look like a bad way to keep your hands occupied.

"Were they having problems?"

She shrugged. "Off and on. No more than any normal couple. A few weeks ago, they had a huge argument, but they'd patched it up... at least that's what Melissa said." Her gaze sharpened. "I thought you were here to get a story or two from me. Why are you asking these other questions? I thought the police investigation was over."

"Oh, it is. And I do want your stories of Melissa. I was just going with the flow. I also heard that Melissa had an affair a while ago—not that I'm putting any of that in. Just my natural journalist's curiosity, I suppose."

"So, you think he did it out of anger?"

"I don't think so." Although, what had that fight been about? Had she started seeing Phil again? But then, their ghosts were happy. Going back and forth with "were they fighting or weren't they" was like being on a manic seesaw. I wanted off. "Everyone seems to think they were happy, that they got over it. I just wondered if maybe the man she had an affair with didn't like that she got back with Tom and that it was all a cover-up."

Her eyes widened. "Surely not. I mean, she did have an affair, but I don't blame her. She wasn't well, and she panicked. I think it was like, you know, some people drink to avoid facing life-changing moments, some people take drugs, and some people have affairs. I just think it hurt Tom more than he let on. He said he forgave her, but maybe he hadn't." She stared at the wall behind me for a moment.

"Did she talk to you about the affair?"

She hugged herself. "Yes, but she wouldn't say who it was with." She shook her head. "Look, I don't want to talk about this any more. Melissa would hate that we're speaking about her mistake. As far as I'm concerned, Tom killed them both. Now, I'll tell you a story of when we were teenagers and went on a camping trip."

Well, that was a vote for Tom being guilty. I was clearly going to get nothing further from her. "Okay, great. Go ahead." I took out my notepad and pen and started writing. Just when I thought I was getting somewhere, it seemed that I wasn't.

CHAPTER 11

Wanting to escape my frustration for more than five minutes, I parked back at home and went to the pub for lunch. Even if Meg was busy, I could still enjoy lunch. They had the best beef and Guinness pie ever. My mouth watered just thinking about it.

The small lunch crowd was buzzing with summer enthusiasm. Well, except for Phil, who was here with his two workmates. He noticed me as I walked to the bar, and anger thundered across his face. Cat's bum. Had he found out what I said to Bellamy? That was something I didn't count on. I thought the police were meant to be confidential about things.

"Hey, Avery." Bailey's greeting stole my attention.

"Hey." I shrugged off Phil's death stare and smiled.

"How's Daisy going?"

"Really well, thanks. I took her to Cramptonbury this morning… well, she took me. No problems at all. Thanks again. I really love her."

He grinned. "I like to please." Hmm, was there innuendo

in there? I wasn't quite sure, but the way his gaze didn't leave mine made it more than fifty, fifty that there was.

Because I was too embarrassed to flirt—what if he was being genuine and I'd misinterpreted it?—I ignored the whole thing. "Is Meg here? I'm going to eat here today."

"She's just in the kitchen, but she's working, so I don't think she'll be able to. I'm sorry."

"That's okay. I'm an adult—I can eat by myself. I'll just say hello when she comes out."

"What are you having?"

I gave him my order and paid, even though he tried to refuse my money. Then I found a table near the bay window and far away from Phil who, by the aggro on his face, was sad I was still here and alive. I wasn't that worried, but the more his personality came out, the more I could believe he'd killed the Downses. Phil wasn't the type of guy you broke up with. Hmm, maybe I should ask around about his history because I didn't want to *assume*. Meg's dad might be able to fill me in. Seemed as if he'd decided to stay in Manesbury for a while longer. Maybe it wasn't as painful to be here without his wife as it used to be?

I purposely had my back to Phil's table. Unfortunately, it didn't discourage him from coming to annoy me. He came around and stood at the other side of my table with his arms folded so he could look down at me. His lip curled up in a sneer. "I don't appreciate you tattling to the police. I had nothing to do with Mel and Tom dying. Mind your own business, or it's going to get you into trouble." He unfolded his arms and punched his fist into his palm. "Comprendo?"

Adrenaline shot through my belly, and I was careful to make sure my voice was steady. "Did you just threaten me?" I pushed my chair back, stood, and stared him down. He was much larger than me and could punch me out in one second, but I didn't want him to know that, that scared the bejesus out of me. "I'm a reporter. I deal in the truth, and if I discover something the police should know, I'll tell them."

"Listen here, girlie," he growled. "Mess with me, and you get what you get. This is your first and last warning." As he stomped past me, I almost put my foot out to trip him. That would've been hilarious, but I probably would've gotten a concussion for my trouble.

Bailey hurried over a tad too late. To be fair to him, it escalated quickly, and he couldn't have heard much of what was said from the bar. "What happened, Avery? Are you okay?"

I took a deep breath and again willed my voice to not shake. "I'm okay. I told the police that Mrs Downs had an affair with Phil, and Phil didn't appreciate it. He just threatened me."

His eyes widened. "You have to call the police. Tell them." When I didn't answer, his gaze implored me. "Promise me, Avery. Please."

I blew out a breath. "Yes, okay. I'll call now."

"Good, and I'm going to throw him out."

"No! He might hurt you."

He shook his head. "Not likely, unless he wants to find himself in jail. We don't take too kindly to people threatening our patrons." Before I could argue, he turned and strode to Phil. After some—what looked like—heated words, Phil stood and stared Bailey down. It looked like it could be on, but after Luke patted Phil's arm and said something to calm him, he stuck his finger up at Bailey and left.

Crisis averted. For now.

Bailey came back. "See, all fixed. Let me know if he gives you any more trouble, and please call the police right now."

I wanted to roll my eyes, but he was right, and it was nice that he cared. "Okay. And thanks for kicking him out. I'm sorry about causing trouble in here." I took out my phone.

His brow furrowed. "What are you talking about? It wasn't your fault."

"Well, it kind of was. I dobbed him into Bellamy."

"It doesn't give him the right to threaten you." He jerked his head around and looked at the bar. "I have to get back to work, but come see me if you're worried. Okay?"

"Okay. Thanks." I gave him a small smile.

As he walked off, Meg came in and walked towards me, carrying what I could excitedly describe as my pie. "Yum, thanks."

"My pleasure." She put it on the table. "How's everything going? Is your new car good?"

"It is, thanks. How's things with your man?" Even though he was moving, maybe she'd made peace with the fact that they'd have a long-distance relationship.

She shrugged one shoulder. "I don't know. Not great. I mean, we're getting along, and I like him so much, but he's still going." She stuck her bottom lip out.

I grabbed her hand and squeezed it. "Things will work out. Besides, Scotland isn't that far from here. Surely you can go over for weekends and vice versa."

She gave a nod. "Yeah, but it's a long way. I can't see either of us doing it that often, and we're super busy on weekends here, but I guess Dad can fill in for me here and there—he's staying for a while now, said he misses Bailey and me."

"Aw, that's so sweet of your dad. I'd donate my time, but you'd lose customers. Half of Manesbury hates me." I laughed.

"Who hates you? Point them out, and I'll deal with them."

I smiled. "You're the best. Well, just before, I had an *issue* with Phil." I told her what happened because Bailey was sure to, and she'd want to speak to me about it. Might as well get it over and done with now.

Her mouth formed a large *o*. "That pig! He's always been a gruff sort of bloke, and I've heard from the guys that he can get a bit rough when he's had too much to drink, but to threaten you? That's horrible. Have you called the police?"

"I was going to, but then my pie came, and it's going to get cold." I gave her a cheesy grin and picked up my cutlery. "I'll call them as soon as I've finished this."

She gave me a "you'd better" look. "Okay, well, I'll check on you later. I've got meals to serve. Let me know if you need anything."

"I will. Thanks."

So, if it was Phil, how would I prove it? And were the police looking into it, or did Bellamy talk to him and decide I was wrong? Well, the only way to find out was to ask him. As soon as I finished my delicious dinner, I went out into the hallway where it was quieter and called Cramptonbury Police Station.

A man answered. "Cramptonbury Police, Constable Fredricks speaking."

"Hi Constable Fredricks; it's Avery Winters here. Is Sergeant Bellamy in?"

"Hello, Miss Winters. I'm afraid it's not his shift. He'll be back on in the morning. Can I take a message?"

"Um, no. I'd like to make a report of a threat."

"Oh, I see. Hang on a moment, and I'll write it down."

I explained what had happened, and the events leading up to it. "I'd also like to ask Sergeant Bellamy why he told Phil

Granger that I spoke to him about the affair. He's put me in danger, and that's not right."

"I can assure you, Miss Winters, Sergeant Bellamy would've done nothing of the sort, but I'll get him to call you as soon as he gets in. Do you feel safe at the moment?"

"Yes, I'm fine. The threat was more if I do anything else, I'd better watch out. Hopefully Phil will go back to work and cool down."

"If you have any concerns, don't hesitate to call 999."

"Okay, thanks."

"Anything else I can help you with?"

"No, Constable. Have a good afternoon. Bye." So, that was a worthwhile phone call…. Maybe I should figure out what to do if Phil attacked me. Getting in first was always a good idea, or running; that was good too. He was a massive unit, so I didn't like my chances of punching him, or even striking with my elbow. He was way taller than me, and I might have to jump to reach. Kicking the side of his knee and breaking it would be best. Right, so that was my plan. It wasn't great, but it was all I had. Here's hoping I didn't need it.

After lunch, I said bye to Meg and Bailey and hurried home. Because I'd parked back at home before lunch, I'd gotten the premium spot again. There was another note on my car.

Just so you know, I sprained my ankle today and had to walk further than I otherwise would have. Cruel woman. Yours crankily and in pain, Vinegar.

I laughed. Very funny. As if he'd sprained his ankle. He was just trying to make me feel bad… right? Hmm. I grabbed a pen out of my bag and edited his note.

Just so you know, I sprained my brain *today and had to* have a scan to make sure it was still working. Wonderful *woman*, I'm sorry for being so annoying. *Yours crankily and in pain, Vinegar.*

I'm so sorry to hear that, Vinegar. I hope your brain starts functioning soon. Lightning.

I sniggered as I put it under his windshield and turned towards my place. Now to avoid Mrs Crabby's notice.

When I unlocked the front door, I was as quiet as possible. I even held my breath to listen for sounds of ambush from my landlady. None came. I tiptoed up the stairs. Only when I'd unlocked my door and put myself safely inside with the door again shut and locked did I breathe properly. Yay! After the day I'd had, it was a relief to avoid further confrontation.

"You're back." Everly stood there, arms folded, neck sliced and dripping. Looked like I spoke too soon. "You look… frazzled. What gives?"

"Do you think you could, you know…" I gestured to my own neck. "…clean it up a bit? I don't really have to look at that when I talk to you, do I?"

"Oh, sorry. I always forget. Besides, no one usually sees me. Other ghosts don't seem to care. I only clean it up if little ones are around."

Yikes. "Do you end up looking like when you died? Or do you get a choice?"

"When you first die and are in shock, you tend to look like your body did when it died, but once you get the hang of it, you can look however you want. Some people choose to look young even if they died when they were eighty. I died young, so I didn't see the point of looking younger, and we can't change size, so I couldn't go back to looking like I was ten or anything."

"So strange since you're not solid."

She patted herself down. "I feel solid to me." She reached

out and swiped a hand through my shoulder. I shivered at the sweep of cold that chilled my shoulder and arm. "You're the one who's not solid."

I smiled. "Ha, interesting. Perception counts for everything. Are ghosts solid to each other?"

"No. Just to ourselves."

I supposed if ghosts were solid to each other, they might as well just get on with life... or death... because they'd be able to have physical relationships with other ghosts. But not being able to touch another being, well, it would get lonely. No cuddles for comfort, no kisses of affection... nothing. And from what Patrick had said, they didn't feel physical discomfort or pleasure either. What was the point? Fear of the unknown was a great motivator. When I died, if I had the choice, would I stay in the in-between or step through? I had no idea. "Quick question. Do you know a Tom and Melissa Downs, or a Phil Granger?" She might've come across them on her travels around the village.

"I don't know the first two, but I knew Phil when I was alive, and I've seen him around the village since I died. Why?"

"Do you think he's the type of person who could kill someone? Mr and Mrs Downs recently died, and he was having an affair with Mrs Downs a little while ago, but she called it off."

Interest lit her eyes. "Ooh, a mystery to solve. You seem to like those. Maybe you should've been a detective."

"I'm a journalist. There's a crossover in what we do, but I have a harder time getting information, and I don't get the satisfaction of throwing the scum in jail at the end of it. But I don't have to put myself in danger every day either, so I can't complain." I cocked my head to the side. "You didn't answer my question."

"Let me think a moment." She moved past me, sat on the

couch, and crossed her legs. As she deliberated, she swung her top leg up and down. "He was about my age—same year at school. His dad was a gruff man, and his mum was a bit of a mouse. It wasn't unusual for him to come to school with bruises, but he gave a bit too. He wasn't the worst of the bullies, but he was definitely into roughhousing with the other boys. Got into a few fights, the usual. Back then, I think all boys were keen for a bit of biff." She shrugged. "I don't think he was worse than most. Could he kill someone? Couldn't we all?"

"Given the right circumstances, yes. I could kill someone if I was fighting for my life, but if a guy broke up with me, there's no way I'd even think of killing him. Heartbreak is awful, but it's not the end of the world. The sun shines again eventually. Murdering an ex is about power and craziness. Do you think he's that kind of person?"

"Just because a person is cranky or standoffish doesn't make them a cold-blooded killer. People who seem kind and caring can also be killers. So I honestly don't know. Sorry." She hugged herself and looked past me to the window, lost in her own thoughts. Had the person who killed her been *kind and caring*? Psychopaths were cunning and could show the world what they wanted them to see.

I bit my bottom lip and watched her. What had she been through, and why didn't she want my help? I wouldn't ask that now because I had enough to do, and she wasn't going anywhere. I had time to coax it out of her, and she might also be the kind of person who took a while to trust someone. If she was murdered by a trusted friend or boyfriend, no wonder ghost Everly was wary of others. "Well, he threatened me. I'm not sure if I should be worried or he was just getting it off his chest."

Her gaze pinged back to me. Concern and a hint of fear darkened her eyes. "Be careful. He may do nothing, but he may hurt you. Don't go out at night by yourself, and check the locks." She eyed the front door, then turned her head towards the back door.

I swallowed a burst of fear. I knew I'd locked the front door, but just in case, I got up to check it. When I was done with that, I checked the back door. "Yep, all locked." Just for fun, I looked out the back window. The yard was clear, and the back gate was locked. Mrs Crabby had placed a padlock on it after the drama with Fiona's killer. Although, the fence was still only chest-high, and if someone really wanted to climb it, they could. The police had suggested security cameras, but she said she wasn't going to turn her whole life upside down because of one incident, and besides, she didn't want to spend the money. I wasn't sure what they cost, but I probably didn't have the funds either.

"Hey, Avery."

I spun around. "Charles! I'm surprised to see you here."

He shrugged, then looked at Everly. "Hello, Ev. Nice to see you again."

"Lovely to see you again too, little man."

My eyes widened. "You two know each other?"

"This is my house, Avery. I made sure Charles knew that when he first visited."

"Right." I wasn't going to argue. It was my place too, but I could be kicked out whenever, and it certainly wasn't my forever home. I was just passing through, but Everly had been here for a very long time and might be here for eternity as far as I knew. Although, what happened when the building collapsed? Buildings didn't last forever. "So, Charles, what brings you here?"

"Just bored. I heard the last bit of your conversation. I'll go everywhere with you and warn you if I see anything. I can be your safety lookout."

Everly smiled. "That's a great idea. You're pretty smart for a kid."

Charles rolled his eyes. "And you're pretty annoying, even for an adult."

Everly laughed, the clear timbre of her mirth spearing me through the heart. Murdered so young. All that promise extinguished. I'd do well to heed her advice. "Okay, that sounds like a great idea. You can warn me if you see Phil lurking around."

"I can watch outside, too, like out the front, if you'd like."

Wow, my own personal bodyguard. I wanted to say no because I didn't want to impose, but he was dead. What else did he have to do? "You don't get tired, do you?"

"Nope. I might get bored though, so maybe I can just watch for a bit of time after your lights go off at night. I'd say an hour or two, but I can't measure time."

"Well, that's better than nothing and far more than I expected. Thank you, Charles."

A smile beamed from his young face. "Think nothing of it."

"I'll certainly sleep better tonight, thanks to you." Trying to stay awake so I could hear if someone tried to break in would suck. At least I'd get a couple of hours' sleep before I likely woke myself up, worrying about someone breaking in and attacking me. Two hours were better than none.

"Right, well, I'm supposed to be working right now, so I might do some research into other articles I can write."

Everly didn't seem too fussed. She looked at Charles. "What do you feel like doing?"

He shrugged. "I don't know. What about visiting Donigal's farm? The horses there like me. They're good company."

Wow, something else I didn't know. "Can all animals see you?"

He nodded. "Yep. I always loved animals, but Dad said they were only for eating or working, and that he'd never pay to feed one."

"Maybe I should look into getting a dog or something?" I missed having a pet.

Everly looked at me, a serious look on her face. "M..." She took a deep breath, although she didn't breathe. Maybe old habits died hard? "Mrs Collins won't allow pets here. I tried way back when, and she said no."

My mouth dropped open. "She was your landlady back then?"

"Ah, yes."

"Was she as cranky then as she is now?"

"Sometimes, but not really. She was strict but fair." Everly jumped up and pinned her gaze on Charles. "Okay, let's go and let Avery get some work done."

With that, they were gone and leaving me wondering what had made Mrs Crabby so, well, crabby. Maybe her husband had died or left her? Loneliness could make a person grumpy, and I didn't think she had any children. At least, no one had come to visit her in the time I'd been here—not that I'd been here long. I would ask her, but she was sure to get offended and yell at me or slam the door in my face.

I made myself a cup of tea—when in Rome... or England, as the case might be. Then I sat at the kitchen table to work. Since I was doing an article on the gym tomorrow, I figured I could cover some health topics, stuff that might also be good for a wider audience. The more credits I could get, the better.

As long as I met my obligations to the *Manesbury Daily*, I could submit extra work for the other papers in their network. I would get paid per article, but if I didn't meet my obligations to the Manesbury paper, I could lose my job. I supposed it ensured you did the work you were paid to do and didn't shirk your contract. Which was more than fair. The contract I'd signed also prohibited me from selling my stories to rival papers. Since they were paying a wage, and it wasn't all contract, that was fine and only fair. Some media bosses were slave drivers or sleazy, so I'd been lucky to land at MacPherson Media—Julian had been a good boss so far.

I spent the afternoon planning for work, and while I was cooking dinner, Meg called to check on me. As I was getting ready for bed, Everly showed up. She was going to keep an eye out inside, and Charles was doing outside, so I was set. Who knew ghosts would one day be the ones helping me get some sleep? Normally, they were the ones scaring people into not sleeping.

As I nodded off to sleep, I realised how truly lucky I was to have been hit by lightning. That one fateful moment had changed my life for the better, and even though I'd found myself in a couple of dangerous situations since I'd gotten here, and there was much adjustment, I'd never been happier. Maybe everything really did happen for a reason.

CHAPTER 12

T he night passed quietly enough, and I accidentally slept in. Both ghosts were gone when I woke up. I hurried to get ready and rushed out the door— without breakfast or a coffee. Gah, what a way to start the day. Not to mention, I was working on a Saturday. I promised myself I wouldn't make it a habit.

Ooh, some good news when I reached my car—there was no note. Double win. Finnegan's car was still there, but my return note was gone. I smirked, imagining his outraged expression as he read it. I'd bet he was already planning his response.

I hopped in my car because I was going straight to the gym at Cramptonbury. As soon as I started my engine, Finnegan walked out of the laneway and smiled. He shook his keys in front of himself, obviously so I had a clear view. Not wanting to encourage him, I left my window up.

I could still read his lips though. "Morning, Lightning." He pointed to his car, then my car. Presumably he was telling me that he was going to move into my spot. I rolled my eyes. Big deal. The only sadness I had at moving was that he would see it as a win, but I didn't particularly care about walking the extra few steps later. Honestly, what a child.

I smiled and waved, rolled out of my spot, did a U-turn, and drove off. What a ridiculous thing to be part of. I shook my head.

On my way out of the village, my phone rang. The road was so narrow, and there was hardly any grass verge, so I had to let it go to voicemail. Gah, I hated when I had to let it take a message. Having to call people back was annoying, and it was Murphy's Law that the phone rang when I was otherwise occupied—like driving or sitting on the toilet—and I would never answer it from there. It might be Bellamy calling to apologise. I hoped he didn't think I ignored it on purpose. I'd call him back as soon as I reached the gym.

I arrived at my destination, found a parking space, then took my phone out of my bag. I dialled my voicemail. Oh, it wasn't Bellamy. It was the accountant from Tom's company. That was interesting. Had the receptionist said something to her? She wanted to talk to me, but not at work, and had left her mobile number for me to text her. Interesting. I sent her a message thanking her for contacting me and saying I could meet whenever and wherever she wanted. Once that was done, I grabbed my bag and conducted the interview with the gym owner, who turned out to be normal. What a shock! *Ha, just kidding.* But still, I was pretty sure she was the first normal interview I'd had since arriving.

After a couple of back-and-forth messages, we arranged to meet for lunch at Meg's pub. The accountant didn't want to accidentally run into Russo, and she was pretty sure he wouldn't be there because it was the weekend, and he didn't live nearby. So after the gym visit, I headed back to the office, and wrote my article. Just before I hit Send to MacPherson, my phone rang. I crossed my fingers that it was Bellamy. "Hello, Avery speaking."

"Miss Winters, it's Sergeant Bellamy here. Sorry I couldn't get back to you earlier, but it's been a hectic morning."

"Not a problem, Sergeant. I'm just glad you called. I wanted to ask about Phil Granger. Did you tell him I spoke to you about his affair? Because he threatened me yesterday."

"Yes, I heard about that. No, I didn't tell him anything, but you spoke to me in the middle of the high street, and anyone, including Mr Granger, could've seen. I want to make it clear that I would never compromise someone's safety like that. He probably saw us talking and made an assumption. I've been to visit him this morning, and he won't be giving you any trouble. I've put him on notice."

The sergeant sounded sincere, and I guessed I'd just have to take his word for it. "Oh, thank you. I appreciate it."

"I take it you had a quiet night?"

"Yes. No trouble."

"Good. Now, let's keep it that way."

I knew it was a waste of time asking, but I couldn't help myself. "So, how did he react when you asked him about his affair?"

He cleared his throat. "I'm not at liberty to say."

I rolled my eyes. "Are you going to pursue that avenue of enquiry?"

"That's not for me to say. Now, I have a lot of work to get through, Miss Winters, so I'm going to bid you goodbye."

I sighed. "Bye, Sergeant."

"Goodbye, Miss Winters."

And that was the end of that. Could I assume they were at

least considering that angle now? Surely if they weren't, the sergeant would've said Granger wasn't a person of interest. Hmm.... Maybe he'd told me more than he wanted by telling me nothing. Wishful thinking on my part? Possibly, but it was all I had.

⊙✄⊙

Shelley, the accountant, was a thirty-something-year-old woman with a tight bun and an easy smile. After making sure Phil wasn't around, I'd chosen a table in the corner where we wouldn't be obvious to everyone else—you never knew who would tell who, and then she'd be busted. If she lost her job because of me, I'd never forgive myself.

I smiled at her. "Thanks for getting in touch. I'm glad you called me. I meant to call you, but I wasn't sure if you'd talk to me, and then I... got busy...." Got carried away with a different suspect, more like it, but she didn't have to know that. I'd spent so much time focussing on Phil, that I'd almost forgotten about Russo. Oops. Phil did look good for it, but so did Russo. They each had a strong motive, and they each had opportunity. Russo could easily have turned up at the Downses' to "apologise" and figured out how to get the poison into the dinner. Granger, of course, could've put the poison in the meat before he gave it to Mrs Downs, which made sense since he thought she was still a vegetarian and wouldn't be eating it. Mr Downs would die, but she'd survive. But then again, she'd likely end up charged with his murder. So Phil wouldn't lose her totally, but he'd punish her. Hmm....

Shelley sipped her lemonade. "Not a problem. I wasn't going to originally, but then... well, Mr Russo has been ridiculously cranky lately, even worse than usual, and I've just about had enough. To be honest, I'm looking for another job. As much as Mr Russo and Mr Downs didn't get along, Tom would always step in when Mr Russo went overboard with the shouting. But now that buffer is gone, it's been hell."

I had my notebook and pen out, and I wrote it down. "Does he ever get physically violent?" Surely they would've called the police if he had.

She took a deep breath. "Well, he's never touched any of us, but let's just say that they've had to have more than one hole in the wall repaired after he punched it or threw something at it. I think he's gone through four staplers this year alone. He only has the same paperweight ball thing because it's metal not glass. It always comes off better than the wall."

Yikes. My brow furrowed. "That's horrific. How do you stay working there? It sounds like you'd end up with PTSD."

She stared over my shoulder briefly, then met my gaze. "Yes, well, that's partly why I'm leaving. My husband said that if I didn't leave, he'd report him to the police, and I don't need that drama in my life. I just want to move on with a good reference if I can."

"I can understand that. If you had reported him, are you worried about what he would do in retaliation?"

"Partly, and partly because how could I look him in the eye and work with him after that? It might stop him being aggressive in the office, but I know for a fact that he's threatened a couple of our clients when they didn't pay. He's also on the outs with our former office manager. He holds grudges, and I didn't want that hanging over my head, not to mention the reference. Don't get me wrong—it's been a great job if you take him out of the equation, but with Tom gone, it's not the same, and Russo's behaviour has jumped up a notch." Well, it certainly seemed like he had the drive to kill Tom and Melissa, but I conceded it didn't mean he had.

I gave her an "I'm so reluctant but I have to do this" look. "I won't write about this, and I certainly won't tell anyone you said anything, but I need to ask you a couple of difficult questions."

"Okay. I'll answer if I can."

"Did you ever hear Russo threaten Tom, and do you think he could've killed Tom and his wife?"

"Yes to both questions. That's why I'm here. I'm not saying he definitely did it, but I think he's capable, and I have heard him threaten Tom… well, his wife. Tom and Russo had a shouting match one day, and Russo said, and I quote, 'Pull your head in and shut that wife of yours up, or I'll shut her up for you.' Tom lost it and threatened to call the police unless he apologised. Russo did apologise, but he didn't mean it. I know he didn't mean it because when he left the office he walked past me in the hallway—yes, I was standing out there eaves-dropping, not that it was that hard because they were yelling— and he mumbled, 'I'll kill both of you bleeps.' I can't repeat what he said at the end there because it was just too rude, but you get the picture."

I'd filled two pages with her information. The pendulum was swinging back to Russo. Argh, Granger or Russo? "Wow, okay. With Tom gone, did Russo stand to benefit financially?" Being the business's accountant, I figured she'd know all about those details.

"Yes, he did. If Melissa was alive, she would've become a silent partner. She'd get Tom's share of the profits every year, but not his wages. But with both of them dead, Mr Papadopoulos and Mr Russo would end up with an equal portion of Tom's shares and would become fifty/fifty partners after a small payout to Tom's estate."

"Right, so he not only had a personal vendetta, but he's benefitted financially."

"Yes." She finished her lemonade and bowl of hot chips. I'd ordered hot chips as well because my budget didn't allow for proper meals out every day. "Look, I wanted to come clean about all this because if he did kill them, I owe it to Tom and his wife, and I saw that stuff in the paper, that it was ruled a murder-suicide—I don't believe Tom would've killed himself, let alone his wife. He was just too nice. I'm not saying Mr Russo did kill them, but I'd believe that before I'd believe Tom did it." She sighed. "If you could keep all this to yourself, at least for the next couple of weeks so I can quit and get a reference, I'd really appreciate it."

"Of course. And if I do have to tell the police, I won't tell them where I got it from. Russo won't know, but I don't want to get Sandra in trouble either, so I'll only tell the police if I can find some other evidence. Okay?"

"Okay. Thank you. And thank you for looking into it. Tom… well, he was a lovely man. I just… there's no way he did it." She gave me a sad smile, leaned to the side, and grabbed her bag off the floor, then stood. "Good luck getting to the bottom of it, Avery."

I stood as well. "Thanks, and good luck finding another job."

"Thanks." She gave me a tepid smile and left.

I sat again, needing time to digest it all. Three men, all of them suspects—if I was going to be logical, I had to include Tom. What I knew could never be put into evidence, and I had to think like the police. As sad as it was to think it, he definitely could've lied to me, and the evidence the police found could be exactly what it appeared to be. But how did he get to go to heaven? Traditional religion taught us that suicide was a no-no, but even if whoever made the rules let you into heaven for killing yourself, surely murder was frowned upon? If the powers that be overlooked lots of bad stuff and let everyone in, Satan would find himself rather lonely, and what would be the point of getting into somewhere *good*? Charles could vouch for that. If he was a good person, why should he have to put up with his abusive parents for eternity? That didn't make sense.

"Hey, Avery. How was your lunch?" Meg stood next to me and looked down.

"Lovely, thank you. You make the best chips."

She grinned. "It's the batter." She winked. "And who was that? A new friend?"

"No. She worked for Tom, but don't tell anyone because her other boss didn't want her talking to me."

"Ah, I see. So, you're still not convinced Tom did it?"

I shook my head. "Nope."

"I'm assuming this isn't about Phil?"

"Nope." I figured I'd save her the questions and just tell her my thoughts. "I'm not discounting Tom, since the police think he did it, but the other two in the running are Phil and Russo, Tom's business partner."

She scanned the room, probably seeing if anyone needed her right then. Satisfied she had time, she sat and leaned towards me. "So, tell me everything."

I laughed, then spilled. Maybe she could help me figure it out. "So, what do you think?"

"Wow, this isn't easy. They all seem good for it."

Well, poop. "Yes, thanks for telling me something I didn't know."

"Which is why I work at a pub, and you do that stuff." She

stood. "I'd better get back to it. My work is never done." She sighed dramatically.

"I know just how you feel. Have fun." I stood. "I'm going to head home and work from there. I'll see you later."

"Ciao."

"Ciao." As I walked across the room, I scanned for Granger again—he was the last person I wanted to run into. Phew, it was all clear. I waved at Bailey on my way through, and he flashed his smile. Argh, what woman wouldn't be charmed by that smile? There was more than one danger around here.

Walking home, I let the new information swirl around and settle with what I already knew. So, if Phil killed them, he wouldn't have needed access to their house—he could've poisoned the meat at the butcher. Russo would have needed to visit. The front door had been open when I arrived. Was that because Russo panicked and left without shutting it properly? Or maybe he didn't want to leave any evidence behind like fingerprints or fibres from whatever he was wearing— assuming he didn't want to touch the doorknob, he would have had to use a sleeve or the bottom of his shirt to shut it. But then again, how would he have known they were having a special dinner there? Maybe he knew because Tom mentioned something at work? So, if he had been there, had he been caught on someone's home security camera? Had the police even doorknocked and checked?

If only Charles would sort things out with the sergeant ghost. Then I wouldn't be in this position. Russo's phone would also potentially place him at the scene that night. Gah! Should I call Bellamy and ask if they'd considered Russo? The sergeant was already annoyed with me for the Phil thing, and probably everything else I'd ever done. And if I was wrong about this, I'd just look even stupider to Bellamy. But how could I gather more proof?

Ooh, I had an idea, one that made me walk faster because the sooner I got home, the sooner I could talk to Charles. Because I was in a hurry, I wasn't as quiet as I could've been, but Mrs Crabby didn't come out to scold me. She must have been out.

I jogged up the stairs, let myself into the apartment, and locked the door after myself. I made sure I did it with intent, so that I didn't forget. Phil might not be over his anger yet, and it would be stupid of me to make a silly mistake like leaving the door unlocked. I'd been dumb enough to let the last killer in. I wouldn't be that naïve again. If I was wrong, well, I could live with people thinking I was an overreactor. It was better than being dead.

Everly wasn't in, which was fine. I chucked my stuff on the kitchen table. Out of the corner of my eye, I noticed a few dark things on the kitchen floor near the back door. *Huh?* I went over there. What in Hades? Three dead rats. I scrunched my face. Ew. My eyes widened, and my heart kicked up a notch. Had someone put them there? Was that person still here? Cat's bum—the key that was usually in the lock was on the floor.

I probably should have run out, but I wanted to know if anyone was here. I didn't grab a knife though, because if someone were here, they'd probably manage to take it off me and kill me with it. Plus, they'd probably have attacked me by now, so there probably wasn't any one here. Nevertheless, I hurried from the bathroom to the bedroom and looked in the cupboards, under the bed, and behind the shower curtain. Nothing.

Maybe whoever had left these did it when I was asleep—

I'd rushed straight from my bedroom to the front door this morning. There was no way I would've noticed the rats then. Fear vibrated through me, and I shuddered. What time had Everly stopped watching out for me? "Ev, are you around?"

She popped into existence in front of me. "What's up?"

"Do you know what time you finished guarding me last night?" That sounded weird, like she was security or something and I was important.

She scratched her head. "I don't know. It was still dark outside. Maybe I was watching you till one, or maybe it was three?" She shrugged. I sighed. "What happened?"

I gave a nod to the rats on the floor and the skeleton key for the back door near them. "The key's come out of the lock, and someone's planted the rats there. I'm sure of it."

She pouted as she stared at the rodents. "They could've just up and died together?"

I raised one eyebrow. "Seriously? And what about the key?" She could be right, but what a coincidence.

She shrugged. "I don't know. Anyway, you seem safe, and I was in the middle of something, so I have to go. Bye." She disappeared before I could say anything. Argh.

More investigation was in order. I grabbed a tea towel, and without touching too much of the knob, I turned it to see if the door was locked. It opened. Fear edged from my chest up my throat. I swallowed it back down. Someone had definitely been here and left me dead animals. It was clearly a message to beware and to stop talking.

I shut the door and locked it—although what difference it made, I didn't know since someone managed to break in quite easily—then called nine, nine, nine. "I'd like to report a break-in." I gave them my details, and they promised to send a car ASAP. Was I misinterpreting the situation, jumping to the worst possible conclusion because Granger had threatened me? *What, Avery, three rats just randomly died in your apartment, and the key had decided to jump out of the lock of its own volition on the same day?* Well, I'd called the police now. I was going to test my theory of speaking up even if it made me look stupid.

About fifteen minutes after calling the police, the security-door buzzer rang. I grabbed my phone off the table, just in case things went south, then answered the intercom. "Hello?"

"It's PCs Patel and Davis. We're here because you called about a break-in."

"Ah, yes. I'm the flat up the stairs." I pressed the button to let them in.

I opened my door so I could watch them come in, make sure they were who they said. If they weren't, I'd lock the door and run out the back. But surely no one would ambush me in full daylight. And I had my phone, ready to take a picture of whoever it was. After that, I could call the police... again. My heart raced as the door opened.

Phew. They were both wearing police uniforms. I also recognised one of them from one of the times I'd been at the police station. My grip on my phone loosened so I wasn't trying to crush it. "Up here." Okay, so I was stating the obvious, but it was awkward that I was staring at them. I stepped back inside and held the door open.

The first officer to reach the landing introduced himself as PC Patel. He was a couple of inches taller than me, with a slim build and of Indian heritage. His calm demeanour banished some of my jitteriness. "Can you show me where they broke in?"

"Of course. Just in here." I walked the short distance to the kitchen. "They left three dead rats too."

Patel joined me, as did the PC Davis, a taller man in his

thirties with fair skin, red hair, and freckles. They both looked at the rats, and Patel eyed the door. "And they came through that door?"

"Yes."

He peered around the kitchen and living area, then at me. "Is anything missing?"

"No. I don't have anything of value, except my laptop, and that goes with me everywhere. Although, it wasn't in my bedroom last night. I'm not sure if the rats were here this morning when I left because I was in a hurry. So they could've done this last night or this morning sometime."

Davis and Patel shared a "we got another crazy one" look. Davis turned to me. "And why do you think someone broke in?"

"I've never seen one rat in here, let alone three, and all dead in the same spot. They weren't here when I went to work this morning, and the key was sitting on the floor, and the door was unlocked. I definitely checked it last night before I went to bed because I was threatened yesterday. Which is why I called you guys. I normally wouldn't worry, but Phil Granger, the butcher in the village, told me to watch out because I'd given the police some information about him that might be relevant to a murder investigation, and he saw me telling Sergeant Bellamy."

Lines appeared in Patel's forehead. "Are you talking about the Downses' case?"

"Yes."

"That's not a current murder investigation. That case was ruled a murder-suicide, and it's closed."

"Maybe it's not as closed as you think." I folded my arms and tried not to feel like a petulant child. I knew I wasn't being one, but I knew they were thinking it. They were laughing at me on the inside. Poop heads. They'd probably go back to the station later and laugh about the crazy Aussie in Manesbury.

Patel stared at the door. He pulled a glove from his pocket and put it on. He carefully turned the handle and opened the door, then inspected the other side of the door, lock, and door-frame. He shook his head. "Skeleton locks are easy to pick. I don't see any evidence of force, but that doesn't mean anything." He looked at me. "I'm sure you have nothing to worry about, but I'll send forensics over here, see if they can get any prints from the door." He looked at Davis. "Can you get an evidence bag and collect those?" He gave a nod to the unfortunate rodents.

"Okay." Davis turned and went back out the front door.

Patel removed his glove. "Have you got a bin?"

"Yes." I opened the cupboard under the sink and showed him the plastic bag hanging from the inside of the door. High tech stuff. He chucked the glove in and shut the door. "I'm going to call this in and have a chat to Sergeant Bellamy. Once Davis has collected the evidence, we're done, but someone will be by to check for fingerprints later today. So don't touch the door. Was there anything else?"

Hmm, I'd touched the door earlier with the tea towel, but I wasn't going to tell him. I felt judged enough as it was. "Nope. That's it… for now." And hopefully forever, but I didn't believe that for a second.

Davis returned, bagged the rats, and they left. I got my notebook out and wrote it all down—who knew, I might need this for my article. If I lived long enough to solve the crime and write it. Which reminded me. I called into the empty room, "Charles, hello? Charles, can you come see me?"

He appeared, concern on his young face. "Are you okay? You sound upset."

"I'm not upset, but I'm not happy. I'm pretty sure someone broke in and left three dead rats as a warning. And by someone, I mean Phil Granger."

Charles looked around the room, then back at me. "That's not good. I'll stay and watch things for you. I won't leave you alone."

Tears burned my eyes. I was betting no one had ever said that to him when he was a child, dying from the cruelty of his parents. *I won't leave you alone.* The poor child. I blinked my tears back because I didn't want to have to explain them. Charles was a proud person, and I didn't want him to feel less than, especially with me. "Thanks, Charles. That's so kind of you. You know, you would've been a good person if you'd lived. You have your own internal moral compass that points in the right direction. You have a good heart." I smiled.

Concern shadowed his face. "Do you really think that, or are you just saying it?"

I smooshed all the sincerity in the world into my gaze. "I really think that. Do you think I'm the sort of person who sprinkles bulldust around when I'm talking to my friends?"

He blinked. "Do you think of me as a friend?"

A huge smile ambushed my face. "Of course I do. I'll admit that I was wary at first, but now, well, if you were gone, I'd miss you. I wouldn't say that about just anyone, you know. I'm picky about people, especially since I've realised my worth. You're a good guy to have on my side. I like you, Charles. You're one of the decent ones, and anyone who says any differently will have to deal with me." I gave a decisive nod.

He stared at me, then scratched his head. "You really mean it?"

"Yes."

"Do you think Sergeant Fox will forgive me?"

"I know you don't believe me when I say there's nothing to forgive, but I think so, yes. Although, I can't promise anything. I can't read minds or tell the future. But guess what? Even if he doesn't accept it, that's okay. I'll still be here for you, and you will get over it. If he won't forgive a child for the actions of the parents, well, he can go jump. He's not worth another moment of stressing about." Oh, how I wished I could give him a hug right now. "But what if he does forgive you? I think we need to at least try."

"You'll come with me?"

I swallowed, knowing I was about to look like a total loon in front of the police if I couldn't think of an excuse to be there and remain there for the time it took for us to convince Sergeant Fox that Charles was a good person. Hopefully Sergeant Fox would meet us in the lobby. At least Charles could do the talking. Or, I could bake that apple tart I'd promised the sergeant. Hmm, that was a good idea. "Of course I'll come with you. And if it all goes south, we'll come back here and figure it out. Okay? I've got your back, Charles. Always."

His gaze locked on mine. "Thank you, Avery. I believe you." He swallowed. "Okay, then. I think I'm ready." He gave me a tentative smile.

I knew, from the old ghost who'd been in the hire car with me on that first day, that Charles could come with me in the car. "Drive with me?"

"Okay."

"Before we go, I just have something to do first." I smiled. I'd bought the ingredients a week ago and fresh green apples yesterday, so it wouldn't take long, and it was probably a good thing to relax me from the earlier surprise. Also, the police managed to come and check for prints, which worked out well.

An hour and a half later, we hopped into my happiness on wheels. I placed the tart on the front seat. Charles appeared in the car and sat on it. I gasped. "My tart!"

"What?"

"You're sitting on my tart."

He laughed and looked down at his lap. "And?"

I laughed too. "Okay, fine. I just wish you were a bit see through. You look so solid, and I can't see my tart."

"I'll keep it warm for you." That set him off into another fit of giggles. It was pretty funny.

"Ha, thanks."

As I pulled out of the parking spot, I tried not to think about the potential confrontation I would have at the station. There were too many variables, so I'd take it as it came. No expectations, just remain calm—I didn't want to get arrested. If they told me to leave, I'd have to. If that happened, I'd just tell Charles to come with me, and we'd try again.

Charles peered around the inside of the Peugeot. "This is nice." He sighed. "I never got the chance to drive, and I was really looking forward to it."

I glanced at him before focussing on the road again. "That sucks. I'm sorry."

He looked out the window. "I'll get over it, eventually." His noncommittal tone was overdone and broke my heart. When I'd first met him, I'd had no idea of his past. He'd seemed so cocky and carefree. The truth was, he was anything but. He'd offered to help me, and I'd accepted it, but maybe he needed my help way more than I did his… and that was saying something. I smiled. He'd come to the right place. I glanced at him again.

We'd get through things together. I'd make sure of it.

CHAPTER 13

As Charles and I walked into the police station, I appreciated that I hadn't had to ask Meg for a lift. I had a car! Imagine that. I smiled to myself until I noticed Charles walking a couple of steps behind me, using me as a shield. I put my phone to my ear and gripped the plate with the tart in the other hand. If I dropped it now, I'd just about cry. "Don't worry. It's all going to be okay. Remember: if you want to pop away at any time, it's all good, and I'll see you back at my place. Okay?"

"Mmhmm." He didn't move to catch up to me. Oh well. Hopefully the meeting would go better. But what if Sergeant Fox didn't come and see us? *Stop worrying. Deal with it if it happens. He's always there.*

I walked in, and the female constable who usually got lumped sitting at the front desk was there. "Hi, Constable Adams. How have you been?"

"Hello, Miss Winters. I'm good thanks. How are you?"

"I'm good. I was wondering if Sergeant Bellamy was in? I

promised him an apple tart because he's been so helpful and kind." Okay, so he hadn't been as helpful as I would've liked, but appearances and all that.

"Ooh, that looks good. You know it's his favourite?"

"Yes. I asked what he'd like. No use baking a chocolate cake if he hated them." I smiled.

A dreamy look fogged her gaze. "Oh, my word, I love chocolate cake."

I chuckled. "I'll see what I can do." I winked. How cheesy of me. Did it look creepy? Argh, I shouldn't have winked, but it seemed like the right thing to do at the time.

At least she was smiling. "Don't go out of your way or anything, but if you ever make one, a piece would be much appreciated."

"Consider it done. You all do such a wonderful job for our community. It's the least I can do for you guys for keeping me safe." And I meant it. If it wasn't for the police putting themselves in harm's way every day, who knew where we'd all be?

She watched me, a pleased expression on her face. "That's kind of you to say. Thank you."

I smiled in response. "So… I'd love to give this to Sergeant Bellamy myself. If he's busy, I can leave it here, but I'd like to say thank you in person, if at all possible."

"He's just doing some paperwork, I think. I'll call him to make sure." Well, that was more than I'd expected. Note to self: make a whole chocolate cake for Constable Adams because she was a lovely person. After a short back and forth, she hung up. "He said he'll see you, but he's busy and doesn't have long. Come through. You know the drill." She smiled.

"Thanks!" I glanced behind me to make sure Charles was still there. Yep, this was the quietest he'd ever been. The poor kid was nervous. "It's okay," I whispered as the door buzzed and unlocked.

"You know the way." She gave me an encouraging smile.

"I sure do. Thanks so much."

"Any time."

As we traversed the hallway, my voice was a touch louder than a whisper. "Sergeant Fox, can we please talk to you?" I held the plate with the tart with both hands now—dropping it at this point would be a disaster—and I carefully crossed my pointer finger over my middle finger on one hand. "Charles has something he'd like to say."

The sergeant appeared in front of me, and I stopped. "What do you want?"

"Charles needs to tell you something, and I'd like you to be fair and listen, and remember he's just a kid." I looked up. Cat's bum. There was a video camera. I couldn't stand here and talk to myself, so I started down the hallway again, shivering as I stepped through the long-deceased policeman. "Just listen to him, please." He made a noncommittal noise, and Charles yelped. I looked back, but the sergeant hadn't touched him. I gave Charles an encouraging nod, and then I was at the end of the hallway and turning into the main open-plan office area. Bellamy's office was at the far side. Patel was at one of the desks, and he looked up from his work. Recognition pinged on his face. I gave a quick, close-mouthed smile and walked faster. I didn't want to get into a conversation with him about the fact that I was scared of three rats and that surely I'd left my own door unlocked.

Bellamy's door was half open. Having no hands to knock and not wanting to try and balance the plate on one hand again, I stuck my head in. "Hello, Sergeant. May I come in?"

He looked up from the papers on his desk. There was no

smile, but he sat up straight like a meerkat scouting for hawks. "Miss Winters. Is that an apple tart I spy?"

I smiled. "Why, yes it is. And it's all for you. I keep my promises." I almost winked again but aborted at the last second because winking at people you hardly knew was creepy. My eye did a weird twitch spasm thing. He gave me a "what's wrong with you" look before I got my face under control. I hurriedly placed the tart on his desk.

He grabbed the tart and slid it to a spot in front and just to the right of the paperwork he'd been reading. He took the plastic wrap off, leaned his face over it until his nose was almost in the thing, and inhaled. "Ooh, this smells delicious." He sat up straight and looked at me. "Thank you very much, Miss Winters. I appreciate you bringing me this. Is there any other reason you've come?"

"No. Just this."

His eyes told me he didn't believe it for a second. "You're sure you're not here to ask me about any of the cases I'm working on?"

I gave him a "who me?" look. "No. Your officers have sent those rats off for testing, so I'll just wait. There's not much else we can do, is there, Sergeant?"

"Ah, no, there isn't. We might get something back from the lab in a couple of days, but any DNA evidence could take a month or more."

"I understand. You have to prioritise things. I know how it works. And those rats, well, they might be just dead rats who wandered in and died at the same time in the same spot. A coincidence, but not impossible. Am I right?"

He cleared his throat. "Yes, Miss Winters. I think you understand our position. Good. In any case, it was kind of you to bring this in, but I have to get back to work."

"Enjoy your tart, Sergeant." *Don't wink. Don't wink.* I gave him a knowing smile and nod, then turned and hurried out of the office before I burst out laughing. *I mean, who could resist a bit of inappropriate innuendo?* Was that reverse sexism? Hmm.... Maybe it had gone straight over his head?

As I approached the hallway, Sergeant Fox's voice reached me. "Your father was the worst type of scoundrel I've ever come across. Usually, the apple doesn't fall far from the tree. If you'd lived, no doubt you would've been a career criminal too. You can't escape your genes."

I slowed my steps because I wanted to see as much of it as possible, and I might want to put in my two bob's worth. The ghosts came into view. Fox had his arms folded, and he stared down at the boy, who, in turn, stared at the floor. Charles's slumped shoulders looked as if they were going to take the whole boy down with them. Anger flared in my stomach. Charles was nothing like his father.

"So, what do you have to say for yourself, urchin?"

I kept my voice low as I approached. "Tell him what you told me. Tell him everything you want to say, how you feel. Even if he doesn't want to be fair about it, you need to say it." My head was down so the security cameras wouldn't pick up me talking to myself, but I raised my eyes enough to meet his gaze and give him a reassuring nod. "You can do this. I know you can." I hoped my gentle smile reminded him that I was on his side.

Because I had to keep walking, I went past, and then I was almost at the door. I needed to stall, so I dropped my bag, face-down, and everything fell out, and by everything, I meant *everything*. If you've never had the pleasure of searching through a woman's handbag, you'll know that all manner of things resided in one, and they're mini Tardises. A lip gloss fell out, my wallet, my phone, six pens of various colours, my notebook, two tatty but clean tissues, a small, old melted chocolate bar (in its wrapper of course), at least twelve paper receipts, two paperclips, a handful of small shells (I wasn't sure how they got there), my plane ticket, a napkin, an Australian two-dollar coin, keys, an old shopping list from Sydney, and last, but certainly not least, a tampon. *Nice job not cleaning out your bag, past Avery.* This was the only time I was happy at the state of my handbag. This clean-up could take a while, giving me plenty of time to see what happened with Fox and Charles.

"Well, boy?" Fox smoothed his moustache.

Charles began his explanation with his eyes downcast, but slowly, he lifted them and met Fox's gaze. He took us back to the day of Fox's death and explained what happened. Fox made a couple of inarticulate grunts. Then, as I was gathering my old plane ticket, he said, "I'm so sorry you died because of me. I didn't know what my father was going to do. I honestly didn't. If I could take it back, I would. I would've warned you and ran away. He killed me after that because I told him it was wrong. He didn't trust me not to tell anyone." Tears streaked his young cheeks. "My father and I, we took you away from your family and all the people you helped. You were a good man, and I'm sorry. I deserve to be in hell for what I did, but I'm too scared. But I'll cross one day… maybe soon, now I could apologise. Is there any way I can make it up to you?"

I hadn't expected that last bit. He really was a good person.

Fox's unsettled face contorted this way and that, mirroring his conflicting thoughts. How long had he held onto his anger at being killed? How long had he hated this child who led him to his death?

Please forgive him.

I didn't even care about the spying bit any more. If Fox didn't forgive Charles, it would hurt the boy, and he'd already suffered enough.

I'd stopped putting stuff in my bag—which would look suspicious on the cameras—and I stared at Fox, waiting as anxiously as Charles was. I was ready to leap to Charles's defence because he deserved a second chance.

Fox smoothed his moustache again, and his chest rose with a breath he didn't really take. Seemed it was harder to let go of the past than I'd thought. He'd been dead a long time, and breathing was optional, yet he still did it. He eyed Charles up and down. He got on one knee and stared directly into his eyes. "Are you truly sorry, boy? I left behind a wife and children. Leaving them to fend for themselves haunts me to this day."

Charles's brows drew down, and lines grooved into his forehead. "Yes, sir. I'm sorry for my horrible part in your death. It was wrong, what my father done... what he made me do. I'm glad he killed me afterwards because I didn't want to end up like him. Pure evil. What can I do to make it up to you? Please tell me."

Fox's head lowered to his chest for a moment. He looked up again. "I forgive you, Charles. It takes a brave man to admit to his mistakes and an even braver man to apologise for someone else's mistakes. Your father was rotten to the core, but I made a mistake—you're not like him at all." He shook his head slowly, and Charles blinked, disbelief on his face. "After all these years, I've held so much anger, but none of it is for you now. I was wrong blaming any of it on you—you were just a child ruled over by a tyrant." He slowly stood. "So, what can you do for me?" He smiled. "You can keep being a good spirit, but you..." His gaze turned to me. "I've heard you can put a message in the paper for me… a letter from the dead."

My mouth dropped open. "H—how did you hear about that?"

Charles wiped his eyes and thanked Sergeant Fox. Then he gave me a small smile. "News travels fast in a small village, even amongst the dead. And, well, I might've told other ghosts about what you did for Patrick."

"Oh." I hadn't expected that. Maybe not many knew because, thankfully, I hadn't had a lot of requests for letters from the dead, okay, any requests, except for this one. I had nothing to lose, and Fox had earned massive bonus points for forgiving Charles. I pushed the remaining junk back into my bag and stood, no longer worried what those watching the security video thought. I smiled at Fox. "Can you leave this place and go wherever you want?"

"Yes."

I hoped I wouldn't regret this. I gave him my address. "I'll invite you over when we get home, and you can tell me everything you want in the letter."

He held his hand out to shake, and I lifted my arm and met the cold thin air of it. "It's a deal."

I wouldn't make a deal with the devil, but a ghost, well, why not?

Why not, indeed.

CHAPTER 14

As soon as we got home—Charles decided to join me in the car—I called out to Sergeant Fox and invited him in. Rather than going all the way to the library to email it, I typed what he wanted me to say and emailed it straight to MacPherson. If he asked where it came from, I'd tell him someone put it in my letterbox. I could plead ignorance as to where it came from, and if worst came to worst, I could ask Meg to handwrite it for me. No one would have any idea of her writing, and nor would they think to check it.

The letter was to his great-grandson, twenty-year-old Lewis Smith. Sergeant Fox knew that Lewis's mother read the *Manesbury Daily* every day, and Lewis still lived with her, so, hopefully, the message would find the recipient. Lewis's nickname was Fox. The sergeant said it was a nod to the Fox family since his great-grandson's mother was the sergeant's granddaughter but changed her name when she married.

· · ·

Dear Fox,

You don't know me, but I know you. I'm one of your ancestors. I died way before you were born, but I'm stuck in-between. I know your mother gave you the medal my wife received after I was murdered. I know it has pride of place on your bookshelf. I also know that you don't believe in God or life after death. I can't answer the question about God, but I can tell you that there is something else, but you're not ready yet.

I know you're struggling and scared to confide in anyone. I saw you call a depression hotline, but you hung up before they answered. And I know you've done this three times. I've heard you in private speak aloud to yourself—you shut the window once when you sensed me and thought it was just the night air. I know you think your parents and sister wouldn't miss you if you were gone. I can tell you that they will. You will break their hearts, and the emptiness you leave behind will forever be like a festering wound for them, and for you. They will feel as if they've failed you, and you will see them hurting and regret it. They don't know, as I do, that you have a plan to do the deed as soon as you have the courage. Please have the courage to live. I wasn't able to be there for my family when they needed me, but because of a miracle, I can be here for you.

We are all proud of you, we love you, and I can tell you that you don't want to come here. To never receive another hug, another touch, well, it's more painful than I can explain. And you will have the added burden of watching the tragedy of them losing you, and there will be nothing you can do about it.

Your uncle P. joined me two years ago. He told me that you once confided in him that you hated the clothes Auntie A. got you every Christmas, but you didn't have the heart to tell her. You confided this to him when you were drunk one night, and no one else knows. He died that night from a heart attack. We had some time together before he moved on to the light, so you might want to tell your mother that he's okay. And just so you know this is from beyond the grave, tell your mother I know about the letter she wrote to you the day you were born. She has it folded in her jewellery box.

Please ask her to read it to you, and please reach out for help. All is not lost.

Know that I will be by your side—watch for the stirring curtains, and feel for a chill breath of air on your cheek on a still night. There may or may not be a god, but there is your great-grandfather. Oh, and that engineering degree you searched up on the library computer a week ago, sign up —you'll be brilliant.

I know you asked for a sign. You asked what eight times seven, minus three equalled, and you whispered it. I'm the only one who heard. I haven't had much reason to do maths here, but I can still remember the basics. The answer is fifty-three. The other answer is life. Please don't choose to meet me yet. You have too much left to do where you are. When I died, it hurt that I couldn't save people any more, but I have one last chance. That chance is you.

Yours eternally,

A long-lost ancestor

That was twice today that the sergeant showed he had a heart. As soon as he told me why he wanted to send a letter, I couldn't type it fast enough. The mental anguish his great-grandson was experiencing was all too common and all too tragic. I hoped this got through to him. I hadn't said anything to Fox, but I might just chase it up later, go and say hello, see if he needed someone to talk to. Even if he refused, he'd know that people did care. Yes, things weren't that simple, but maybe for once, they would be. When we held secrets, fears, heart-breaks close to our chest instead of sharing them, they grew until they blotted out the sun and darkened our view of reality. The people who wanted to help Fox were smothered by that shadow, waiting for a glimpse of light to reveal them.

After everything that had happened, I didn't want to ask

Sergeant Fox if Charles could have access to the police station. It would be awful if he thought everything that we'd done was because of that. Besides, I had a new plan. One that wouldn't help us for future cases, but it might help us now.

The sergeant left, but Charles stayed. "So, Charles, I have a new way we might be able to get information, but I don't know if you can be bothered with it. It's going to be time-consuming and potentially very boring."

"But weren't we going to ask about hanging around the police station?"

I sighed. "Yes, but I didn't want Sergeant Fox to think that's why you apologised."

"But isn't it?" He wasn't even being facetious. His face was like, "huh?"

"Kind of, but not really. I mean, we needed things to be fine for you to be there, but when I saw how devastated you were about everything with your dad and the sergeant's murder, well, that became way more important. Seeing you happy was way more important." I smiled. "I meant what I said—you're a good person, and you deserve to be happy and not feel guilty for something you weren't responsible for. So, do you want to hear my idea?"

"Sure."

"I know you can't go everywhere, but you can go some places, like all the public ones and offices. I was wondering if you could spy on Russo for a day on Monday. Follow him around and listen to what he says. He might let slip to someone something about the murder."

His top lip hitched up on one side. "But I thought you thought that butcher guy did it?"

"Well, he might have, but Russo might have too. Even if Phil—the butcher—didn't do it, he could still be trying to scare me. So I haven't ruled either man out. They both had the motive, and they both have anger issues."

He cocked his head to one side. "Okay. That sounds easy enough."

"Great, thank you!" I needed to gather information as fast as I could now that someone—assuming Phil, but one could never be 100 per cent certain—was targeting me. It could've been Joyless for all I knew, but the timing was fishy. If it quacked like a duck and waddled like a duck....

"You know I'm not good with time, so can you call me on the Monday morning? I'll come here, and you can tell me where I'm going."

"Okay. Thanks."

"I'd stay, but I have something to do. You don't mind if I go, do you?"

I didn't feel totally safe, but I wasn't going to tell him that. He might have existed longer than me, but he was still a kid. "Of course not. Good luck with whatever you're doing."

He gave me a small smile. "Bye, Avery."

"Bye."

Late-afternoon sun shone outside. It had been a lovely day, and I wouldn't stress about my stalker until it got dark. I could call Everly and hope she could come and watch out for me until the sun rose. Even if I hated bothering people and ghosts, I wasn't stupid. If someone tried to break in, I wanted to know before they managed it. I was going to sleep with my phone under my pillow too. If I couldn't get hold of Everly, I'd put a chair in front of the front door and sleep against the back door. If anyone made a peep on the other side of it, I'd wake up. Sleeping on the floor wouldn't be comfortable, but I'd probably get more sleep there than cowering in my room waiting for someone to sneak in. Besides, if I was on the floor,

I knew a great take-down move that would have them crashing to the ground in two seconds.

Feeling better about my situation, I put my running shoes on to go for a jog and try and enjoy the summery afternoon. After the day I'd had, I'd totally earned it.

CHAPTER 15

On Monday morning, Charles came by, and I explained where Russo's office was. I had no idea if he'd even be in, but the ghost would go and check it out. If he was in, he'd shadow him all day, as long as he didn't go anywhere that Charles was banned. This probably worked out better than spying at the police station because this time, they had no idea. They weren't looking into what I was, so maybe me having to come up with another plan was a blessing in disguise.

After catching up with Charles, I walked to work and stopped at Heavenly Brew to grab a takeaway coffee. Finnegan was nowhere in sight, but Joyless wasn't alone—Anna, her boss, was there. Anna smiled. "Morning, Avery! How are you?"

I returned her smile. "Great, thanks. How are you?"

"Smashing. So, what can I get you?"

I gave her my order, and she passed it to Joyless, who raised her eyes to mine. I would describe the look she gave me as the look given to your own shoulder after a bird poos on it. She wasn't happy to see me. Not. At. All. Maybe I needed to bring Finnegan with me every time, just so I'd get a warm reception. I snickered to myself as I took a step back and waited. Joyless's eyes widened slightly. Not the reaction she was looking for? My smile grew into a grin. Her lips pressed together, and she looked down at what she was doing. I kept an eye on her in case she spat in my coffee.

Anna looked at me. "Oh, I wanted to tell you before, but I forgot. That article you did on Ian and his fiancé was adorable. I'll admit I don't get it, but you covered it with empathy and a touch of humour. Well done."

I didn't want to spoil her assessment that I'd been super empathetic. It had been an effort not to make fun of him in my article. I mean, I was all for accepting people as they were, but when someone wants to marry a tree, surely we should be allowed to acknowledge that they were, well, off their tree? Or was that on their tree? "Ah, thanks. He was strange but nice."

Anna chuckled. "I think that's true of most of us, don't you think?"

"Hmm, maybe not quite to Ian's extent, but yes. We all have weird things about us that others would look askance at." *I see ghosts. What's your party trick?* On second thoughts, I didn't want to know.

"We do indeed."

Another customer came through the door, and Anna turned away from me to greet him and take his order. By then, my coffee was done, so I put the exact change on the counter (I'd been prepared for Joyless to take it), grabbed my beverage, and left.

I used my new key to get into the office. How refreshing to not buzz and be ignored.

"Wait!" Finnegan had hurried along behind me without me noticing. I reached out and stopped the door from shutting. Bethany looked up from her desk and smiled brightly as he came inside. "Good morning, Finnegan. How was your weekend?" *Argh.* I rolled my eyes. Not wanting to be there for the syrupy conversation, I headed straight for the office upstairs.

Carina was at her desk with a takeaway cup. "Mornin', Avery. I heard d'ere's been some trouble at your place. Are you okay?"

I put my things on my desk and had a sip of coffee. Ah, that was good, even if Joyless had made it. I could dislike her without hating her coffee. "I'm fine, thanks. I woke a couple of times last night, but it wasn't too bad." *Because I had a ghost keeping watch….* "I'm thinking it's a warning not to be a pest rather than someone who's actually going to hurt me."

"Aye, but you need to be careful. Did you tell Sergeant Bellamy?"

Finnegan must've been listening just outside the door because he came in, stopped in front of my desk, and hopped straight into the conversation. "Yes, she did. But it doesn't sound that serious." He looked at me as I sat down. "You could've just had three rats up and die. Mrs Collins probably poisoned them, and they stuck together until they carked it. I don't know that calling the police was warranted."

I cocked my head to the side. "Oh, so you're saying I overreacted?" My voice was a dangerous kind of light, one that more men should see coming but never do.

Maybe he noticed the sharp glint in my eyes because he stepped back. "Ah, possibly. At least the sergeant thinks you did." He backed away, turned, and went to his desk where he promptly sat and got busy with his laptop.

I raised a brow, and Carina snorted. "You really don't

value your life much, do ya, Finny?" He grunted something unintelligible, and Carina laughed. "I t'ought so." She looked over at me again. "Don't worry, love. Men don't know the trouble we lasses have with safety. I totally understand."

"Thanks, Carina. I appreciate it." I slid my laptop out of my bag and opened it. Argh, why was I so worried about what he thought? "Look, Vinegar, I know you don't understand, but I was almost killed just the other week. I don't like making a big deal out of nothing, but I figured it was better to be safe than sorry. If I didn't say anything and ended up being attacked, everyone would've said 'oh you should've said something.' Honestly, I can't win. And, just so we know, when was the last time you were threatened by a huge man because you dobbed him into the police for something?" He looked at me. His mouth writhed as he figured out how to answer. "Yes, I didn't think so. When you've been through what I've been through in the last few weeks, then you can tell me how much of an overreactor I am."

He stared at me for a few beats. "Okay, sorry. You're right. It just… it just doesn't sound like much, but I can see why you wanted to be careful."

He so didn't deserve my gratefulness, but I wanted to keep things civil. "Thanks. Anyway, I've got to get stuck into this work. It'll be nice not to think about all that stuff for five minutes." On cue, my phone rang. I was scared to see who it was. Was it Bellamy confirming I was in danger of being killed, or was it just my mother making me wish I was dead? I took it out of my bag. Bellamy. "Hello, Avery speaking."

"Hello, Miss Winters. The tart was delicious, so thanks again. My wife says it's the best she's ever tasted, except for hers, of course." He chuckled, then cleared his throat. "But that's not why I'm calling. The full analysis from the rats isn't due back for a few more weeks, but the lab has confirmed a few dog hairs on two of them. We've matched the dog hair to a pure-bred German Sheppard."

"So, whoever put them there probably has one?"

"Yes. I don't know any circumstances where two of the rats would have that on them—they're fastidious about their cleanliness. I'm sending a pest guy over to check for any rat nests on your property. If we can't find one, it will support the theory that someone put them there, and if we can, we can confirm what nesting materials they've used. Can you be home in an hour?"

"I suppose so. Thank you. If we can't find a nest, what are the next steps?"

"I'd rather not say, but we will be making further enquiries. Call me if they don't show up by ten thirty."

"Okay, thanks, Sergeant. I appreciate it. Bye."

"Goodbye, Miss Winters."

Carina had watched me during the whole phone call. "News?"

"They've found dog hair on the rats. They're coming to check the place for rats' nests, see if they can narrow down whether someone put the rats there or not. They obviously think if someone did put them there, they have a specific type of dog, and they're trying to narrow it down to unlikely or likely. At least they believed me." I threw a "see" look at Finnegan.

He put his hands up. "Hey, I'm just playing devil's advocate."

"Yeah, yeah, tell that to someone who believes you." The backpedalling would be impressive if it wasn't so annoying. "Anyway, we'll see what happens. Maybe you're right, and there is nothing to it. We might find a cute little rats' nest filled with dog hair in my walls." I wanted to add that, because I knew I couldn't be sure. In fact, I hoped I was wrong. "I'd be so much happier if you were right, Vinegar. I really would."

His expression changed, and within it, there seemed to be genuine compassion. "I hope I'm right too. Forget I was an idiot. If anything happens, you can always bash down my door. I'll try to be more understanding."

I almost fell off my chair. "Ah, um, thank you. I guess I appreciate it." I gave a small laugh.

Carina clapped. "Isn't d'is lovely. We're all friends again!"

Finnegan and I both laughed. She was pretty funny. "Well, until next time…." Okay, so I couldn't help it.

Finnegan smiled. "Yes, Lightning, until next time. But, in all seriousness, I don't know what dog they think it might be, but Phil Granger has a German Sheppard."

I blinked at him. The statement surprised me, but it shouldn't have. It's what I'd suspected, right? That he'd planted those rats. "Oh, um, that's what kind of dog Bellamy said it was." There was no point keeping it a secret since Bellamy would probably tell Finnegan anyway. He stared at me but said nothing. What was there to say? Be careful? Don't worry? Those words meant nothing because they couldn't change anything. I just had to let the police do their thing. "Right, well, I suppose I'll go home and work from there this morning. He said they should be there in an hour." I packed all my things up again and stood. "Right. I'll see you guys later."

Carina pointed at me. "Don't forget to let us know what they find. And be careful!"

I smiled, even though I wasn't feeling it. "I won't, and I will. Don't worry."

Finnegan's voice was subdued when he said, "Bye, Lightning, and good luck."

"Thanks. I'm going to need it."

While I waited for them to arrive, then waited another two hours for them to look through my flat, in the roof cavity, Mrs Collins's apartment, and the backyard, I researched an article I wanted to write to go with the gym one I'd just done. It was going to be titled *Great Low-Impact Exercises for Bone Health*. I hated articles that said *Exercises you Must do After you Turn Fifty*, or *If You're not Doing XYZ, You're Doing it Wrong. What not to Wear After Forty*. Seriously, name an article with a should or shouldn't do, and you could guarantee I wouldn't read it. I hated being told what to do, and I gave my readers the same respect.

Bellamy had sent a police forensics specialist as well as the pest guys. He came to tell me when they were done. The forty-something-year-old was tall, thin, and bald, but he had a friendly smile. "We're all done, Miss Winters. I have a couple of questions. Who cuts the grass here, and do you know the last time it was cut? It looks fairly recent."

That was one question I could answer. "I don't know if you noticed some goat droppings out there, but the neighbouring farmer—the one who owns the fields this backs onto —sets two goats in here once a fortnight. They get the job done pretty quickly, which is why the bushes don't have foliage close to the ground."

"Hungry little animals, aren't they?" He laughed.

"Very, but they're cute." My forehead wrinkled. "Why would you be asking? Are you looking for someone to cut your grass, or did you find something?"

"I might have found something, but I can't discuss it with you yet. If it leads to anything, Sergeant Bellamy will let you know. Have a good afternoon, Miss Winters." He turned and walked out the door. His heavy footsteps thudded on the stairs as he descended. I blew out a big breath. I was the victim here. Surely someone could give me some information. So frustrating.

I shut the door and turned around. And screamed before getting control of myself. "For Zeus's sake, Everly. Why would you do that?" I sucked in a deep breath. Having fright foist upon one was a workout.

She stood about one inch from me, and I'd turned to be face to face with her. She grinned. "I told you; call me Ev."

I rolled my eyes. "No respect. Seriously."

"Are you going to ask how my day was?"

Huh? Since when did I have to engage in niceties with a ghost? What could she possibly do all day? She was dead. "Okay. How was your day?"

She smiled, clasped her hands together, and held them to her chest. "Great! I helped a woman come to terms with her cancer death. It's only taken, well, I'm not sure, but it's been a long time. After our session today, she walked into the light."

I blinked. There was more to this young woman than I'd thought. Underestimating people... or ghosts... had become a theme in my life. Was I a huge cat's bum, or was it because my experience with people had been so limited, and most of them had been horrible? I smiled, and warmth spread through my chest. "That's excellent news! Congratulations! Are you like a ghost counsellor or something?"

She smiled. "I was in my first year of psychology at university when I was killed. I hadn't learned much, but since I've been dead, I sit in on classes. I've learned a lot in the last twenty or so years. When I first died, I spent a lot of time in my old lecture halls. I didn't know where else to go. And now I go every now and again. They've changed the course quite a bit since I was first there—or added to it, I should say. There's been a lot of advancements in treating mental illness. Not enough, if the suicides I see coming through are anything to go by, but it's meant I've helped a lot of ghosts who were stuck."

"Is that why you don't want to go onto the next place?"

She shrugged, a carefree, childlike movement. "Partly. I feel like my work here isn't done."

"Well, good on you. You've made your life worth something." I gave her a gentle smile.

She looked at me, as if she'd only just realised what I said was true. "You're right. I died too young, but I've still made a difference. Maybe it doesn't matter when we get the chance to change things for other people?"

"Maybe it doesn't."

She skipped to the kitchen and shoved her head through the fridge door till only from her waist down was visible. *What in Hades?* She popped her head out again and spun to look at me. "I always used to do that when I got home from school. Well, I couldn't stick myself through the door, but I'd check out everything and then tell Mum there was nothing to eat. Mum would shake her head and laugh, then hand me a plate with a piece of cake on it. We'd sit at the table together—she with her tea, me with my cake." She sighed. "Those were the days."

"Where's your mum now?" I wasn't sure if that was too personal a question or something that would upset her. Maybe I shouldn't have asked. *Avery, putting her foot in it for as long as she could remember.*

She looked at the ground, and her shoulders fell. When she looked up again, sadness had tempered her bubbly energy. I was betting that when she was alive, she'd been a lively person. "She never got over my death. I'd rather not talk about it, if that's okay."

"Of course. Sorry to ask. And I'm sorry. I bet if she knew what you were up to now, she'd be so proud."

She gave a limp shrug. "Maybe. So, do you need me to keep a lookout tonight as well?"

"Would you mind? If it's a hassle, you don't have to."

"I love to help." She smiled, shoving off her glum demeanour. If you'd ever told me someone could be a dead survivor, I would've told you, you weren't making sense. But there she was—a survivor who no longer walked among the living.

"Thank you. If there's ever anything I can do to help you, please let me know."

Contemplation impregnated her gaze. "Not right now, but one day, I'm sure I'll have just the job for you." She smiled.

I got the distinct impression she already knew what she wanted me to do. I just had to wait to find out.

CHAPTER 16

T he next morning, because I'd tossed and turned all night, I was tired and left home later than normal. So many thoughts competing for attention as well as fear had kept me awake. Charles hadn't gotten back to me yesterday about Russo. Had he forgotten, or was he busy with something else? Maybe there was nothing to report yet?

It was already nine thirty-four when I lined up for my coffee at Heavenly Brew. This was becoming a habit, despite having to face Joyless every time. Was I building a thicker skin? Either I was braver than I thought or stupider. I'd leave the final verdict up to you.

Two sixty-something-year-old women were standing in line in front of me, one with a miniature poodle in her arms. Their colourful activewear showed off toned legs. These ladies weren't aging without a fight. I hoped I was still active when I was their age. In fact, I just hoped I reached their age. The way I'd been going lately, I was only one annoyance away from getting killed.

The woman without a dog turned to her friend and lowered her voice, but funnily enough, it was still more than loud enough for everyone to hear. I smirked. She was pretending to be discreet, but she clearly wanted to be the bearer of this particular village gossip. "Oh, Layla, did you see the kerfuffle at the butchers this morning? The police took Phil away in handcuffs." My eyes popped open. Zeus's pyjamas! What had they found in my backyard? Had they linked the dog hair to his dog? I desperately wanted to pull my phone out and call Bellamy, but I wanted to hear the rest of the conversation.

"Phil Granger?"

"Yes!"

"No!"

"Yes!"

"My word! You never really know a person. You know, he could be dangerous. He's very good with all those knives. I mean, it wouldn't be a stretch to go from carving up a cow to carving up a person."

Oh, wow, they were getting off the track rather quickly. Looked like the rest would be insinuation. I didn't want to wait any longer to speak to Bellamy. I left without buying my coffee and hurried to the office. Carina and Finnegan were in. I normally wouldn't want to have this conversation in front of them, but they wanted to know what was going on, and who knew, I might need the moral support? I said hello, then pulled my phone out. "I have a call to make. Apparently Bellamy arrested Phil this morning."

They both widened their eyes, and Carina's mouth fell open. She looked at Finnegan. "Oh my goodness! You don't know yet? Ha, the world must be ending. Someone else got the police scoop before you did." She laughed.

"I'm hoping he'll tell me what's going on, especially if it's related to the rats." I dialled the station and asked to speak to him.

PC Adams answered the phone. "Oh, Avery, I'm so sorry. He's in the middle of something. We've had a crazy morning."

"That's why I'm calling. I heard he arrested Phil Granger, the butcher. Did they link him to the break-in at my place?"

"Hang on a minute, Avery. I don't know if I'm allowed to say anything about this arrest, but I'll speak to the sergeant. Just a moment." I swallowed as I waited and tapped my foot. Did this mean he was more likely to have killed the Downses?

"Miss Winters."

I started, not expecting Sergeant Bellamy to come to the phone. I recovered quickly. I didn't want to muck around either, and he was too busy for me to drag this out. "Hi, Sergeant. Did Phil's arrest have anything to do with my break-in?"

"Yes. We've matched the dog hair to his dog, and he left boot prints in the mud outside the back fence and one in the middle of your yard. You're lucky it rained before he came for a visit."

My heart raced. I'd been pretty sure someone had left those rats there, but to have it confirmed…. I shuddered. He'd been at my place. If he'd wanted to hurt me, he easily could have. "Oh." Wow, after all the kerfuffle I'd made about it, and now I had nothing to say? "Um, thank you, Sergeant. Now what happens?"

"He didn't attack you, so it's unlikely that we'll hold him for long. But he's got a court time for this afternoon. We can hopefully get a restraining order then so that he can't come within five-hundred foot of your home or work. He won't be able to speak to you or contact you."

"You mean won't be allowed." The number of times I'd heard of a woman getting a restraining order against an ex and then getting attacked or killed anyway. It was a piece of paper, not a bullet-proof shield.

He sighed. "That's the best we can do at this stage. Let me know if he makes any attempt to contact you. Now, I have to get back to work. Call us if you have any concerns. Good day, Miss Winters."

"Thanks. Bye." I hung up and plopped into my chair.

Finnegan came over and sat on my desk. Carina, still sitting in her chair, wheeled herself to me. She leaned forward and grabbed my hand. "What happened?"

I repeated everything Bellamy said. Carina squeezed my hand. "Wow, love. D'at's terrible. I'm glad you went to d'em straight away."

Deep lines appeared in Finnegan's forehead. "When's he getting out?"

"I don't know. He's in court this afternoon, so I guess if he gets bail—which Bellamy said is likely—he'll be out by tomorrow morning." My stomach flipped, and not in a good way. "Even if they take out a restraining order on my behalf, it's just a piece of paper." Now I knew what a sitting duck felt like. It was like waiting for another lightning bolt to hit. I clenched my jaw.

Finnegan blew a rush of air out of his nose. "Right. We'll look out for you. Why don't you go stay at the pub tomorrow night? Or you can stay in my spare room." Carina's eyes widened. He looked at her. "What? I'm not a total ogre, you know. I might be the worst guy in the world to date, but I'm a damned good friend, I'll have you know."

Carina smiled and patted his thigh. "Yes, you are, Finny. What you did for Alfie last year was top notch."

"What did he do?" Okay, so I wanted to know. Sue me.

"One of our friends was homeless. Finny let him stay in his spare room for three mont's, rent free, while he got back on his feet. He even helped him get a job as a labourer for a local farmer, Mr Donigal." She looked at Finnegan. "How's he getting on, then?"

He shrugged. "Good. We have a pint now and then. He's still working, paying his rent. He would've gotten there without my help. Someone else would've stepped in."

"Ah, but d'ey probably wouldn't have. He was homeless for a mont' before you took him in."

"Well, anyone would do the same. I'm just saying that I'm happy to help. I promise not to be an annoying git if you stay with me for a few days."

Oh lord, one of the hottest men I'd ever met—who was also well aware of his hotness—was offering to have me live with him for a few days. Of course my hormones were screaming at me to say yes, but my brain threw a bucket of cold water over them. I smiled. "That's a ridiculously generous offer, but I can't accept. I should be okay at home. I promise if I get worried, I'll come and knock on your door. How does that sound?"

His mouth quirked up in a lopsided smile. "If it's at two in the morning, that sounds terrible. Wouldn't it be easier if you were locked up safe in my spare room? Then I wouldn't have to be woken at 2:00 a.m."

Carina waggled her brows. "Kinky stuff." She smirked at me. "He wants to lock you in his spare room. Maybe Phil isn't the one we should be worried about."

Finnegan rolled his eyes, and I sputtered a laugh. Trust Carina to lighten the mood. "Ah, Crazy Carina. You know just how to cheer me up." I gave them both a grateful smile.

Carina winked. "You know it, lady."

"You're both awesome. Thanks for offering help. I won't take it for now, but if I do freak out, I'll move in for a few days, but I'd rather try staying on my own first—he's in jail tonight anyway, so I'm safe. I don't want to give someone else that power over me. I hate that he's scared me and I have to change my life because of it. Living in fear, well, it makes me angry."

Finnegan stared at me, his gaze fierce. I almost looked away—the intensity was too much. "We'll keep you out of harm's way—your new Manesbury family. I'll have a word with Meg and Bailey. With the four of us"—he gave a nod to Carina—"looking out for you, we should be able to keep you safe."

It took a moment for me to absorb his words. "I can't ask you to do that. Everyone's busy. You don't have time to babysit me. Besides, during the day, won't he be at work? Maybe I should just work from home so I don't have to walk past the butchers? And, honestly, I don't think he'll hurt me. He could've hurt me before, but he just wanted to scare me."

Carina folded her arms and gave me a stern look. "We aren't taking no for an answer, young lady. And if you won't stay somewhere else, maybe we can all take turns spending d'e night at your place. I've got a fold-up bed on wheels I can leave d'ere."

"Great idea." Finnegan smiled. He held up his hand to Carina, and they high-fived.

Erin appeared on the other side of my desk. "Are you okay?"

I blinked. I couldn't exactly answer her, so I nodded, then subtly jerked my head towards my colleagues. Erin giggled, waved, and left. That was nice of her to check in. Maybe I really did have a new family here? I smiled. "Thanks, guys. Maybe rotating people staying with me would be better. Then I don't feel like I'm imposing as much, but we'll see. I'll think about it tonight."

Carina smiled. "You know we'll just keep bugging you till you give in?"

"Is that the way it works around here?"

Finnegan nodded. "Yep. You can run, but you can't hide. We know where you live."

"Fine. I'll let you know tomorrow."

"Stubborn little t'ing, aren't ya." Carina shook her head. "I have to get back to work, but if you need anyt'ing, shout out."

"Okay. Again, thank you both." I'd say something else, but I wasn't used to being super friendly or mushy with anyone, except my ex and my sister. My ex, well, we all knew how that turned out, and my sister, she had the same kinds of issues I did. We didn't express our feelings much because putting yourself out there at my parents' place usually resulted in having the rug metaphorically pulled from under you. My sister and I loved each other, but we were still wary, especially since my parents always pitted us against each other—pretended to be nice to one to get information on the other. Totally despicable behaviour. How I put up with them as long as I did, I had no idea. That lightning strike finally illuminated my situation enough that I couldn't pretend not to see it any more.

Finnegan stood. "I guess we should get back to work." He wandered back to his desk. Carina pretended to be whipping herself on the bum like a racehorse as she rode her chair back to her desk. I shook my head and laughed. Such a larrikin.

Time to focus on something other than my personal problems. I went through my emails. There were three articles I was supposed to cover over the next couple of days, so I rang up the one I thought I could deal with today—an adorable dog called Champagne. He was a golden retriever, and a smart one at that. He was apparently an internet sensation, and after watching the videos of him doing clever things like getting a beer out of the fridge for his owner and carrying a bag of shopping home, I'd have to agree that the title was well-deserved. I might have even followed his TikTok account.

The house was in the village, so I walked, spent thirty minutes there—ten minutes videoing and interviewing, and twenty minutes playing with him. *Ahem.* When I was almost back at the office, a familiar face approached me. She wasn't in her white coat though. "Dr Bickford." *Please don't get angry at me for something*—the week I'd been having, it wasn't out of the question. She might even be wondering where that article was. Just waiting on more information....

She smiled. Phew. "Miss Winters, I'm so glad I've run into you. I was going to see you at your office, but here you are."

I smiled and stated the obvious so as not to stand there looking like a moron. "Yes, here I am." Hmm, now what?

She put her hand in her pocket and picked out a piece of red string, then held each end of it between thumb and forefinger and twirled it around one finger, then the other. "Well, this is a bit of a sensitive topic." She bit her bottom lip. "You see, well, I, ah, I wanted to tell you that you have nothing to worry about from Phillip Granger. If he could apologise, he would, but he can't from jail, obviously."

I scrunched my forehead. "Why are you telling me this? How do you know him?" It was a forward question, but under the circumstances, I felt it was fair.

"Well, he asked me to smooth things over. He swears that he didn't put those rats in your place, but he is sorry for threatening you. He thinks maybe someone overheard what he said at the pub, and they have it in for him, so they've framed him. He said his car was hotwired and his boots went missing that night." Well, anyone could make up that story.

And she'd only answered one question. "Did you know him through Melissa?" Even though she claimed to not know who Melissa had the affair with, maybe Melissa had introduced them, or maybe she'd lied to me because she didn't want to put him in it as far as the article was concerned? My cheery mood had as much cheer as Joyless had joy. Bye, bye playing-with-a-dog afterglow.

Her brow furrowed, and the red string snapped. "Not through Melissa, no. We used to be married. We were together for ten years, divorced three." She shrugged, back to nonchalance after breaking her string. Interesting. "We're still friends though—I feed Burt when he's away, that kind of thing. We just weren't meant to be together, but I still love him. He's not a violent person, really. You just got him on a bad day, and I know that he absolutely hates being accused of something he didn't do, and when you went to the police insinuating that he might have had something to do with Tom's and Melissa's deaths, well, he was livid." She frowned. Her gaze held sadness. "It's been hard on me, on him too. We were all good friends… well, before the, you know. After that Tom cut him out of his life."

Zeus's pyjamas. She knew who Melissa had the affair with and had lied to me. "Can you blame him?"

She wound and unwound that red twine over and over. Must be a stress-management thing. "No, I can't. Anyway, I just wanted you to know that he swears he didn't do it, and if he didn't, then someone else must have and framed him for it." She leaned closer. "I think maybe you should just watch out, that's all, because whoever did it isn't who you think." She shook her head. "And, honestly, the police have closed the case. Why would you go to them with that information? You're just prolonging the agony for the rest of us. This whole thing has broken my heart, and while you're stirring up trouble, their families and I can't move on." Her eyes glistened with moisture. Argh, I was just trying to get to the bottom of things, but I wasn't going to tell her that Tom's mother had asked me. The last thing she needed was more grief.

"As you know, I found the couple. I just… well, I just have a gut feeling that maybe someone had it in for them. I'm just a reporter trying to get to the truth, and something I saw there made me think it wasn't voluntary." I couldn't tell her they walked into the light and denied killing themselves. She'd just have to take my word for it. Should I remind her that she'd denied knowing Phil was Melissa's lover? Maybe she was just trying to protect him in the first place but since she now knew that I knew, what was the point of pretending differently? I blew out a breath and rubbed my forehead. A dim throbbing beat behind my temples. I was obviously thinking too hard. My brain needed a break.

"You're barking up the wrong tree. No one had it in for them. I just think Tom wasn't handling things well." She took a deep breath and sighed it out. "Anyway, I have to get back to work. I just wanted you to know that Phil won't give you any problems, and he never did anything in the first place." Hmm, she'd used a dog reference. I was fairly sure she wasn't insinuating anything about me…. "Bye, Miss Winters."

"Yeah, goodbye." That wasn't super polite of me, but I was trying to process. Phil wasn't supposed to contact me, but his hearing hadn't happened yet, so he could still ask someone to contact me on his behalf. Should I believe her? And if it wasn't him, who had it been? And if it was him, how dare she come see me on his behalf. I let my head drop back and stared at the cloudy sky. Why did everything have to be so complicated?

I kept on to the office and went upstairs. Everyone else had left, so I sat down and got straight to work. This article was a good one for the internet because I had video as well as pictures. The only caveat was that I was in the videos. The owner wanted me to give the dog instruction to prove that the dog was smart and that anyone could tell him what they wanted. It was a lot of fun, but watching myself back was embarrassing. Meh, the things I did for a story. I finished typing it up, linked all the dog's social media. Then I laughed because that dog had way more followers than I did on Instagram. I wondered what he would think if he knew. It was a crazy world we lived in, and my life was just another piece of the ridiculous puzzle. Weirdly, that was somewhat comforting.

When I'd sent everything to MacPherson, I headed to the pub. Most of the lunch crowd should be gone, and I wanted to talk to Meg, see what she thought about my surprise visitor. As soon as I walked in, Bailey waved from behind the bar. "Hey, Avery. I heard about what happened. Are you okay?"

Argh. I went to the bar. "I'm fine, thanks. Phil's in lock-up for tonight at least. And it's not like he hurt me. He killed some rodents, which probably isn't very nice, but I figure if he wanted to hurt me, he could have." How many times had I had to explain that today? I was tired of hearing myself say it. "Is Meg around?"

His gaze held concern, but he smiled. "Yeah. She's buzzing around here. She just took some plates to the kitchen. Go back there and find her."

I smiled. "Thanks." My payment for that was a sweet, swoonworthy smile. Hmph, that was a sneak attack. Totally mean. Or maybe he didn't even realise. *Seriously, Avery, just stop.*

I hurried into the kitchen, which was a white-tiled affair with commercial stainless-steel workspaces and ovens, and large iron gas hobs. The chef and two kitchen staff were washing up, and one was standing around talking to Meg. "Hey, Meg."

She turned her head and looked at me. "Avery!" She hurried over and threw her arms around me before standing back. "I heard what happened. You can stay here. No charge, of course."

I shook my head vehemently. "No, no. That's not why I'm here. Can we have a quick chat? I just need to run something by you."

"Of course. Come on." She grabbed my hand and led me across the hallway to the main office.

Her dad was sitting at one of the three desks on his computer. He smiled. "Hello, ladies." After another moment of appraisal he asked, "Do you need me to make myself scarce?"

Meg looked at me. I shook my head. Maybe he'd have some insight? "No, that's okay. I could use more than one opinion."

"Sit." Meg pointed to an office chair in front of the desk next to the window. She grabbed the other chair and sat. "Now, tell us everything."

I started with the conversation with the sergeant about the evidence and Phil's arrest and finished with the visit from Catherine. "I mean, should I believe her? And why would she risk me going to the police and complaining? They've been divorced for quite a while. She claims they're still friends, but seriously, who cares that much about their ex?" God knew, if Brad was arrested for something, I'd be calling them to add more fuel to the fire.

"She's not a bad woman, that one," Meg's dad offered.

"But their divorce hit her hard, and she's been chasing him ever since. She'd do anything for him. I suppose she doesn't want to see him go to jail."

"Well, she'll get her wish in the short term. Bellamy said he'll likely get bail and be out in the morning. Even if she cares about him, why does she care if I'm scared or not?"

Meg tapped her nose. "She probably doesn't. Maybe she's trying to prove to him that she loves him? Or maybe she wants the restraining order dropped because it'll make it hard for him to move freely about Manesbury. It could just be that she really doesn't want him incarcerated later. If she can get you to back off, his problems will go away."

"But if he killed the Downses, his problems are only just starting."

Meg's dad's eyebrows shot up. "You really think that?"

I shrugged. "It's a possibility. I'm still not convinced that Tom killed them both, and I have two suspects right now—Russo and Granger. I mean, if Phil still loved Melissa and she kept pushing him away, which it looks like, he wouldn't be the first man to kill after being rejected."

Meg's dad shook his head. "Stay out of it. You're putting yourself in harm's way. Let the police deal with it."

Meg focussed on her dad. "It's her job to uncover the truth. I think it's noble of her." She gave me an encouraging look.

I smiled. "Thanks." Then I thought of something. "Granger lives in the village, right?"

"Yes," Meg's dad confirmed.

"Will he have to move? Maybe she's just worried about all the hassle he's going to go through?" That didn't sit right with me, but I had to think of all angles. Something didn't seem right, but then again, it might just be because I could never imagine helping out an ex, especially one who dumped you. That had to have hurt. Hmm…. "Does she live in the village too?"

Meg nodded. "Yeah. She actually lives on the block that backs onto the Downses'. I guess she wanted to be close to her best friend."

I grabbed my phone and pulled up the photos I'd taken the day I found the couple. I scrolled through to the kitchen photos. Argh, what a mess. I zoomed in and moved the picture around so I could study each pile of mess. I stared at the floor for a moment. Maybe it was nothing, but the goosebumps on my arms said otherwise. "I just need to ring Bellamy."

"What's up?" Concern filled Meg's gaze.

"I'll tell you in a sec." I called the police station. PC Adams answered. "Hey Constable Adams. It's Avery here. I was wondering if I could speak to Sergeant Bellamy. It's rather urgent."

"I'm not sure. I think he's in with someone. Just a moment, and I'll check."

"Can you tell him it's super urgent?" Just in case she missed it the first time.

"Yes, of course. Are you in any danger?"

"Not right at this moment, no, but I could be."

"I'll be back in a moment."

Meg and her dad stared at me, their concern turning to alarm. I shook my head and mouthed, "I'm fine." I hoped I wasn't like the boy who cried wolf and that Bellamy would take this call.

"Sergeant Bellamy speaking. What is it, Miss Winters?"

I breathed out. Thank goodness he agreed to take my call. "Sorry to bother you, but I need you to answer some questions. Is it true that Phil Granger's car was stolen that night and his boots too? Do you have security footage of him driving to my place?" I chewed my lip. I'd look like a right idiot if I was wrong, and he'd probably never take a call from me again.

Silence. Then, finally, words. "Who told you about the security footage?"

"No one. I guessed. But is that common knowledge? Did you tell him, and if you did, has he had time to tell someone other than his lawyer? And what about the boots?"

"Blimey, Winters. This is confidential information."

"Please tell me. I'm beginning to think he didn't leave those rats."

"What?!" I winced at his raised voice. "You told me it was him, and we found the evidence. We arrested the man, for goodness' sake. I don't know what you're playing at, but—"

"Just tell me, please. I promise that if I'm wrong, I'll never ever, ever call you again. Ever." A monetary bribe wouldn't work, but I was sure this would.

"Ever?" Hope rang loud and clear in his voice.

"Ever. Even if a hundred dead rats show up at my place and I'm on fire and someone is punching me at the same time."

He coughed—trying to cover a laugh maybe? "Okay. This is the last time I tell you anything about a case. His boots weren't stolen, and his car wasn't hotwired. We got his boots from him, and the dirt on the bottoms matched that from your yard. He wore different shoes to work, so they were still well preserved in his hallway. Inside. And his car was where he parked it the night before."

My stomach dropped, and a swarm of nausea smothered me. "I think I can prove Catherine Bickford killed Tom and Melissa and set up Phil. I'm not quite sure why she did it, but I have a rough idea." Meg and her Dad gaped at me, their eyes wide. Meg mouthed a swearword, which was about how I felt. Now I just had to wait for the information to sink into Bellamy. Ten, nine, eight, seven, six, five, four—

"Did you just say what I think you said?"

"Yes. The vet, Catherine Bickford. The woman scorned, not once but twice. First, her husband breaks up with her; then her best friend has an affair with him, likely knowing how she still felt about him. I mean, Meg's dad even knew she still loved him, so I would think Catherine's best friend did."

"Meg's dad? What?"

"Ah, never mind."

"Look, Winters…" Oh, dear, he'd dropped the Miss. "You can't just go around accusing people because you have a theory… an unproven theory with no evidence. I'm afraid I'll have to give you a warn—"

"Did you check any security video to make sure no one came in the front door of Tom and Melissa's that night?" I wasn't going to give up that easily.

"Well, yes, of course. And no one went inside that day, other than those two."

"Catherine lives directly behind them, does she not? She could've gone through the back door. I'm not sure why she was there that night, but I think she was. She has a red piece of string she likes to fiddle with. When I went in there and saw the Downses were dead, I took photos of everything, just in case they would help with my story."

"You did what?! You better not have published them anywhere. We can have you arrested for—"

"Please just listen. In the photo of all the mess of cooking, there was a red piece of string, the exact same colour as the ones I've seen her twirling around her fingers. What if she'd gone there that night and 'helped' cook the dinner? And she told me she feeds Burt when he's away, so she probably has a house key, and I'm assuming Burt is his German Sheppard. She could've let herself in and taken his car if he was fast asleep, same with the boots."

"Send me those photos, dammit. And don't say a word to anyone. If you're wrong, you've just defamed someone who can sue you. She's well-respected in this community."

I eyed Meg and her dad. *Oops.* "I wouldn't dream of it. If I'm wrong, I'll look like a right idiot." I hoped I wasn't wrong, but I didn't think I was.

"You'll be the death of me, Winters. I swear. Now we're going to have to go back over everything in that house again." He grunted. "Is that all?"

I thought for a moment. "Yes. I'll email you those photos."

"That you shouldn't have taken."

"But you're glad I did?"

"Don't push your luck. Goodbye, Winters."

"Bye, Sergeant."

Meg's mouth was open wide. "Oh my God, Avery! What?!" Why was everyone saying that to me today?

"So, that's my theory. I might as well show you the pictures. But don't look at more than the two I show you. I took photos of their bodies too."

Meg's dad raised a brow, and Meg paled slightly. "Ah, yeah, no thanks."

"Don't tell anyone what you just heard either. Bellamy will likely throw me in jail if he knows I told anyone. I'm casting aspersions with no proof, and if they can't prove she did it, I could get sued. Not that I have anything for Catherine to take, but they might just take my wages for the next twenty years."

Meg's dad finally weighed in. "Wow… that was… a lot."

"Tell me about it. I hope they haven't thrown that evidence away."

"I hate to be the one to say it, but what if you're wrong?" Meg's dad had to go and be the party pooper, but I couldn't blame him for stating the obvious.

"I'll look like the world's biggest idiot, and I can never speak to Bellamy again." And if I ever solve another crime, they won't listen to me. I'd used my "get out of jail free" card. This was it. And I'd be failing Mrs Downs senior. If I'd made a mistake and Russo was guilty—please no, Avery—there was no way I could posit *that* theory. I'd just used, to employ a cliché, my last roll of the dice.

"Now what?" Meg asked.

I swallowed the nerves clambering up my throat and emailed the photos to Bellamy from my phone. "I guess we wait, and I cross my fingers."

"And toes." Meg's dad was such a bundle of support.

I gave him a deadpan look. "Thanks for the vote of confidence."

He chuckled. "It's in the hands of the gods. Best thing you can do now is pray."

Boy, was I in trouble.

CHAPTER 17

Bellamy didn't get back to me that night, and Charles came and told me he'd shadowed Russo all day, and the only thing he was guilty of was being a huge cowpat. No news there.

I didn't sleep. I couldn't help but think I'd peaked too early. Was I wrong? Had I ruined Tom's mother's chance at finding out the truth? Or did we already know it, and I was just a nutcase? Maybe I wasn't cut out for journalism any more? Could I make a promise to myself not to interfere, just report the stories and not care about them? I had to do something. I was off the rails. Making my mind up about things without solid proof. I had to admit that most of that stuff with Catherine was conjecture. I didn't even know if she really had a key to Phil's place.

It was only half past five in the morning, but I got up. There was no way I was sleeping. I dressed in my workout gear and went for a walk in the calm breaths of a morning still half-asleep, its eyes only beginning to open to a new day. I listened to her changing rhythms as her rosy skin slid from between sheets of grey. A rooster crowed, a light turned on in one house, now another. I imagined people wiping sleep from their eyes, boiling their kettles for their morning cuppa, sliding bread into the toaster for breakfast. One of those people would be Mrs Downs, hoping a new day brought news exonerating her beloved son. She would have no peace until her wishes melded with reality. Had I ruined everything for her?

I pondered it until I returned home forty-five minutes later. I went inside and made a coffee, but it was too early for me to eat. I couldn't stomach food first thing in the morning, especially when the time had a five or six in front of it, but coffee was a must. When the coffee was ready, I placed it on the table and sat. Everly appeared in a chair across from me. "You look deader than me, and that's saying something."

I raised a brow, then yawned. "That might be because I didn't sleep, and I still need it. Unlike other people I know."

"Ha ha, you're a comedian. Good to see your sense of humour's still alive."

"If I ever lose it, just kill me."

"Deal." I smiled, which took me by surprise. I wasn't sure anything could make me smile this morning, but there I went, being wrong again. "So, what gives?"

She hadn't been here last night, so I hadn't caught her up on my dramas. As I sipped my coffee, I talked. "And now I have to wait. It's like waiting to go to the gallows."

"You don't think you're overreacting? So what if you look like an idiot in front of people? Does it matter?"

"Kind of, yes. It's not just that. I'm letting Mrs Downs… down." I shook my head and moved on. "And I'll never get information out of Bellamy again."

"But you hardly got any before from what you've told me."

I pressed my lips together and pushed them out. "Hmm, you make a good point." I smiled. "And I suppose I still have a chance at getting Charles in there to spy. But the problem is… I've lost confidence in my ability to make sound decisions. I thought I had a good gut, but what if I don't? What if I've just been lucky this whole time, and I'm really an idiot who shouldn't be investigating serious crimes? Maybe Brad was right all those times he criticised my work." My sigh was proportionate to my self-loathing. To be clear, the sigh was huge.

She folded her arms. Her voice was measured and stern and insinuated I was a silly child. "Are you quite finished with your pity party?" She unfolded her arms and leaned forward, placing her forearms on the table. I'd have to ask her later how she didn't fall straight through. I still had no idea how everything worked in the other plane of existence. "Do you know how lucky you are to be alive?" She waved an arm in the air. "All this other stuff, it's unimportant. Did you do your best?"

"I guess so? I mean, I tried." My defeated tone was even starting to annoy me. It reminded me of past-Avery, the one who cowered and did her best to please everyone, even when their requests or orders were ridiculous. Feeling bad about myself and deferring to the opinions of others was a habit I needed to break…. Although, this time I had a good reason. Didn't I?

"Why did you get involved?"

"I saw their ghosts. Tom asked me to help find out who did it. He and his wife both went into the light. Surely they couldn't have if he'd killed her? I believed him when he said he didn't do it. I believed in their love when they smiled at each other. And, logically, without all that, it didn't make sense. They had plans, and she was getting better. But maybe it was just me and my wishful thinking, wanting to believe the best in people?"

"You're right, Avery. He wouldn't have gone into the light if he'd done something like that. I know from watching those around me. Even the ones who finally understand why they did what they did and choose to depart, they don't all go into the light." She frowned, and divots appeared between her brows. From what she'd told me, she helped people come to terms with their lives so they could move on, which meant she inadvertently sent some people to be consumed by the shadows.

"That's not your fault, Ev. You didn't make their mistakes for them. You just helped them heal, or realise, or whatever. Maybe where you go after your stage is also temporary? Maybe we hop back on and do it all again? Who knows?" My eyes widened. Had she done something in life that she thought would get her sent to the bad place? "I actually thought, from what Charles said, that the shadow took you even if you weren't ready?"

"No. I mean, it can, and so can the light. You have to be quick on your feet when you die, but many people don't realise what's happened, or at least, the implications of it. They don't know they might have a choice, so they go along with what's put in front of them. I'm sure not everyone gets a choice, or even what difference it makes for them to stay in the in-between for a period when the outcome is predetermined... or is it?" She lifted her hands in a "who knows" gesture. "It is what it is, and I don't try and figure it out. I want to keep what little sanity I have, thank you very much." She smiled. "So, you have very good reasons for what you did, and, for what it's worth, I think you're right... at least about the police being wrong."

"But I pulled the trigger too quickly. I should've tried to find more out." Cat's bum. I should've waited and had Charles spy on Catherine and Phil, see what they said to each other. Now it was too late. Argh.

"Stop it, Avery. Chastising yourself before you even know if you were right isn't going to help anyone, especially not you. Just chill."

"Easy for you to say. You're eternally chilled." I pressed my lips together to stop my smile from forming. It seemed like a good joke at the time, but maybe death jokes were offensive for dead people?

Everly chuckled. "Ha ha, good one."

I let my smile loose. "Phew. I thought you might be offended by that. I should've checked with you first. Are you okay with death jokes?"

"Of course. I made fun of you too. Same, same. I'll tell you if you've crossed the line. Don't worry." She stood. "I've got things to do, places to go, etcetera. Are you going to be okay?" For someone who'd come across as unpredictable and silly at first, she was actually a kind-hearted soul.

"I'll be fine. Thanks for the chat. Today, well, until Bellamy gets back to me, I'll focus on work and do my best not to think about all the ways it could go wrong."

She laughed. "What am I going to do with you?" She shook her head. "I'll see you later."

"Bye."

She disappeared. I was alone, and I felt it.

I checked the time. Six forty-two. I rolled my eyes. This was going to be the never-ending day. Might as well get started trying to ignore the elephant that would be following me around all day. I stood. Without anything better to do, I decided I'd have the cleanest apartment in the whole of England. Toilet brush and bleach, here I came.

❧

By 9:00 a.m., I was ready for bed. Instead, I was walking into the office. Before I'd had a chance to put my stuff on my desk and sit, MacPherson raced in, out of breath. He surveyed the room. Seeing no one else there, his gaze landed on me. "You're the only one in."

I looked around, then back at him. "Seems like it."

"You're not the ideal person for this job."

"Tell me what you really think." My eyes widened. *Darn it, mouth! I didn't tell you to open.* Lack of sleep was a dangerous thing.

It must've been my lucky day because MacPherson laughed. "Funny one, Winters. You've got a dry sense of humour, but I like it. I wanted someone to cover a police investigation that's going down right now. It's not that I don't think you're capable, but, well, you might be a bit close to this one." He ran a hand through his hair, and his gaze pinged around the room again, just in case something had changed in the last ten seconds. He looked back at me. I was still the only other person here.

"What is it?" I could probably guess that it had something to with Phil. Maybe he wanted someone to cover his getting out of jail. "If it's Phil, I obviously can't cover it with the restraining order. Although, no one's told me whether it was granted."

"They moved his hearing to this afternoon."

I scrunched my forehead. "What? Why?"

"New information came to light, apparently. Which is what

brings me to this—asking you to go to Catherine Bickford's place. The police are executing a search warrant right now. If it wasn't so urgent, I'd wait, but…."

Oh. My. God. Bellamy listened to me. My heart beat faster. I wasn't missing this for anything—it was my story. "Of course I can go. But why wouldn't you want me to?"

"You're still related to the case. She's his ex-wife. Who knows? Are you okay with it? If you're not, I can cover it myself. It's been a few years since I was in the field, but it's not that hard."

I chuckled. "No, it's not. Thanks for minimising my job."

His mouth opened, shut, opened. "Ah, sorry, Winters. You know what I mean."

I smiled. "Yes, I do. I'm on it. Oh, what's the address?" Whilst I knew she lived directly behind the Downses', I didn't know the place well enough to find the street from memory. I'd been to many places since I'd arrived, and it was all new. My brain would take time to get its bearings.

"I'll text it to you." He slid his phone from his pocket and sent it. My phone dinged. He handed me a plastic lanyard attached to a silver clip. "Proof of your employment. That's our media pass, in case the police move the public on. Good luck."

I took the pass. "Thanks." The only person I might have a problem with was Bellamy. If he ordered me to leave, no pass was going to save me. I blew out a huge breath, mentally pulled on my big-girl pants, and left. So much for ignoring the elephant. At this point, I'd mounted it and was riding to my doom.

It was a seven-minute walk, but I decided to take my car because if I needed to leave in a hurry with the hounds of hell chasing me, I could. So I power-walked home and got into my cute car. Every time I saw her, I was surprised she was mine. I happy sighed as I started the engine. *See, Avery, good things can happen. And you do deserve it.* Maybe one day I'd get the hang of self-affirming talk. Baby steps.

I used my map app to get there. Because it was a live scene, I decided to video it and watch it back later. Often things could happen in the moment that you'd miss making notes because multiple things were occurring simultaneously. And, yes, I'd learned that lesson the hard way when I first started out.

I pulled over and parked a few houses away from the scene. A crowd stood out the front of her home, gawking, and a news crew was already there, what I was assuming was their van had a large 4 News on its side. One police car blocked off the road near where I parked. I donned my lanyard, got out, and walked along the footpath.

Her house was easy to pick, even without being able to see the number. Along with a police officer guarding the front gate, police tape in front of the fence, uniformed police and plain-clothes ones entering and exiting the front door, as well as the nosy public, Catherine stood out the front of her house, arms folded, face tightened grimly.

I took my phone out and filmed, panning the scene. At least Bellamy had taken me seriously. This was only now sinking in. He would've had to have more than my word for this to happen. What evidence or information did they find to take it this far?

When I reached the scene, Catherine noticed me. I kept filming but lowered the camera to hip level—I didn't need to film people's faces, and this was more for me than anyone. She narrowed her eyes. "What are you doing here?"

"I'm a reporter, remember? And just so you know, I'm

recording this… I mean, not just our conversation, but my boss asked me to cover this for the paper. It might be nothing, though, and I doubt the police will talk to me, so the only thing I might have to report is that the police are searching this house. Do you know whose it is? And how are you going with Phil's hearing being moved?" I didn't expect her to think I didn't know whose house it was, but if I played clueless and friendly, maybe she'd be less wary of me.

"You don't know whose house this is?"

"No. My boss was in a hurry when he sent me the job." I shrugged. "He just said there's a police operation at this address, and to hurry up and get my bum over here."

She stared at me, but I held my innocent expression. "It's my house."

My mouth dropped open. "Oh my! Why are they searching it? Is it something to do with Phil? Did he threaten you too?"

Her brow wrinkled. "No. You're not too bright, are you? I think I misjudged you."

I frowned. "That's not very kind. I thought you were nice. I think I misjudged you."

She pressed her lips together. "The idiot police think I had something to do with Melissa's murder. It's insane. If Tom didn't do it, which I think he did, it must've been Phil."

"I thought you didn't think he was capable of killing anyone? Or did you just say that because he's so attractive and you love him?"

"You think he's attractive?"

If I could play to her jealousy—which was probably what got Melissa killed—hopefully she'd talk and spill what she'd done… if she had, indeed, done what I thought she had. "Well, unfortunately yes. I think I have a thing for bad boys…

or men, as the case may be. My ex was a total piece of you-know-what." Ha, that much was true. The bad-boy thing, not so much. "I had my eye on Phil when I first interviewed him at the butcher, but then he threatened me, and it put me off, but then you insisted he didn't do it, and I started to reconsider. I'd have a good chance, don't you think? Men tend to go for younger women." I stuck my chest out a bit, not that there was that much to stick out, but they said a handful was enough, didn't they? It was probably enough to drive a jealous woman mad.

"You, what?!" She gave me an incredulous look. "Are you crazy? He's old enough to be your father." Her nostrils flared.

"Well, can you blame me? He's a catch—you still love him, and Melissa had her turn as well, which is pretty disrespectful since she knew you still had a thing for him, and he was your ex-husband, oh, and she was still married. None of that kept her away." I shrugged.

"No, it didn't." She clenched her teeth and her fists.

"That must've hurt. She was your best friend, wasn't she? So disrespectful. Phil must have a huge—"

"Someone had to stop her! Phil was still panting after her, for God's sake, after all this time. If it weren't for her, he would've come back to me. It was all her doing. She didn't care, and she shoved it in my face, went on and on and on about him and how kind he was, and how he bought her flowers and how he loved her, even after she knew how heart-broken I was at losing him. I couldn't wait for him to forget her any longer. Argh!" She screamed. Yikes.

The crowd stared at us, and the policeman at the gate put a hand on his belt. Maybe he was considering whether one of us needed handcuffs applied.

"So, did you come and prepare dinner for them that night,

or did you slip something into the roast when Melissa wasn't looking?"

Her self-satisfied smirk highlighted the crazed look in her eyes. "She thought I was being nice, offering to cook their dinner so they could have a romantic evening. She might have thought she was better than me, but she wasn't nearly as smart." Hmm, not as devious maybe? Smart, not so much, since she'd just admitted everything on a recording I'd told her I was doing.

I licked my bottom lip and turned to the policeman at the gate. Our gazes met. I gave him a look, like, just give me one more minute. He gave a nod and mumbled something into his walkie-talkie.

Catherine pulled out her red string and started playing with it.

I looked at her. "Why did you frame Phil for the threat, then try and get him out of it?" That was the thing I couldn't figure out, and one reason I wasn't a 100 per cent on my theory.

She grinned. "Punishment for rejecting me and being upset that she was dead. You know he called me and bawled on the phone... bawled!" She pressed her lips together and gritted her teeth, her jaw muscles bulging. "And I was there for him. Always. He used me, but I took anything from him I could get. I didn't care." Her shoulders slumped, and she looked at the ground for a moment. Then she raised her eyes to mine. I held myself back from recoiling. A weird combination of lost, loopy, and righteousness filled her gaze. "He promised if I could get you to drop any charges, that he'd see if we could work out again."

"Wow, so manipulative of him." A spec of sympathy dirtied my vision. I cleared it away because she'd murdered two people in a premeditated fit of jealousy. What a waste of so many lives, even Catherine's. All those animals who needed her that she'd never treat. All the good she'd done over the years had been obliterated within a few weeks. And all over a man? I shook my head. It so wasn't worth it.

"Yes, he was." Her face blanked. Had she only just realised the futility of her actions?

I turned to the policeman and gave a nod. He had a female officer with him now, and Bellamy stood behind them. The two constables moved forward, and I stepped out of the way.

As one pulled her arms behind her back, the other said, "I am arresting you for the murders of…"

I turned my back on them and went to Bellamy. This time, I shut off the recording. I didn't think he'd appreciate me recording our conversation. I was pretty sure I could remember it. "I've got it all on here if you need it."

Expression stoic, his gaze held… was that respect? "Yes, we will need it." He regarded me a while longer in silence. "Come on. Follow me." He turned and made his way to her front door.

Zeus's pyjamas! He was letting me into the inner sanctum. I couldn't help but grin as I went through the front door after him. "Can I take a couple of photos?"

"Yes, but don't show the officers' faces, please. And I'll have to okay any you want to include in your exposé. I expect you to not beat up on us too much."

"If you could help me out a little more on my cases, I'll even spin it the other way. I don't need any credit."

We were in the kitchen already, and he stopped and turned. He blinked, then shook his head. "You've turned out to be nothing like I pegged you for when we first met. Well played, Winters, well played."

"Thank you, I think. So, can you give me a few details? Did Catherine have a key to Phil's house?"

"Yes. It was just as you thought. She borrowed his car, wore his boots, returned everything knowing we would find it. We still had the evidence from the Downses' as well, and her string was there, as were her fingerprints."

"You would think she would've worn gloves."

"That would've been hard to do if her friend was there. How would you explain that? My guess is that she knew we wouldn't take prints from the scene since it seemed cut and dried. We don't have unlimited resources. I expect her to say her fingerprints were there because she was their friend and visited often, but we also found them on the two phones in the bedroom that were turned off."

"She did that so they couldn't call for help?"

"I would say so, yes. We're retrieving information off those phones as we speak. So, you managed to get a confession?"

I smiled. "Yep, and before we talked, I told her I was recording, so I've covered my bases."

He nodded. "Nice work, Winters. I thought your sleuthing skills were a fluke last time, but it seems you've proven me wrong."

I grinned, relief and happiness making me feel like I could float. "Thanks. That's my favourite thing to do, you know… prove people wrong." I winked—against my better judgement— and smiled, so he knew I was kidding… well, maybe half kidding. Goodness knew that I'd spent my life being underesti-mated and underappreciated by most people. With a bit of work, in time, I'd prove that negative voice in my head wrong too. *You did good, Avery. You did good.* Now it was time to call Mrs Downs and tell her the news. And that was the best thing of all, giving a woman back her peace of mind. She could be proud of her son again and grieve him properly, secure in the fact that she did know her son as well as she'd thought. He *was* the person she'd brought into the world, knew, loved, and had to see leave it.

This one's for you, Mrs Downs.

CHAPTER 18

I was still floating on my cloud when I returned to the office, but it didn't last long. The office was empty, and a yellow sticky note stuck to my desk said, *Come see me as soon as you return. JM.* Okay, it was obviously from the boss. I would like to think it's because he was congratulating me, but he wouldn't have heard the news yet. Was I in trouble for something?

I left my stuff on my desk and headed to his office. I knocked. "Come in!"

"Hi, Mr"—he stared at me with a warning look, cutting me off. "Ah... *Julian.* You wanted to see me?"

"Yes. Please have a seat." His serious expression wasn't encouraging, and my pace slowed. It made for a long, torturous walk to my chair. "Do you have a sore leg?"

"Ah, no."

"Why are you walking so slowly?"

"No reason." I normalised my pace and sat.

"Where are you getting these letters from the dead? The

last one we printed earned us a complaint from the person's mother… the person it was aimed at. She said we'd embarrassed her son and made things worse. I promised I'd follow it up and see who was behind it. Do you have any ideas?"

Cat's bum. My cloud dissolved and unceremoniously dumped me on the floor. *Ouch.* "Nope. They just turn up in my inbox, and when I search the return address, it's usually hijacked from someone else. Technology isn't my forte." But lying is.

"Well, here's her address. Placate her." He slid two twenty-pound notes across the desk. "Take her some flowers from us. Apologise and tell her we're deeply sorry. As I see it, you caused this issue, so you can fix it."

I swallowed. There wasn't much I could say to that. Looked like my days of helping ghosts with messages was over… at least in its current iteration. "Yes, sir. I'll do that right now." I grabbed the money and stood. What a failure. Instead of making things better, I'd made them worse.

"Good. Let me know when it's done."

"Will do."

I went to my office, grabbed my bag, went to the flower shop, and bought a bunch of happy flowers—yellow and mauve—and drove to Cramptonbury. I wasn't sure if it was possible, but I called out to Fox as I drove. He appeared in my passenger seat, looking as surprised as I felt. "Winters?"

"Hi, Sergeant."

"How did you do that?"

"Do what?"

"Make me come here. One minute I was in my office, the next, I pop out here. I don't much care for being kidnapped."

I laughed. "I didn't kidnap you, and I have no idea why that happened." I had no energy for investigating what just occurred, and I was almost at the house, so time was short too. "My office received a complaint from your granddaughter. She said we made things worse, and I'm going there to smooth things over. I figured I might need you to help. And, before you complain, I'll basically be telling them I can talk to the dead, which I don't want people to know, so you're not the only one put out here. But I need you for backup. You need to tell me things only you or someone in the family would know."

He smoothed his moustache. "Okay, but I don't give you permission to call on me again. If you want me for something, come to the station."

I rolled my eyes because this was all under my control. Seriously.

I pulled up at the house, a brick bungalow with a pretty garden and detached garage. I looked at Fox. His brow furrowed. "What are you staring at?"

I looked down at his lap. "Um…. I need to grab the flowers off the front seat, and I know you're not really there, but reaching for your crotch is still, well…." I shuddered. Shock burst over his face—even his moustache seemed to jump—and I laughed until I snorted.

He disappeared and reappeared on their front porch. I grabbed the flowers, locked my car, and joined him. Déjà vu anyone? I knocked, waited the appropriate amount of time and knocked again. There was no bell. I sighed. "Looks like she's not home." Why hadn't I called first? Why hadn't MacPherson? We were so inefficient.

Fox listened. He looked at me. "Wait here."

"But you can't go in. You haven't been invited."

He smiled. "This used to be my home."

"Oh. I did not see that coming."

He disappeared. After a minute, he materialised in front of

me. "Get in there now! He's hanging himself. He's got the rope tied to a ceiling beam. Hurry!!"

"Oh, Jebus. What the hell? Can you call the…" Argh! I dialled 999. "Hello, I'd like to report an attempted suicide ongoing at 12 Delphinium Street, Cramptonbury. He's trying to hang himself. Yes. Thank you." I hung up.

"Hurry up! Get inside!"

My head jerked around as I looked for an entry point. There was no way I could break the front door down. No matter how much hapkido I'd done, I was still way too small and light, and I didn't fancy breaking a leg. I left the flowers on the porch and ran around the pretty front garden. Heart racing, I grabbed a brick out of the garden border and went to the front window that faced the porch. I was about to warn Fox to look away but then remembered he was a ghost. Doh!

I grabbed the end of the brick and turned my face away, protecting it with my other arm, as I struck the window with the other end of the brick. It smashed. Small fragments of glass stung my arm. I opened my eyes and set to work clearing the remaining glass with the brick. When it was all gone from the frame, I climbed inside. "Where is he?" I'd entered into a snug, as the English called it. A cosy room with a couple of armchairs and a pot-belly fireplace.

Fox walked back through the wall next to the smashed window and jogged to a closed door. I opened it and followed him through, down a short hallway, and into another living area that looked like a more modern addition. Thick wooden beams hugged the tall sloping ceiling and crossed the expanse. A young man was on a ladder, the noose around his neck. He was just about to step off.

"No! Stop! Fox, you can't kill yourself."

He turned to look at me, his eyes bugging out.

My heart thudded quickly, each beat reverberating in my ears. I ran to the ladder and held it so he couldn't kick it away. If he wanted to jump off, I'd bloody well move the ladder, climb it, and cut him down if I had to. "If you try, I'll save you. I'm not going to let you die." I looked at Fox senior. "Can you find a serrated knife? I might have to cut him down."

"Okay." He hurried off.

"Who are you talking to, and who the hell are you?" One of his hands held the ladder, the other the noose around his neck. His hair was long enough that it just rested on the rope at his nape. Crap. I tamped down my panic. *Keep it together, Avery.*

"I'm Avery Winters from the *Manesbury Daily.* I'm the one who put that letter in the paper, the one from your great-grandfather. I came to apologise to you and your mum for upsetting you. We wanted to make things better, not worse. And when no one answered the door, your great-grandfather —who's a ghost by the way and wrote you that letter for real— came in and saw you. He told me to get in here quick smart. I've already called the ambulance, told them you were hanging yourself. Sergeant Fox is here."

Right on cue, he returned. "I've found a serrated knife. There's a timber block on the kitchen bench shaped like a hedgehog."

The young man scowled down from the ladder. "You're nuts."

"I'm not…. Well, maybe I am, but that's not the point. Your great-grandfather came to me because he was worried about you. He doesn't want you to do this."

"Did my mother put you up to this?"

"No, of course not."

"Well, you're stuffing this up, just like the rest of my life is stuffed up. And you've broken in because the door wasn't open."

"Your life isn't stuffed up."

"Don't tell me what my life is or isn't!" Anger flashed in his gaze.

"Once you do this, you can't go back. You're going to break your parents' hearts. Don't do it."

"Tell him he needs to go back on his medicine."

"Your great-grandfather says you need to go back on your meds."

He narrowed his brown eyes at me. "Stop lying!" Yikes. I was doing this all wrong. He wasn't supposed to get aggressive—he was supposed to realise he should live and get off that bloomin' ladder. I looked at Fox for inspiration.

"Tell him it's not his fault Jack drowned."

"Who's Jack?"

"His cousin. They went boating when they were six."

"What did you say?" The anger had leeched out of the young man's eyes, and he stared down at me.

"Your great-grandfather—who I'm going to refer to as Sergeant Fox from now on because it's a pain in the bum to say—said it wasn't your fault Jack drowned. So I asked who Jack was. He said he was your cousin, and you went boating."

He breathed the words out. "How… how did you know? Did you read up on me?"

"No. I didn't know anything about it till right now. Hang on a sec." I turned back to Fox. "What else happened that day that I wouldn't know?" Fox relayed the information, and I looked up at his great-grandson again.

"This wasn't in the paper, but Sergeant Fox was there, so he saw it all. He said you stood up because you were excited about catching a fish, and a wave hit at the same time. The boat tipped over. Everyone fell out, but your cousin was trapped underneath it. Your dad saved you, and when he went to get your cousin, he was already gone. You had on your favourite red socks that day. Before it all happened, your cousin sneezed, and your dad said gesundheit, and you asked what it meant."

His hand dropped off the rope, and his eyes regarded me with despondency that radiated through a sheen of tears. I tried to swallow my own sadness at the look on his face, but tears still burned my eyes. "It wasn't your fault. It was a freak accident. You were so small, that just you standing would never have tipped the boat. That wave did it. You weren't to blame... no one was."

His voice had lost its power, and as he spoke, it dwindled to almost silence. "Dad told me not to stand up. He told us before we left. I forgot. If I hadn't...."

I took a liberty and grabbed his dangling hand. "Please don't blame yourself. Would your cousin want you to be suffering like this? If it had happened to you, would you want him to suffer as you have? Would you have blamed him?"

A tear tracked down his cheek. "No, of course not."

Fox said something else to me. I nodded and sniffled back a sob. "Fox saw him the day he died, and they had a chat; then Alby went into the light. His grandmother was there to take him. He told Fox that he was only worried about his Snoopy teddy. On the day of the funeral, he tried so hard to tell his mum to give it to you, and by some miracle, she heard him. He knew you'd take good care of it, and he said he loved you, so it was right that you minded it for him until later."

He took his hand out of mine and covered his mouth. Tears cascaded down his face and mine. This was too much.

But I needed to turn off the waterworks. I wasn't a very good support person if I was falling apart.

God, I hoped I was getting through to him through the years of guilt that had formed an impenetrable barrier between him, happiness, and feelings of worthiness. Fox disappeared. Argh, great time to leave me.

He let his hand drop again. "Are you telling the truth? Like really telling me?"

I nodded. "Yes. I swear on my life." He eyed me, still not ready to give in.

Fox returned. "His Snoopy is hidden in his cupboard, under an ugly Christmas jumper."

A smile broke through my melancholy. "Sergeant Fox has just gone to check, but he says the Snoopy is hiding in your cupboard under, and I quote, 'an ugly Christmas jumper.'"

Fox Junior barked a laugh, then sniffled. "Okay, you got me. My mother doesn't even know about that. I told her I threw it away so she wouldn't make me wear it, and I keep my door locked, so she never comes in any more. I've shut a lot of people out of my life." He paused and stared at nothing. Processing, deciding? Finally, his hand lifted to his throat, and he removed the noose.

I took a shuddering breath. Thank God. My stomach muscles remained clenched until he'd made it to the ground and was standing in front of me. His sad eyes stared into mine. "I don't know where you came from, I mean, you know, in life, but thank you. You saved my life."

"It was my pleasure. But please don't go back to where you were. You were a kid, excited, vibrant. Punishing yourself every day, killing yourself, it won't solve anything, and if you killed yourself and met with your cousin in the afterlife, he'd be devastated to know what you'd been through. He'd probably blame himself, and then the whole thing would start again." I gave him a sad smile. "Can I give you my number? In case you ever need to talk, or want to chat to your grandfather? I'm sure he'd love to keep in touch. Just don't tell people I can talk to ghosts. I have enough trouble with people taking me seriously as it is."

He smiled. "Okay, that sounds good, and I'll keep your secret."

"Cool." Sirens wailed outside. "Looks like the cavalry's arrived. They might want you to go in for an assessment."

He shrugged. "That's okay. I probably should start talking to a professional. I've refused this whole time because I felt so guilty, and I didn't want anyone to know it was my fault. My father never told them what really happened. He said a wave swamped us, which is what was in the paper." So, he did believe me. I couldn't have known.

As the authorities pounded on the door, I took one last look at Fox Junior. "Promise me you'll call if it gets too much for you?"

"Yes, Avery. I promise I'll call. You'll be my personal angel on speed dial."

Banging came from the front door. "Good. I guess I better answer that on my way out. And give them an abridged version." This time I let my eye have its way and wink. Goodness knew I deserved that one silly gesture without feeling like a weirdo.

We gave each other a brief hug, and I ran to the door and opened it before they broke it down. I pointed the way to the living area, and the paramedics hurried through. "He's okay now," I called out as they passed. A policeman followed them in. I gave him my side of the story, minus all the ghost stuff, grabbed the flowers from the porch and placed them on the hallway table, then left, Sergeant Fox at my side.

When we were back in the car, he turned to me. "Nicely done, Winters. The force could use someone like you."

I chuckled. "Have you been talking to Bellamy?"

He looked at the sky. "I wish."

I grinned. "Maybe I can help you with that."

Haunting Avery Winters

(Paranormal Cosy Mystery)

A Killer Welcome #1

A Regrettable Roast #2

Book #3 coming April 2022

The Circle of Talia

(YA Epic Fantasy)

Shadows of the Realm

A Time of Darkness

Realm of Blood and Fire

The Rose of Nerine

(Epic Fantasy)

Tempering the Rose

ABOUT THE AUTHOR

USA Today bestselling author, Dionne Lister is a Sydneysider with a degree in creative writing, two Siamese cats, and is a member of the Science Fiction and Fantasy Writers of America. Daydreaming has always been her passion, so writing was a natural progression from staring out the window in primary school, and being an author was a dream she held since childhood.

Unfortunately, writing was only a hobby while Dionne worked as a property valuer in Sydney, until her mid-thirties when she returned to study and completed her creative writing degree. Since then, she has indulged her passion for writing while raising two children with her husband. Her books have attracted praise from Apple iBooks and have reached #1 on Amazon and iBooks charts worldwide, frequently occupying top 100 lists in fantasy and mystery.

Printed in Great Britain
by Amazon

40962669R00138